EROS CRESCENT

EROS CRESCENT TRILOGY VOLUME TWO

RICHARD LEE

Dedicated to a world in need of
love and imagination.

If you only read the books that everyone else is reading, you can only think what everyone else is thinking.

— HARUKI MURAKAMI

CONTENTS

PREFACE

After a year in Positano on the Amalfi coast finishing his second novel, Roger left Italy and returned to London. There he learned that he and his stepsister Jackie had inherited a large Edwardian house opposite a beautiful park in Eros Crescent in their native Sydney. Roger and Jackie and her partner Miranda, move back to Australia and discover the sensual delights of their neighbours.

Meet the new residents of Eros Crescent, Roger and Caroline. Discover Rosa's network of women friends and lovers young and old, all of whom she is happy to share both with her husband and with each other. Rosa maintains that the kiss is the most important part of sensuality, alongside anticipation of what might happen next, and that there should always be loving intent when expressing ones affections. Enjoy the adventures of Rosa's friends, Maude, Helen and her husband Frederico and their step daughter Alice and her friend Freya. Enjoy the neighbours, Mary and her niece Sophie along with Mary's enigmatic admirer, the hyper-sexual Janice.

1

ROSA RETURNS

Rosa Bennett had been home from an extended stay in hospital for just a few days. The mysterious malady that had kept her there had been judged by the doctors to be non life-threatening but they warned her that, even though she might be only sixty-six and youthful in her outlook, she must lead a more sedate life and resting regularly.

Her husband Bertie, now seventy-one, had been told that he must not exhaust her. Bertie had smiled and said that he would do his best. But Rosa had very different ideas.

Twenty years earlier, Rosa and Bertie had drifted apart and Rosa had taken a lady lover. Then, unusually, Rosa had seen Bertie in a different light and had fallen back in love with him, since then she had occasionally brought home a new lady lover to share with him.

Such was the Bennetts' unusual but obviously successful relationship and over time Rosa's sexual and loving proclivities had reached out to close family friends. These included her first lady lover's daughter Helen and Helen's husband Freddie and, more recently Freddy and Helen's stepdaughter Alice, a student now living in the cottage behind the Bennetts' house.

Coming home from her stay in hospital at last, Rosa knew that life was going to be a little different. Things had happened while she was away, things that pleased her but nevertheless might change her home routine from now on.

There had been a time in hospital when she thought she might not live for much longer and she had worried about her husband's likely lack of female companionship. She had prevailed on Helen, who she knew had had, even from adolescence, a long-time crush on Bertie, to engage with him physically.

Rosa knew that their boarder, Alice had accidentally discovered Bertie's huge and willing cock one morning – what Rosa called his "Morning Glory" – but she foresaw the day when Alice, being so young, would leave university and quite likely travel overseas and if she was not around, then Helen would be was the one who could best look after her husband's sensual needs.

There was also another thing for Rosa to think about: Bertie's seeming loss of memory and the possibility of his having dementia. It was still unclear what was going on in Bertie's head. All Rosa knew was that Bertie seemed to see things differently to most people and his responses to intimate or sensitive matters could cause surprise and confusion to those close to him.

Before she had been diagnosed and sent to hospital, she had developed a code of short instructions relating to hers and Bertie's extensive range of sexual activities to which Bertie had quickly responded.

Rosa had named this code the Fifi Code. She needed a key word that could not be confused with anything else and that, when spoken, would trigger the necessary parts of Bertie's brain so that he simply responded by fulfilling her request.

The word "Fifi" came from a postcard Rosa had given Bertie many years before which depicted a French maid in a black costume and white apron and with a "come hither" look on her face. Bertie had liked it so much that he had pasted it inside his wardrobe door, where it remains today.

Now Rosa only needed to pick a code she fancied, or thought that Bertie would enjoy. For example, if Rosa said the words, "Fifi wants it over the back of the sofa", it would result in her being escorted to the lounge room, bent over the back of the sofa, her panties removed, and

Bertie giving her an excellent shagging; all without the slightest confusion!

She had written down her long list of Fifi codes, everything one needed to know about the sexual antics that gave her and Bertie pleasure and had given copies to Alice and then to Helen.

All of this was fine, except Rosa was now mostly fit and well and back home and confronted with fitting in her own and Bertie's sensual enjoyment with the lovemaking of two other people. Even though all three women were intimate, some sort of roster might be necessary. The more Rosa thought about it the more she reasoned that she should discuss this with Alice and Helen.

In the meantime she told Bertie that she would be getting up very early on Wednesday and Saturday mornings to do her yoga in Alice's spare bedroom in the cottage.

"Someone else will have to hop into bed with you Bertie. Alice or Helen perhaps."

Bertie seemed happy with this arrangement.

"Well, all right darling. I'm sure everyone will manage. Just don't overdo the exercises. You know the doctor wants you to take it easy."

Helen called Alice and said she wanted to come over, and Alice said she would be working at home on Wednesday and suggested that Helen pop in after she had visited Bertie.

"There is so much we need to talk about, darling. Rosa phoned me and said she had told Bertie that she would be getting up early on Wednesdays and Saturdays, supposedly to do yoga in your spare room, but obviously to make way for us."

"Should we get Rosa in to discus things perhaps? We need to get ourselves properly sorted, don't you think?"

"I agree Helen. Why don't I ask Rosa to join us on Wednesday late in the morning after you and I have talked?"

Helen and Alice embraced and kissed each other, then got on with the business at hand.

"It was to be expected that things would change, Helen. So how do we still have – or not have – the freedom we've enjoyed with Bertie now that Rosa is home? Perhaps we should just stop visiting him? I'm sure we'd both miss having him but well, it was great while it lasted. And Rosa's needs must come first."

Alice had made coffee and they were sitting at Alice's kitchen table. Alice instinctively slid a hand onto Helen's knee and caressed it. Helen closed her eyes momentarily, then reached out and put a hand on Alice, letting it creep up a little bit under her skirt. They leant towards each other and kissed.

"Oh, Alice darling! I so love you."

As they began discussing the situation, there was a knock at the front door. Alice answered it.

"Rosa! Come in. Helen is here and we're just discussing asking you to come and talk to us. So you've come at the right time. Coffee or tea?"

Rosa kissed Alice and then Helen then sat down at the table.

"Tea please, Alice my love. Not allowed coffee any more.

"Now, you two. You are both wondering how my return home is going to affect the two of you in your adventures with our dear Bertie. Am I right?"

The two looked at the well-dressed, petite and beautiful wife of Bertie.

Rosa had, over the course of the month, become intimate with both women during their visits to her in hospital.

The first time with Alice, had happened when Alice was about to leave the hospital after visiting and leant down to kiss Rosa goodbye. Rosa had let her hand wander up Alice's leg and touch her crotch and Alice had responded by thrusting her tongue into Rosa's mouth, then slipping a hand onto Rosa's breasts.

When Helen, a long time family friend, had confronted Rosa about why Rosa had never allowed the two of them to become close, Rosa had confessed to being the lover of Helen's mother and related to her the sad details of how the love affair had ended and why she didn't want to hurt her lover's daughter, being fearful of hurting her as she thought she had hurt her mother.

Then Rosa had told Helen that she thought she might die soon and that Helen was the best person to look after Bertie's physical needs. She had told her how she knew that Helen had always admired Bertie, even when she was a teenager.

When Helen had agreed and indicated that she would try, Rosa's mood suddenly changed and she reached for Helen on the hospital bed, saying that she and Bertie always shared their lovers and so, now that Helen had agreed, she, Rosa would have her first.

Within moments Helen's skirt had been round her neck and Rosa's lips and hands had been busily enjoying her beautiful body.

"Yes, Rosa, we have talked about the situation but only briefly, and we've sort of come to the conclusion already, this being that we should both stop having a relationship with Bertie and let things return to what they were before you went into hospital.

"Alice is even prepared to move out of this cottage and find a flat elsewhere if it makes things easier. In the event of Bertie asking after her whereabouts, they would all have the same story: that Alice had moved for reasons to do with her work."

Rosa lifted the cup and sipped her tea.

"Now you can both listen to me. Even if I were one hundred per cent fit, I would want you both to continue with your loving attention to my husband. His pleasure is also my pleasure. And if Bertie was here he would say the same as regards my pleasure in pleasing him.

"It will not be difficult for the two of you to carry on. The reality is that my doctors are insisting on my leading a quieter life and restricting some activities. They've given me a list of things I can and cannot do and, believe it or not, they've even put a limit on how many orgasms I'm allowed in a week."

Alice and Helen exchanged looks and they both laughed.

"With respect Rosa, how would they know?"

Rosa eyed the two with a bemused smile.

"Because I have to fill in a diary. The doctors agree that orgasms are good for people generally, but not more than a certain number if you've got a heart condition like mine, whatever that is."

Rosa reached for a chocolate biscuit.

"That's my third biscuit today. Mustn't forget to write that in my diary."

Everyone chuckled and Alice poured more hot water into the teapot and went to the kitchen for more coffee.

"I've talked to Bertie about it."

Helen and Alice both stopped what they were doing and stared at Rosa.

"And? What did he say, Rosa?"

"Well! He said that if I was prepared to remain in bed with him when one of you called in, he would be happy to continue with the arrangement. If I wasn't happy about it, then he was prepared to forgo his sessions with – in his words – 'those delicious girls' and also forgo his 'morning glory' with me to prevent my having an orgasm. He insisted that my health was what mattered and he was sure that you would both understand."

There was silence in the room as Alice and Helen digested what Rosa had said.

"How would you feel about being in the bed at the same time as one of us was enjoying Bertie's attention? Mightn't you find it awkward in some way, Rosa?"

Rosa laughed.

"Oh you funny sexy things. I would love it! I might not be allowed to orgasm, but I'm certainly allowed to be the randy happy voyeur. Just don't touch my clit though, or I might come. The question really is whether you two would be comfortable with me being there?"

Alice and Helen looked at one another.

"Rosa darling, just how many orgasms are you allowed?"

Rosa looked at Helen and grimaced.

"The experts have decided that my limit is to be just four orgasms each week, and that if they are 'multiple orgasms' they can only be multiples of not more than three.

"I've thought about it carefully and I think I can manage that. I am feeling that I should slow down a little bit anyway, so these rules will help rather than hinder. As I get older, I can enjoy watching others. Becoming a touchy voyeur won't be hard for me! Just be aware that my fingers will enjoy themselves, so you should both be ready at any time to indulge your older lady lover."

Helen and Alice smiled and looked at each other with a special look.

"Well Rosa. I think I can speak for both Helen and me when I say that we look forward to all parts of this special touchy voyeur touching us. In fact, I think I want your hand on my leg right now, Rosa."

"Me too?" asked Helen.

Rosa looked at her two beautiful lovers.

"I suggest we head into the bedroom girls. I can feel a big touchy feeling moment coming on right now."

2

ROGER IN ENGLAND

AFTER A YEAR in Positano on the Amalfi coast, Roger left Italy and returned to London. He had completed the novel and stayed long enough to fulfil his publisher's requests for small changes to the manuscript and to enjoy for the last time the pleasures afforded him by the many artists and writers and others whom he had met and, of course, the beautiful landscape. Roger would miss it, but he now looked forward to having a few months in England.

Roger's stepsister had offered him a room with her and her partner in south London for a period of three months, after which they would rent out the apartment and move to Australia. Both were highly qualified and had well-paid jobs at home and abroad.

Their flat was close to transport, which would provide Roger with easy access to the wonders of the British Library, the British Museum, bookstores and the theatre. These three months in London would allow him to liaise with his publisher and make himself available for book promotions such as magazine or radio interviews.

Jackie would of course interrogate him about his personal life as she always did. At thirty-three and five years his junior, she could not understand how it was that at six feet tall and with such good looks and possibly "even a little intelligence" that he could possibly still be single.

"There are so many beautiful women around who would willingly waste themselves on a man like you, Roger," she would say teasingly as her partner Miranda looked on, enjoying the banter. Miranda rarely had the opportunity to see Jackie's side of the family, and considered Roger to be the only member.

"Okay, okay!" Roger would reply, trying to defend himself. There is just too much to do Jack. I can't fit everything in."

"You can't fit everything in? My god, if the glimpses I've had of your life style in the past is any guide, dear brother, I have a good idea how many women you manage to 'fit in'. What is wrong with you, that not one of them chooses to hold you down in the bed long enough to become part of the furniture? And what about us? How long do we have to wait to become aunts?

"Miranda and I are planning to start a family the year after next and that will give you 'uncle' status. I don't want our kids to have an 'old rake' for an uncle with some poor young bimbo wearing a Mother Santa miniskirt, balancing on six inch heels and hanging onto his arm, arriving for a family Christmas dinner."

Jackie's attacks would always be the same and Roger could never provide acceptable answers for her questions. She was too sharp, too honestly confronting, so that he always had to hide behind unsatisfactory answers.

"Jack, I would love to have children and make you an aunt. The right woman just hasn't come along yet. After all, it took you and Miranda time to find each other, didn't it?"

Jackie would become steely in her gaze and when this happened Roger knew that he was in big trouble.

"Dearest brother, how many women have you had sexual relations with in the last twelve months? Answer me that. That's if you can count past fifty."

"Dearest sister, when does a respectable man every talk openly about such things? Sufficient to say that for some mysterious reason, women enjoy my company and I enjoy theirs. And it's not as though we break up fighting. In fact. in most instances we remain friends.

Some even invite me home to dinner and introduce me to their husband."

And then all hell would break loose and both Jackie and Miranda would jump on Roger and drag him onto the sofa and pummel him and call him unspeakable names. He recalled that once Jackie called to Miranda to go and get a knife from the kitchen "so that we can fix him for good".

And then, only when he had offered a brotherly promise that he would earnestly consider making her an aunt in the next two years, would they let him get up.

"The clock is ticking," Jackie spat as she straightened herself up.

Later, when things quietened down and civility and even humour had been restored, Roger would ask them about their plans and if they would consider returning to Australia some time in the future.

"Of course Roger. That is where we want to bring up our families. What about you, brother, will you settle there?"

"It's most likely that I will. However, being a bloke as I am, I have noticed that women who settle down to have children usually want to stay close to their mothers and families. This being the case and with the clock ticking as you threaten, I'd best be sure to fall in love with an Aussie woman; otherwise your and my kids may never get to spend time together.

"Needing to fall in love with an Australian, and ideally one from Sydney, will of course greatly reduce the size of the pool of likely eligible candidates and impinge quite negatively on my love life but, dear sister, I will do this for you."

This brought general laughter from all of them and peace descended once more.

Roger's longer-term plan was to return home to Australia, find pleasant accommodation in a quiet sleepy tree-lined Sydney street and write the next book. He was already a long way into the plot and story in his head, and now looked forward to a life without distractions so that he could work.

Really big surprises are rare in life and so for Roger and Jackie, being left a large Edwardian house in one of Sydney's better suburbs by a spinster aunt was not something they had ever imagined would happen. Aunt Dorothy was the older of two unmarried sisters. However, unbeknown to them, the younger sister, Mabel, had unexpectedly passed away just a month earlier, leaving them both as the next of kin.

Roger and Jackie mourned for their two aunts and celebrated their surprise inheritance in one big dinner party at Le Bistro Clos Maggiore in Covent Garden. Jackie and Miranda invited a small number of their friends and Roger asked his agent and her husband.

Everyone was excited to learn of their inheritance, and when Roger announced that the house was at number twenty-one Eros Crescent, they all fell about laughing, making snide jokes about "coals to Newcastle" and how suitable it sounded for "a single man who is known to enjoy life's important pleasures".

"I've been to Eros Crescent," a woman called above the noise.

The crowd at the table became quiet and looked at Caroline, a friend of Roger's sister.

"Believe it or not, my mother and father actually live there now, but they took me there on a Sunday drive when I was a teenager.

"It was quite lovely. There are houses on one side only, and the Crescent sweeps around a beautiful little public garden and there is a hug bush park at the back. There is a little statue of Eros in the gardens, supposedly paid for by a famous Sydney Madam after she was refused permission to open a brothel in that prestige suburb. It is said that it was her way of reminding local residents of what they were missing out on.

"Mum and dad eventually moved to live at number one. You'll be neighbours."

Caroline was one of Jackie and Miranda's girlfriends and originally from Sydney. She was in publishing, a very attractive and intelligent stereotypical executive type who had worked in London for the past couple of years. Caroline and Roger's agent Larissa, had plenty to talk about.

This gave Roger time to get to know Alistair, Larissa's partner. It turned out that Alistair knew a lot about Edwardian houses, so by midway through the evening Roger knew more about plaster cornices and ornate ceilings in grades one and two heritage-listed buildings, along with Edwardian doorknobs and window fittings than he ever intended to ingest into his knowledge base of less=likely-to-ever-be-used facts.

He was just beginning to wish he hadn't spoken the words "Edwardian houses", when Caroline turned and leant across in front of Larissa and, with the smile of someone experienced in the pitfalls of dinner party conversations and making sure that Alistair understood her request, asked if Roger would be available to talk to her during dessert and in quite a loud voice said that she urgently needed to ask him something before he left to go to Sydney.

"I'd be delighted to talk to you, Caroline, over my baked Greek yogurt cheesecake with white chocolate and mandarin sorbet," he replied, taking advantage of his earlier appraisal of the desserts menu.

Caroline and the others laughed.

"Are you always so forward thinking in what you want next?" Caroline asked.

"It always helps to know what is on the menu," he replied.

Caroline and Roger at last got to talk to each other, but only briefly. Due to the shortage of time, not to mention the rising noise levels as everyone drank a little more, Caroline asked if she could call on Roger one evening at Jackie and Miranda's flat.

"They are going to France for a few days next week. Why don't I call you and make a time and meet you then?"

"Fine by me, Caroline. Look forward to seeing you."

Roger messaged Caroline his telephone number.

Whenever his stepsister took him to task over his failure to enter into a serious relationship, it was not unusual for Roger to think about his early development, in particular his early romantic experiences with women. It was no accident that so many women, especially older women, found him interesting.

When Roger first met a woman, he would present as an attractive and genuinely pleasant and interesting male. As well, it was easy for any of the more perceptive ones – and those who might be so inclined – to register that Roger would be a willing respondent to any need that they might have for a physical encounter, not just because of his ability to flirt or offer mental stimulation or humorous titillation.

How this came about was interesting. Early experiences are central to the person we eventually become and Roger's early adolescent sexual experiences, more often than not, had involved older women.

His mother had become ill and passed away when he was twelve. His father had immediately employed a housekeeper so that the household could continue its routine. Edward worked as a solicitor in the city and Roger attended grammar school, also in the city. The loss of his mother was a shock to both of them but, as so often happens with men, male stoicism meant that they did not dwell on her passing but rather carried on with life as they believed they would have if she were there. Each mourned her loss in his own silent way.

From the age of around ten, Roger had regularly spent his winter holidays with his mother's brother and his wife, who lived on a rural property in southern Queensland. This ended the year his uncle Tom suffered a stroke and not long afterwards, died.

It was understandable that this holiday routine should stop, but a few years later his father announced that Aunt Ella had suggested at the end of a telephone call, about some minor legal matter, that Roger might like to resume the holiday arrangement and visit the farm on his next term holiday.

Roger had very fond memories of both his aunt and uncle and also loved being on their sheep property, The Pines: horses and dogs, chickens and guinea fowl along with a host of native wildlife and of course the old quad bike that they both were happy for him to ride.

Roger had just turned sixteen, and was excited about the opportunity to revisit The Pines.

Aunt Ella and Fred, the elderly farm handyman at The Pines, collected Roger from the station.

"He's bloody grown up since I last saw him," said Fred in his raspy smokers voice. "Are you sure we've collected the right fella?"

"He certainly has, and yes it's him all right." replied Ella, laughingly inspecting Roger from head to toe. "He's going to cost a lot to feed while he's here. Might have to slaughter a beast Fred. Not sure we have enough meat in the freezer!"

Roger stared out of the window at the pastoral vista, enjoying their friendly down-to-earth banter.

Fred had been at the farm even before Roger's uncle and aunt bought the place. He shared a cottage with his grown-up daughter Sheila. Sheila's husband had been an interstate transport driver but had been killed in a road accident years before Roger started going to the farm for holidays. Sheila was the housekeeper and general farm hand and her cooking was another wonderful feature of his holidays.

The farm had not changed in any way that Roger remembered, except for the absence of uncle Tom. Even the chicken flock in the orchard looked to be the same chickens as he had known four years ago.

Maisie the old kelpie bitch was still there, but now so obviously older. She barked and wagged her tail and staggered from her comfortable kennel near the back door as the utility pulled up. A younger kelpie came bounding out from behind the sheds and jumped up and tried to lick Roger's face. Fred yelled and the dog quickly backed off.

Roger called out his thanks to Fred as Fred limped off to his quarters on the pretty little gardened block behind the machinery shed.

"See ya later, lad," Fred called back.

"Okay Roger. Let's settle you in. You remember where your room is I imagine? It's a bit more cramped since you were here last. We put in a double bed for Maureen and her husband when they visited. They got married shortly after your last visit. They asked to have a bedroom a bit further away from ours. Can't think why."

Ella gave a little laugh, seemingly the result of a private thought. She went on telling him of the changes he might notice about the place.

"We no longer keep a sow, as it was more work than we could manage."

The orchard hadn't been pruned, so it was looking very overgrown. Jenny the bay pony had foaled and the now two-year-old mare had just recently been broken in by a local horse breaker, but his aunt wasn't sure whether he should try to ride her yet.

"She's still a bit skittish," she said.

Roger thought that aunt Ella seemed to treat him a little differently from the way she did on his previous visits but he couldn't be sure. When you are just a kid, grown ups seem to take it for granted that you will just follow on whatever they do. Now Ella seemed intent on seeking his opinion and approval. And she was keen to find out more about him and the things he thought about.

"Do you think Edward will ever remarry? Renata has been gone a few years now and your father is a very youthful and attractive middle-aged man. And I must say Roger, you are looking more like him than I would ever have thought possible."

"He doesn't say much about those sorts of things, Aunty, but I know he does get mail that has a strong perfumed smell which makes me wonder if there is someone that he likes. He will say something when he's ready, I guess."

"And what about you, Roger? Do you have a girlfriend?"

Roger felt himself blushing with embarrassment and Ella noticed. It appeared to amuse her greatly. She unexpectedly took his hand and looked at him intently.

"Oh Roger, I think you're not going to tell me even if you do have a girlfriend. But surely you must know that these are things that women love to know about. Perhaps I'll find a way of getting you to tell me before you go home."

She eyed him with a joyous look in her eyes and a smile that was mysteriously bewitching, even to a sixteen-year-old.

She slipped her other arm around Rodger's waist and pulled him tightly against her.

"So glad you are here Roger." She squeezed his hand, then headed off to the kitchen to see what Sheila had planned for dinner.

Fresh air and exercise, along with a plentiful supply of excellent home cooking makes for a very healthy young man and Roger revelled in all of it.

Horse riding was a favourite activity. He saddled and rode Jenny, which caused her daughter – as yet unnamed – to call out and run up and down the paddock fences whinnying loudly to her mother. He cleaned out the henhouse and took the manure to the vegetable garden, which Fred appreciated very much.

"There's nothing so good as manure for growing vegetables," said Fred.

With lessons from Fred, who was no longer able to climb ladders, Roger began the biggest job of all: pruning the trees in the orchard. At morning tea time Sheila would appear with a basket of sandwiches, fresh scones and thermoses of tea and soft drink.

Roger noticed Sheila well before she arrived where he was working, watching her saunter down between the rows of apple trees. For a reason he didn't understand he found her intriguing. She seemed to hover above the ground as she carried her long thin body along the path to the orchard.

At sixteen, Roger was not at all experienced nor – until now – particularly interested in watching or looking at women, yet Sheila seemed to suggest some other way of living; she seemed to live suggesting she live a life seperate from that of most of the people he knew.

From the little he did know about Sheila, it appeared that, since the loss of her husband many years before, and she being now in the later part of her forties, he had not seen nor heard mention of any man visiting her, and the weekly visit to town to shop was always in the company of Fred or his aunt, or both.

"How is it all going Roger?" Sheila asked, smiling. "You haven't fallen off the ladder yet, then?"

Sheila looked up at Roger atop the stepladder. The tall, slender woman wore pretty much the same clothes all the time. A work shirt; this one was red and green and black check, and hung loose outside her Bombay shorts, which reached down below her knees. She wore brown leather sandals on her small brown feet which, like the rest of her tanned body, signalled someone who enjoyed the outdoor life.

She gave the impression that nothing bothered her and that everything she did was exactly what she wanted to do. She seemed very much her own woman.

"No, I haven't fallen off yet, Sheila, but there is still plenty of time for that to happen. The main threat seems to be from old rabbit holes hidden in the long grass. I've twice managed to stop the ladder falling over after one foot of it suddenly went down into a subsiding bunny burrow."

Sheila laughed. "It seems like you are doing a very good job. I'm sure your aunt will make a fuss of you when you finish. Nothing excites Ella more than seeing a job well done. She will want to reward you somehow, I bet." She laughed in a way that suggested she was sharing a secret with herself. "Now come down and have something to eat."

Fred arrived and parked the little tractor with the grass cutter on the back. He was clearing the long grass ahead of Roger and was nearly done except for the outer perimeter. Roger figured that at the pace he was pruning, he wouldn't finish for another three days. But that was fine. He was enjoying the challenge.

Sheila laid out a cloth and then the food and drink.

"Now I must tell you, in case you don't already know, that today would have been your Uncle Tom's birthday. Ella always celebrates it at dinner by dressing up most elegantly, as she would have for her husband on his birthday. I always serve Tom's favourite dishes, including a pavlova desert. She also likes to remember him with a drink or two, usually a red wine. Ella will probably inform you later but I'm telling you this so you won't be taken entirely by surprise."

"Sounds great. I love pavlova," Roger replied.

"My one piece of advice, Roger is don't drink too much. I don't want to have to put two people to bed afterwards." Sheila smiled again in that mysterious way that suggested she knew something.

When Roger eventually arrived back at the house, his aunt was nowhere to be seen and he presumed that she wouldn't be far away;

and remembering Sheila's words, Ella could well be sorting out her wardrobe for that special dressing-up ahead of dinner.

He went to his room and stripped off. Then he grabbed a towel and headed for the bathroom. A hot shower at the end of a long day's work or a game of Rugby was truly wonderful, and he had been told by Ella that, because it had been an especially wet year in these parts, there was lots of water available; so longer showers were allowed.

Roger soaped up all over and applied shampoo to his hair. As always, despite attempts to stop it happening, soap or shampoo got into his eyes and so he kept them closed while he continued soaping himself. When he at last began to rinse off the soap and opened his eyes, he wasn't prepared for what he saw. Ella was standing in front of the shower staring at him or, rather, at a particular part of him.

Roger rushed to cover his cock, which was luxuriating in the soap while obviously enjoying his careful cleaning techniques, which was probably what caused it to stand enlarged and at half-mast.

"Aunty! I'm so sorry. I didn't hear you come in."

It was Roger's turn to stare. Ella was wearing a see-through shift with nothing underneath. The nipples of her large shapely breasts pushed out at the top and front of the shift and her wide hips pushed out the sides, making it a very tight-fitting, flimsy covering. Ella's solid but shapely legs tapered gently down to a pair of pink bedroom slippers with raised heels and adorned on the fronts with little white fluffy pom poms and which Roger thought might be rabbits' tails.

Ella watched him looking at her, all the while smiling and running her tongue lightly over her upper lip.

"That's all right, Roger. We are family of course, and we will soon get used to seeing each other *au naturel*. Are you okay with that, darling?"

Before he could answer, or perhaps not expecting an answer, she turned her back on Roger and stepped over to the edge of the bath.

"When you get out darling, would you be so good as to run the bath for me? Just turn on the hot tap. I'll take it from there. I'm putting in some bubble bath. Once you are out I will come and have a soak before dinner. It would have been your uncle's birthday today and so I like to dress up a little bit in memory of him.

"I will wear an outfit that he loved. And Sheila is making a wonderful birthday dinner, so we will have a great time."

She had now bent over to pour in the bubble bath flakes and Roger's eyes could not move away from her barely-clad body. As she bent forward, Ella's large buttocks pushed outward, filling the robe with the most exciting view of womanhood a young man of his age could possibly see. Until now, he had never seen a woman's bottom and this sudden introduction to such an exciting and beautiful vision was electrifying. Aunty Ella's rear end was stupendous: it seemed huge; sexy beyond belief. A giant white orb with a shadowy crack down the middle, and what appeared to be a substantial quantity of pubic hair visible between her thighs.

Roger wanted to stare at her backside forever and prayed she would never move. But Aunty did move, turning quickly and looking straight at where his hands were now holding and attempting to cover an even bigger instrument, which he could not prevent from peeping out between his fingers.

Ella did not try to hide the fact that she was staring at Roger's not-so-shy penis and what she was looking at caused her to smile appreciatively.

"I'm so looking forward to our dinner date tonight, Roger. It will be wonderful having you stand in for my dear Tom. I so want you to enjoy it, exactly as he would have enjoyed it."

Aunt Ella gave one of her most beautiful smiles and looked directly at Roger. Then she pouted her sensuous lips and with one hand blew him a kiss, while with the other hand she slowly cupped and adjusted the position of a breast beneath her tight shift. Then she turned and left.

No matter how hard he tried, Roger could not get the vision of Ella's lovely backside out of his head. And it seemed that his fully erect member couldn't either.

He stepped out of the shower and reached for the towel. Then he turned on the hot tap in the bath and left.

Getting to his bedroom, he locked the door and fell onto the bed. Holding his very stiff erect penis in his hand with the view of Aunty's delicious rear-end in his mind caused the two joining forces to make a very satisfying conclusion to his ablutions. His sex education had truly begun. Roger's life from this day on was going to be very different and dinner with his aunt was looking to be much more than just a tasty meal.

Sheila had everything under control in the kitchen when Ella wandered in to check on things.

"Kitty hasn't arrived yet?" asked Ella.

"Yes, she has. She's just putting her things away in the staff quarters. She will be here in a minute or two."

"How is the girl? Does she seem any different from when she was here a month or so ago? I know we both thought she had matured quite a bit then."

"Interesting you ask. Yes, Ella, I think she has matured even more. I got the impression that life for her had moved on a bit. She said that they'd had her city cousins come and stay and that it had been great fun. A boy and a girl around her own age. That would have been good for her, I'm sure. She leads such a sheltered life at home with her mother."

Kitty lived on her uncle's property with her mother, thirty kilometres or more up the road. Ella was able to offer her casual work on the farm during the year, helping during the sheep shearing or picking and bottling fruit and vegetables alongside Fred and Sheila. They all enjoyed having the teenager stay. She was always happy and full of fun and at the same time a very dependable worker.

At that moment, Kitty came into the kitchen.

"Hello, Mrs Elliott. Thanks for asking me to work. My goodness, Mrs E. that is an amazing outfit you are wearing. So sexy, if you don't mind me saying so. Wish I could wear something like that. I just don't have the figure for it."

Ella exchanged amused looks with Sheila.

"Kitty, you don't have to have a special figure to look sexy. People are sexy simply because of who they are and how they think and act. Sheila and I both agree that you have all the qualities a young woman would ever need to enjoy every aspect of life as an adult."

"Oh, thanks, Mrs E. But do you think I will scrub up well enough to get a bloke? I think about it a lot, but then I worry about my weight."

Sheila smiled and passed Kitty a tea towel and nodded towards the sink and the dishes.

"Kitty! We both love it that you are Rubenesque. We think you are definitely sexy."

Everyone laughed and then Kitty asked, "What does Rubenesque mean, Sheila?"

"You tell her Ella."

Ella moved and stood at the sink beside Kitty, taking the pots and pans and stacking them as Kitty washed and scrubbed them.

"Rubens was an artist who painted in the seventeenth century. He was famous as a painter, particularly for his paintings of naked larger ladies. The paintings often showed a group of ladies enjoying themselves in a woodland setting. You can see pictures of his masterpiece 'The Three Graces' in many art books. I can probably find one in one of my books in the library. Remind me some time and I'll look for it.

"Many artists who painted women depicted them in the popular form of the larger woman. Renoir painted women and one of his works was called 'The Large Bathers'. Someone even described it as 'a great celebration of abundance'."

Sheila looked at Kitty and then at Ella.

"And as for scrubbing up for blokes, well in my opinion, what blokes like in a woman can be as different as there are personalities and body shapes. And by the way, Kitty, many women and men are attracted to both men and women in a sexual and loving way and they are not concerned with body shape. In other words, there are more than enough differences among people to go round, and definitely someone for everyone."

Ella looked across at Sheila, who had paused to look across at her. Ella winked and nodded her head up and down, suggesting that what she had just told the seventeen-year-old was okay. Sheila looked thoughtful, then relaxed and nodded back in approval.

"My cousin likes girls," answered Kitty suddenly.

"What's his name, Kitty?"

"Her name? Margaret. She told me one night that she liked girls. Then she kissed me.

The silence that followed seemed to go on forever and Ella and Sheila stared at each other behind Kitty, who was standing at the sink. Then, before either of them could speak, Kitty followed with another shock statement.

"I liked it and kissed her back. Apparently I seem to like blokes and girls. Is that weird, do you think?"

Sheila decided to answer before Ella could. Giving an assuring laugh, she said, "You're like me then Kitty. Liking boys and girls is called being bisexual, bi meaning both ways. I'm bisexual."

Kitty stopped washing the dishes and turned and stared at Sheila.

"Well, that is interesting Sheila. You've made me feel much better. I was a bit worried it would bother people. Now I can just relax and be who I am. This is really a great relief. You've made me feel really good about myself."

She turned back to the sink. Again Sheila and Ella stared at each other, smiling.

"Well, if we are telling each other our secrets, I should tell you Kitty, that I too am bisexual and it is a wonderful thing. I discovered these feelings much later in life, in fact not long before my husband died. It has been a comfort to me ever since."

Again Kitty stopped doing the dishes. She turned and stared at Ella's face; then she let her eyes drop to survey Ella's elegant body sheathed in its tight skirt and her black-stockinged legs and heeled shoes.

"Well, I'm really surprised at what you have both told me. I think my world has changed."

"For the better, I'm sure," said Sheila. "Now Ella, we will be ready to serve in twenty minutes, so perhaps you could go and organise the drinks and let young Roger know dinner will be served quite soon."

As Ella left the kitchen, she heard Kitty's voice. "Who's Roger, Sheila?"

Dinner was wonderful. Roger's appetite had improved dramatically during his stay at the farm, mainly due to the huge amount of exercise he had from working in the orchard and roaming the farm on foot and sometimes riding Jenny.

Sitting next to his delightful aunt was a bonus. Part of him was still reliving seeing Ella almost naked in the bathroom earlier. Roger's senses were on fire and he could hardly avert his eyes from his aunt's laughing face. Only occasionally did he look away to search the food that Sheila and Kitty kept adding to the table.

Ella had already had a couple of drinks and was now enjoying regular sips from her glass of red wine. She wasn't drunk, just slightly tipsy and very happy.

Every once in a while, Ella would lean towards him to tell him some little story and when she did so, she placed her hand on his leg and moved it up and down his thigh, pausing when her hand came close to his crotch. This resulted in Roger's penis being erect, or at least semi-erect throughout the meal. He longed to reciprocate and reach out and touch his aunt's thigh through her tight skirt, but he managed to control himself.

While introducing Roger to Kitty when she first entered the dining room with extra plates of chicken slices and roast vegetables, Ella's hand reached right up to his crotch and he felt her fingers exploring further than they had before.

"Roger, this is Kitty. Kitty lives on a farm some distance up the road and comes to The Pines when we need help. She's brilliant in the kitchen and in the shearing shed. She is good at everything. Kitty will be with us for a few days.

"Kitty, this is Roger, my late sister-in-law's son, who used to visit here regularly before Tom passed away. This is his first visit in four years and we are amazed at how much he has grown. Which is exactly what happened to you, Kitty. Neither of you are the kids Sheila and I first knew. Now you are young adults."

Kitty looked long and hard at Roger's face. Seeing someone her own age and a male was most exciting.

"Pleased to meet you, Roger. Hope you're enjoying your visit. There's so much to do at The Pines. I love it when Ella invites me over.

She and Sheila are so good to me. I guess we'll catch up around the farm. I'm here for the rest of the week."

Roger stared back at Kitty's lovely face and noticed that she was sturdily built. Her low-cut blouse gave him a peep at a cleavage that caused his penis to twitch only slightly, but enough to cause his aunt's hand to press more forcefully at the bulge in his trousers.

"So good to meet you, Kitty. I look forward to catching up some time soon. I'm working in the orchard for the next three days at least, but I'm sure we will come across each other somewhere."

Ella sighed and said, "Oh to be young again," as Kitty left the room.

His aunt was now revelling in her situation, occasionally becoming both morbid and then cheerful as she talked about her late husband and about life generally. She regularly mentioned things that Tom had liked.

"On his birthday I always rubbed his leg under the table, just like you are letting me rub yours, darling." Ella confided in him.

She looked deep into Roger's eyes and he felt himself disappearing into hers.

"There were lots of little things Tom loved me doing for him on his birthday. I've just thought of one of them now. He loved it. Here we go! Oops! How silly of me, I've dropped my napkin, Tom. Be a darling and get under the table and retrieve it for me would you, sweetie? I have had too much to drink to do it myself."

Ella stared at Roger with an air of expectation. Her last sentence sounded more like a command than a request.

"Sure, Aunty, I can get it."

Roger slid to the floor and looked around in the shadowy world beneath the table, shielded from the outside world by the large table-cloth hanging all around. He looked for the napkin and spied it well tucked back under Aunty's chair. But something far more interesting grabbed his attention.

Ella's dark-stockinged legs and black shoes and the hem of her black skirt slowly revealed themselves as Roger's eyes grew accustomed to the shadows. He stared. Ella's legs where spread wide apart and he found himself looking up into an abyss at the end of which – past the white flesh above her stocking tops – he could just make out his aunt's secret hairy parts. Then Ella's voice called out, pretending to address her husband.

"Tom! I hope you are all right down there darling? I suppose it is quite dark. Can you see anything? You might have to feel about, my love. Don't hurry. I'm very comfortable up here."

Roger suddenly experienced a rush of what used to be called Dutch courage but which anyone else would call a surrender to lust. He moved forward on his knees so that his head was between his aunt's thighs. He placed a hand around each of her ankles and then ran his fingers up behind her calves to the backs of her knees.

"Oh Tom. You darling man. This is always my favourite part of your birthday dinner. Do whatever you want, my love. What you see is yours for the taking."

Roger glued his lips to the soft bare flesh on a thigh. He could smell his aunt's sex, sweet and perfumed and he moved his face further up her skirt until his nose brushed the hairs on her sex. Then he opened his mouth and instinctively stuck out his tongue and nestled it into the mound. He was in heaven. Wetness suddenly covered his mouth and Aunty's sex opened up and found his tongue and let him lick her warm wet vagina.

"Oh Tom! You lovely man. Don't stop. It's your birthday. Have whatever you want, darling."

Ella lifted her legs and slid forward a little so that Roger's face pushed further into her.

It was at that moment that Roger heard another voice, quite low.

"Oh Ella, you are a lucky girl. I can see you've got what you wanted."

Roger recognised the voice of Sheila.

"Can I have just a tiny touch?"

He heard Ella sigh and utter a few words. "Of course my sweet. Just don't put him off his stroke. It's divine."

Suddenly a hand appeared above Roger's head and fingers firmly rubbed a spot at the top of the now wide open pussy. Then two wet fingers pushed themselves into his mouth, before returning back to where they had been before.

The hand withdrew and as it did so Ella orgasmed, grabbing Roger's head by his hair and pulling him tightly to her.

Then he heard Sheila's hushed voice.

"Beautiful Ella! I hope you will let me have him later?"

"Any time darling," replied a gasping Ella. "You know Tom loves to have you shortly after me. A delayed two-in-one he called it. You deserve it."

Then Ella addressed her husband beneath the table.

"Oh, darling. That was wonderful. Now Tom, if you've had enough, you'd better get up here as soon as possible. Sheila is about to serve the pavlova."

Roger moved backwards, taking in the view of his aunts shapely legs and feet and the extraordinary pink wet rose in the midst of her fluffy bush. He gently rubbed both of her stockinged legs with the palms of his hands, then picked up the napkin and wiped it across his lips and face. He resurfaced and sat back on his chair just as Sheila entered with the dessert.

Both women stared at Roger with loving smiles. It was as though the young man had passed a secret test and that he was now a member of an exclusive club.

Ella became quieter. She seemed to have gone inside herself. She was obviously happy with everything and looked lovingly at her nephew, but said very little.

After Roger had enjoyed second helpings, he helped himself to pavlova and fresh cream. If he had thought about it – and maybe he did – life for a sixteen year old couldn't get much better than this.

There came a time when Roger could eat no more and his aunt could drink no more. Every so often Ella would reach out and touch his arm or run her hand softly up and down his cheek or sometimes his thigh, and tell him how wonderful he was. Emboldened by what had happened earlier, Roger now felt it was safe to reciprocate and let his fingers slide up and down on her stockinged leg beneath her skirt. Ella seemed not to notice, and if she did she did not object.

Sheila came in and announced that it was getting late and asked if anyone needed help getting to bed, a question obviously addressed to the very tipsy Ella.

"I think I could do with a lie down, darling. If you would be so good as to point me in the direction of my bedroom, it would be much appreciated."

Roger and Sheila both laughed and together they helped Ella from her chair and guided her down the long carpeted passage to her room.

Once Ella was safely sitting on her bed and Sheila had begun to undress her, Roger thought it appropriate that he say goodnight to the pair and head off to his own room.

Roger bent over to kiss his aunt goodnight, at which point, she gathered herself together long enough to insist that he must kiss Sheila goodnight as well. "Like you really mean it, you young stud!" Then Ella flopped over onto the bed and to all intents and purposes, passed out.

Roger looked at Sheila. "Well, Sheila. Thank you for a wonderful meal. Everything tonight was most enjoyable."

Sheila laughed out loud. "You lovely young man. Now you must kiss me goodnight as your aunt said, like you really mean it."

To Sheila's surprise, Roger slipped into the same lustful mode he had discovered in himself when he moved in between his aunt's legs earlier. He reached out and clasped Sheila in his arms and kissed her lovingly, then turned her and leant her back onto the bed so that she was lying at right angles to the supine body of his aunt. Sheila gasped.

It took only seconds for Roger to unzip and open up Sheila's waitress skirt and pull down her knickers over her ankles. He dropped his own trousers and pants to the ground and buried his penis between her legs, which opened up, her vulva sucking him into her wet secret place.

"Oh Roger! I never expected this. Please push into me. Yes, bang me hard, Roger. Really hard. I want to feel you right inside me."

Neither of them noticed that Ella had woken up and had propped herself up on her elbow.

"Yes, Tom, you wonderful man. Fuck Sheila hard my love. I love her so much. I want her to have everything I have and more. She deserves it."

With encouragement from two beautiful women, Roger needed no further instruction. He was wild with desire and was dangerously close to hurting Sheila. He ripped open her shirt and bit her tiny breasts. He buried his teeth in the flesh of her shoulder, all the time shagging her tight pussy with such vigour that he thought he would never be able to stop. Sheila suddenly thrust her long legs skyward and screamed and came, but her arms held him close so that he could not escape, and then she came again and a number of times after that. He held on to her skinny legs and pushed into her even more. And she screamed again.

When Roger had ejaculated for the second time, he withdrew from this extraordinary creature. He looked down on her excited and slightly haggard face and kissed her passionately. When he stopped, Sheila burst into tears and wept.

"Thank you," she whispered between sobs.

Roger held her tight for some time and when Sheila's heaving had abated, he said goodnight and headed off to his room.

In thinking back to his early sexual experiences, Roger could not help but question his proclivity for liaisons with the more mature woman, and how younger women and girls his own age failed to excite him in the same way. If he visited the homes of friends and who had teenage sisters, it was more often his friends' mothers who attracted his attention.

What was it? he wondered. Did they exude a desire to mother him? No, it couldn't have been that, because most times he would notice that their reaction was in some ways like that of a teenage girl or a younger woman. It was only in tiny ways, but it was perceptible to his rapidly expanding senses, which took in the real needs and desires of people.

When Roger tried to think of an example, he could only think of the different way that his mates mum might ask him if he would like vanilla or chocolate ice-cream with his fruit salad. A motherly attitude would simply say, "Vanilla or chocolate, Roger?" without lifting her head or making eye contact. The response he drew would more often be "Roger? What ice-cream do you prefer? I can offer you vanilla or chocolate. Or are you a some-of-each sort of person, or maybe someone who thinks deeply before deciding what he likes? What do you think?" And all the time they would retain eye contact, and often with a youthful and knowing smile.

Always their response to him left open the possibility of a further exchange. And Roger often thought that they knew what lurked in his head when he gazed at them appreciatively and that they simply played along with those deeper feelings. But of course they also knew their limits and most times simply enjoyed this opportunity to flirt within the safety of their domestic lives, knowing there was no chance of any sort of complicated consequences.

It wasn't that Roger didn't find younger women physically attractive. Indeed, he did. However, it was a rare occasion when one of those younger nymphs excited him sufficiently for him to want to know her better.

Roger figured that the physicality of young women gave them premium space in the realm of a man's desires and these young things knew that fact instinctively, and from an early age.

Most men created a fantasy world in which a young woman would easily slip into the role of the central character; and once there, a man would happily, and some might say foolishly, become their slave.

Older more experienced women usually understood all this but their life experiences had moved them on past that young time in their lives.

An older woman was likely to better understand that the loving interaction between a man and a woman could be a mutually beneficial arrangement, a give-and-take of desire and intellect, but that this situation was not easily achieved. As he grew older and more experienced, Roger was happy to help satisfy the needs of those older women.

As he moved through his teens and entered his twenties he found that although he had occasionally enjoyed sexual relations with young women, most times these relationships had been fraught with moments of angry despair for his partner, mainly brought about because of his reluctance to commit to a long-term relationship.

And what young woman wants to look ahead without seeing sign-posts leading to security and motherhood?

To the beautiful young things, Roger was a disappointment.

When Roger eventually got to talk to Caroline, he was intrigued to find that she was indeed a delightful and surprising woman, extremely well read in the areas that interested him. She was also a recognised water colourist and had recently shown at one of the major London galleries.

It was also a pleasant surprise to discover that Caroline's family and a couple of her friends lived in Eros Crescent.

"That is amazing, Caroline. Do you know them well?"

"Yes Roger, and I'm sure you will become friends. Helen and Freddy are in their late forties and are very open, warm and worldly. In fact every time I see Helen, I just want to go to bed with her. You will love them, I'm sure."

Caroline laughed. She had confirmed her bisexual nature. Roger knew about her close relationship with his sister Jackie and partner Miranda, and he was happy about that.

Relationships between women made sense to Roger, who had spent a lot of time observing men and couples and had concluded that, in a sexual relationship, a woman could provide much more. Men were limited by their conditioning, he suspected, and their single mindedness and physiology appeared to limit their sensual expression.

Roger had invited Caroline to a spaghetti dinner. He was good at preparing this dish, having been taught by a wonderful chef in Italy. Roger's sister and her partner were away for a few days, so he had the flat to himself.

Roger found himself fascinated by Caroline's maturity. Put another way, he was impressed that a younger woman – Caroline was in her early thirties – could exude the sensuality that he usually found only in older women. He was suddenly more interested in this woman than he had expected to be.

But he wasn't prepared for what Caroline said next.

"Roger, I have a proposition, a request for help, I suppose. Can I tell you what it is?"

Caroline laughed as she spoke and her eyes sparkled.

"I just hope you don't go running from the room when I tell you."

Roger looked eagerly at Caroline.

"I think dear lady, you have captured me. I simply can't move. If I wasn't so worldly wise, I'd say that I'm in love with you already. I suppose a weekend in Margate wouldn't interest you?"

They both laughed at his attempt at flirtatious comedy. Margate was a coastal town where the masses went for long weekends, but it was also the centrepiece of a well-known joke about where some people went for a dirty weekend.

Caroline laughed at his audacity and replied "No thanks". Then she looked serious and seemed to change her mind.

"Well, maybe it would."

Roger looked at her quizzically.

"Hear what my proposal is Roger, before I get even more confused."

She told him how she had spent quite some time with Roger's sister Jackie and her partner Miranda. She described how his sister Jackie sometimes talked about her step brother and in particular how Jackie wished he would find someone and settle down. She always seemed genuinely concerned for his welfare.

"We would also discuss returning to Australia and Jackie and Miranda mentioned starting a family once they had settled.

"Of course it was speculation and fantasy when we talked about it, but it seemed real enough. But now, with this inheritance of a Sydney house, the possibility looks a lot more promising for all of you and I'm looking forward to talking to them again about what might happen."

Roger put his hand up.

"Caroline, sweet lady, please tell me what the proposition is. I'm so hoping it will take us to Margate."

They both laughed at Roger's innuendo and joke.

"Well, Roger, here it is. I believe that you and I should have a baby together."

Caroline stopped talking and took a deep breath.

"We could solve umpteen problems in one go."

She smiled a wicked smile.

"Well, actually it might take more than one go."

She laughed, but Roger didn't see the joke. He was trying to get his head around Caroline's proposition.

"You see Roger. I want a baby. I want to live in Australia. Your sister and partner both want to have children and live in Australia. They want the children's uncle's children to live close by. I want to live close to friends I love. And to top it all off, I do not need any financial support. I am well provided for in my own recent inheritances and with my publishing career."

Caroline paused again and looked at the stupefied Roger.

"Every which way looks like a winning situation, Roger. And if it helps my case, Roger, yes, we could go to Margate, although maybe a cottage in the Cotswolds for a dirty weekend could be preferable."

Roger's head was bursting. This super-attractive woman was offering him herself at a price which seemed not only negligible, but with bonuses that would help him change his ridiculous and basically unproductive lifestyle to one that people might more easily respect.

He was trying hard to think of the negatives in the offer. Surely there was a hidden catch. He quickly thought of one, then another. Did Caroline expect them to live together as a couple? Would there be an expectation of fidelity? And what if Caroline met another man or woman she wanted to be with instead of him? And what are fathers meant to do anyway?

Roger felt himself being sucked into a vortex of immense proportions. Maybe deep down, he wanted to be partnered. Coupledom might be where he should really be heading instead of just talking to his sister in terms that made out that he wanted to be part of a couple but knew that he could never achieve that lifestyle.

A hand reached out and took his hand and Roger looked up into the angelic face of Caroline.

"I don't want you to feel pressured, Roger. And I want you to know that if you decide against the idea, I'm still likely to be up for a trip to Margate with you, although hopefully it would be the Cotswolds."

Then she leant forward and kissed him gently on the cheek and moments later he was looking into her eyes and crafting his reply.

"Maybe we should spend a little time together doing ordinary things, Caroline. Movies, picnics, gallery openings, shopping. I have many questions about how you see this working. I've only just thought of what making a baby entails and what a father's responsibilities might be. I confess I'm a bit taken aback by your suggestion. However, I do want you to know that, from the bottom of my heart, I am seriously considering what you have suggested."

Caroline looked at him with a look of hope in her eyes and an appreciation of his seriousness.

"May I propose that we start dating, if that's the right word? And, Caroline, let's leave Margate off the list until we've discussed things in more detail."

Caroline smiled.

"Sounds like a plan. I love a man with a plan, Roger. With your approval I declare us girlfriend and boyfriend, if you agree with that?"

Roger laughed and nodded his consent.

"And Roger?"

"Yes, Caroline?"

"If the mood takes us, we don't have to travel all the way to bloody Margate. My place is very comfortable."

Roger stared at this incredibly modern woman. Then he stood up and went round to Caroline's side of the table, took her hand and lifted her up. The two embraced and then kissed.

Then he took her hand and rested it agains his trousers where a large and happy erection was pushing upward.

"Oh my God! Did I do that? I'm such a clever girl."

"You don't have to be clever to do that, Caroline, just the beautiful sexy woman you are."

Caroline pressed against him and moved her body gently up and down.

"Can you take me to Margate now, Roger? Please? You are entitled to try before you buy, and I'm still on the pill so I promise this will not lead to entrapment. And let's use your sister's bed. I'll feel quite at home there, darling man."

"Now you're being clever, sweet Caroline. You lead and I'll follow. I've had fantasies about getting into Jackie and Miranda's bed."

3

ROGER IN AUSTRALIA

It was during his first weekend in the new house in Eros Crescent that there was a knock on the door at mid-morning. Roger was making coffee in the kitchen and wondered who it could be. Who would know he was there?

A smiling woman dressed all in black and with a full figure beamed at him when he opened the door.

Hello. I'm Maria and I live over the back, on the far side of the bush park with my daughter Serina. I should mention that we had the job care-taking your house for the few months before you arrived, so we both know your house very well.

"We clean and cook for people in the area. I was wondering if you might be looking for someone to help in the house. I heard you were on your own and so thought it wouldn't hurt to call and ask. I'm happy to work just one day a week, or more if you wish."

She stopped talking and handed Roger a piece of paper with her name and phone number.

"Well, Maria. It's lovely to meet you and you're right. I will need someone just to vacuum and keep the kitchen tidy. And I'm prepared to hire you for a day a week right now. Choose your day and hours. I'm Roger Robertson by the way"

Maria smiled and Roger noticed that beautiful thing he so often saw in older women that he could never properly describe. He put her age at around fifty but with that lovely healthy southern European skin colour it was difficult to know.

"You certainly make up your mind quickly, Mr Robertson. Well, how about Tuesdays starting at nine and finishing at two? Is that okay?"

"Sounds good to me. Here, I'm sorry, do come in Maria and look around in case you have questions."

"It's a big house, Maria, as you must already know, but I'm only using the kitchen, the lounge and a bedroom and bathroom upstairs. The rest of the house is not used, so don't worry about cleaning it. Eventually, when my sister arrives later in the year, she and her partner will occupy the house and I will move into the cottage at the back."

"It all looks good to me, Mr Robertson. Will I start next Tuesday?"

Maria wandered around the kitchen as she spoke and Roger couldn't help noticing her curvy body in her tight black short skirt and skivvy and stockings.

"Yes, Maria, that would be good. Oh! I should tell you that I mostly work at night, so you might not always see me until late in the morning or even the early afternoon. Because of that, I will give you a key and I will leave your money in the cutlery drawer in an envelope. Now how much should I leave?"

Roger usually worked late on Monday nights, so rising early was not something he ever did on a Tuesday. It was a habit he'd acquired when working as a night watchman to provide a little income while waiting for the first decent royalty payment from his first novel, published two years earlier.

With bedtime usually around 2 or 3 am, nothing could wake him until around ten or eleven, but glancing at his diary late at night, Roger saw that Maria would be coming in to work for the first time the next morning at nine o'clock, so he took the precaution of closing the bedroom door in anticipation of the sounds of the vacuum cleaner and the laundry equipment.

Roger had warned Maria of his sleeping habits but didn't want her feeling that she had to creep around trying not to wake him. And she knew that money had been left for her in an envelope on the kitchen dresser, so it wasn't necessary for him to speak with her before she left at around two o'clock.

With the above arrangements in place, Roger felt secure in falling asleep without any concern for the domestic matters of the day. Oblivion would be easy and he would wake up to a clean house and clean washing. So it was something of a mystery to him later when he awoke and found that he was able to recall an incident that had happened earlier.

Roger could only guess that it had occurred quite early in the morning. He was aware that the bedroom door had opened and someone had come and stood beside the bed, seemingly to look at him in repose. He was not cognisant enough to open his eyes or move in any way, but on reflection he remembered a faint smell of perfume.

The person, whom Roger realised could only be the new home help, had then retreated, closing the door softly as she went.

So what was it that had brought her into the bedroom? Was there something she had considered required his urgent attention but then, on seeing him fast asleep, she changed her mind?

It would remain a minor mystery for now, but it did get Roger thinking that he could not have a home help whom he never saw. It might seem all right to have a magic genie fix the house while he was asleep, but he could see that Maria might have regular questions and enjoy some contact with him.

Roger resolved to set an alarm for ten thirty next Tuesday morning and to make an effort to become a more sociably responsible employer.

The following Monday night, Roger got to bed a little earlier and set the alarm. He would rise and shower and dress and be down for breakfast at around ten forty-five. He would be able to be a sociable person and available for any domestic matters or other things that Maria might like to talk to him about. It would also give him an opportunity to ask questions about the area where he was now living and perhaps learn something about his neighbours.

It would be good for him, he mused. Maria was an attractive woman, and seemed a very likeable person, and also, in his rush into the writing of this new novel, Roger ran the risk of returning to a habit of spending too much time alone.

Certainly, one needed peace and quiet, but equally one benefited from contact with people, however simple these interactions might be.

As interactions go, what happened the next morning was most unexpected. Roger's deep sleep was only slightly disturbed; so slight as to allow him to offer no visible indication that he was awake or aware of what was happening.

His usual happy dream state had morphed into a great physical pleasure when he became aware that his cock was standing to attention and being licked, and that fingers were lightly touching his testicles. And a very faint perfume close by was a clue to who might be doing it.

Roger lay very still, not wanting to break the spell. If this was only a dream, why would he want to interrupt it?

Gentle fingers wrapped themselves around his shaft and moved up slowly until they reached just below the crown, and it was as much as he could do not to quiver or shake as a soft mouth enclosed the top and a tongue slid around below his knob and then went back to the top and lapped at his urethra, likely finding a small night emission.

Roger's head lay to the side pointing in the direction of the door and, also, the enchantress with her head beneath the sheets. He decided to open one eye just a tiny amount to see what might be visible to him.

There, within inches of his face was a large shapely backside sheathed in a tight black skirt, which had pulled itself upward as the wearer had arranged herself on the bed.

Roger had not failed to notice her more than adequate posterior when he had first met Maria, but her beautiful smile and youthful countenance and remarkable shining eyes, not to mention her sufficiently partially uncovered bountiful chest, had probably got to him first. He remembered thinking that this widow must surely have many admirers.

Not wanting to move his head for fear of disturbing her, Roger let his eyes travel as far as they could along her body. Where her skirt ended, the end of a suspender peeped over the smooth white skin of her thigh and clasped the top of a black stocking, which then ran smoothly down her leg to a smallish foot and a low-heeled black shoe.

Suddenly the mouth gave a long but gentle suck as it dragged itself up Roger's shaft and away from his member. Then Maria removed her head from the bed, rolled gently over, got up and left, softly closing the door behind her.

Roger lay without moving, not wanting to lose these recent thoughts and sensations. But then he was forced to wake up to address this extraordinary event, turning it over and over in his still dazed mind.

This amazing woman had had her way with him secretly, or so she thought, and for now Roger would give no hint to his lovely visitor that he knew about it.

A huge clap of thunder interrupted Roger. He was seated at his desk writing, early one Monday afternoon. He watched through the bay window as rain poured down much heavier than he could ever remember seeing it.

His first thoughts were to close windows and check the upstairs rooms and the balconies for leaks or problems with gutters and drains – anywhere that water was meant to escape.

Suddenly, an enormous wind blew across the property and he heard a deafening crack and a thump as part of a large tree blew down somewhere nearby.

As the wind eased, Roger heard the sounds of fire trucks and alarms in the distance. He thought that this must have been an extreme weather event. These were becoming more common around the world as the effects of climate change became more noticeable.

Later, the television news reported that a mini tornado had swept across Sydney and that emergency services where flat out trying to sort out fallen trees and dangerous debris.

• • •

It was Tuesday and Maria had not appeared. Roger rose earlier than usual so that he could inspect the property outside. When he came back in, his phone rang. It was Maria.

"Sorry I'm not there, Mr Robertson. A huge tree crashed onto our house and the whole roof has collapsed along with some of the walls. Things are a bit chaotic as you can imagine. I might not get in until later in the week."

Roger thought how good it was of her to even think to call, given the circumstances.

"Thanks for calling, Maria. I'm so sorry. Don't come in until you've sorted everything. If I can help in any way, don't hesitate to ask. Oh, and Maria? Do you have somewhere to go until the house is repaired?"

"Not yet, Mr Robertson. I have a sister we can go to but she is way down in the south-west of Sydney, too far to travel to work every day."

Roger thought quickly and replied.

"It might not suit you, Maria, but we've got an empty self-contained granny flat here at the back of the property which I would be very happy for you and Serina to use until your place is fixed. It's surprisingly large, three bedrooms but only one bathroom. Think about it and call me."

"Thank you so much Mr Robertson. That is the only bit of good news so far today. I'll talk to Serina and get back to you soon."

Maria had accepted Roger's offer of accommodation, and she had moved her family and things in within a day of the violent storm that had swept across the city.

When the final furniture and essential household stuff had been delivered, along with Maria's daughter Serina and Maria's late husband's elderly father, Alberto, and Maria's boarder, Giorgio, the newly arrived distant relative of Alberto, they accepted Roger's invitation to come over to the house for coffee and cake.

The significance of this new and sudden change of events seemed like a coming together of members of a tribe. Roger smiled as a beaming Alberto tried to correct his attempt at conversational Italian, watched by a bemused Maria and her hauntingly beautiful daughter

Serina, while a totally confused non-English-speaking Giorgio looked around, trying to make sense of all of it.

Knowing that these people were now ensconced in the cottage made Roger very happy.

"Maria! Do feel free to use the kitchen here, if and when any of you need to. You are all welcome to use this house, especially as the cottage is really only designed for a couple. You might find the sitting room handy too. You are welcome to come in day or night to watch the television or play music or read or whatever. And I rarely use the downstairs bathroom, so please use it should you find the cottage facilities inadequate."

Maria thanked him, as did Serina. Roger felt that Serina was watching his every move, almost to the point where he thought he should say something to her, just to break the spell.

"So Serina! What do you do each day to pass away the time? Sorry! I meant to ask of you were working or studying or something?"

Roger felt foolish and Serina continued to stare at him. Then she spoke.

"Well, Mr Robertson, I work as a housekeeper, alone mostly but sometimes with mum. We often get work, catering for parties or events. I manage to keep busy Mr Robertson."

She aimed a disarming smile at Roger.

Roger suddenly realised that he had meant to say something earlier and had forgotten.

"Maria and Serina and Alberto. I would like you to call me Roger from now on. I think we can forget the mister bit. It's not as though we're living in England, is it?"

Roger's unwitting attempt at social levelling and humour met with little reaction.

"Thank you, Roger. From this moment on, we will call you by your first name, except when we forget."

They laughed and Maria eyed her daughter with what Roger thought was a knowing mother-daughter smile.

That night, Roger called Caroline in London. He had thought long and hard about her proposal and before he left for Australia, had accepted Caroline's offer to father her child.

Now they needed to work out a real plan of action. They had already agreed that Caroline would visit Australia for a month fairly soon to visit her parents, Rosa and Bertie, and to have what the two now affectionately referred to as "Margate time" with Roger. In the meantime, Caroline said she had already stopped taking the contraceptive pill and, hopefully, during her visit "the seed would be planted" as Roger would happily transmit to her over the phone in a loud country yokel voice.

"I've told Jackie about us Roger. She was totally surprised and then excited. Looks like you've given your sister a present that was so unexpected, but very welcome. No doubt you will hear from her soon. I asked her not to mention it to any of our friends, at least not until we can announce lift-off. Of course she can and will tell Miranda."

Roger enjoyed listening to Caroline's beautiful voice and felt very confident that, in agreeing to her proposition, he had done the right thing by everyone including himself.

"Well Caroline. I suppose a quick trip to Margate is out of the question, considering the twelve thousand miles that separate us, and telephone sex doesn't do it for me, but I want you to know that I am really looking forward to us being together soon. And Caroline, I'd like to say that I love you. It feels okay to say that."

There was a silence and for a moment Roger thought that they had been disconnected.

"I love you too, Roger. I really think what we are doing is a wonderful thing and I'm so happy that you made it possible. Thank you sweetheart."

They said their farewells and Roger went to his study to write.

Maria's daughter Serina knocked on the study door early one afternoon, just a couple of days after the family had moved into the cottage. Roger called "Come in". He thought that it would be Maria.

"Hello Serina. Nice to see you. Don't know that you've ever been into my writing room. There is not much to see, but what is here does the job. Is this just a social call Serina or was there something you wanted to ask me? Is everything all right in the cottage? That easy chair might be better to sit on. Sitting on the chair opposite me and the desk feels sort of formal, doesn't it?"

Serina took the seat. She was dressed neatly in a skirt and blouse and little shoes. At their first meeting he found her a little unnerving. He figured that she was somewhere in her late twenties or early thirties. He knew that she had been married briefly because Maria had mentioned it.

"I just thought I should ask if everything was all right, Roger?"

Roger noted that the question sort of inferred that things might not be all right. "Why yes, Serina. All is well. I assume you're thinking about your mother and her working here one day a week. If that is the case, yes, all is fine so far as I am aware. Should I be concerned? Have I maybe offended her? What are you thinking, Serina?"

There was a long pause and Serina actually stopped staring at him for the first time and gazed out of the window instead.

"I know she still misses Dad."

Roger relaxed back into his chair, relieved that this was not about him.

"He died nearly four years ago and Mum hasn't shown any interest in any other men since then. They had a strange married life in some ways. Over the last twenty years or so Dad worked night shift, getting home at around 3 am and sleeping until midday. Mum worked at a shipping company cafeteria and left home around 7.30 each morning. They spent very little time together."

Real-life stories were of particular interest to Roger as a writer. They helped provide background and substance to his work, often just in small unrelated ways.

"When I was around fourteen or fifteen, I would often find it difficult to sleep and would wake up and go and get into bed just before dawn, beside Mum. She always felt so warm and reassuring and welcomed her little girl with a hug and a kiss.

"I began waking up most mornings in their bed. Dad never really knew I was there. I would be well and truly gone when he woke up.

"It was then that I discovered something unusual about my

mother. Most times I'd wake up as mum left the bed to go to work. Occasionally, when I felt her body moving, I would become semiconscious and aware of her movements."

"One morning, I was sufficiently awake to notice mum moving in the bed. Usually, when this happened I would just doze off. But this morning I didn't and to my surprise, I discovered that mum was very gently sucking my dad's cock. Then after a short time she simply left the bed and headed off for breakfast and work.

"From then on, I observed her doing this on most mornings. It seemed that my father never knew what was going on and she obviously didn't want to wake him."

Roger stared at her in disbelief. Could this be a clue to what was happening to him, early on Tuesday mornings?

"I worked out that Mum and Dad were almost totally separated by their shift work and so rarely, if ever, had the opportunity to be sexually active. It appeared that mum had discovered a way of satisfying herself, at least partially, and it seemed like it was working for her."

Roger looked closely at Serina. She seemed to be totally absorbed in her story.

"After Dad died, life went on pretty much as usual. I still climbed into Mum's bed in the early mornings and cuddled up to her.

"One morning, only a short time after Mum had left the bed, I remembered I needed to work on something before school, a test or something, so I got up.

"Mum wasn't in the kitchen and I wondered where she was. Then, as I walked barefoot to the bathroom, I noticed that grandpa's bedroom door was open. I glanced in and couldn't believe what I saw. There was Mum with her head moving up and down under the duvet sucking on my sleeping Gramps' cock."

Roger was still staring at Serina, trying to take in all that she was telling him.

"And your grandpa? He didn't wake up either?"

Serina smiled.

"Grandpa usually watches television until late, then reads Italian newspapers, drinking his vino and laughing and calling out things in Italian. "In vino veritas" was his catch phrase. You would never see

Grandpa up and about until late in the mornings; and he slept like a log."

Serena paused, staring out the window and obviously reminiscing.

Roger took advantage of this moment of silence to order his thoughts. Why was Serina telling him all of this? Did she know something about what was happening on Tuesdays? Was she warning him of something he hadn't thought of?

"So Serina? How does this affect me and why are you telling me?"

Serena turned from staring out of the window.

"There is something I haven't told you, Mr Robertson, sorry, Roger. It would seem that what happens when mum starts her day in the early morning, is that she is likely to visit you. She may have already, but you don't know about it. Now that we are living in the cottage and with easy access to your house, I'm thinking that you will almost certainly have an early morning visitor."

Roger was silent. Should he tell Serina that this had already happened? But then he had only discovered it by accident really, and Maria didn't know that he knew. Keeping quiet seemed the better option.

"There is one more thing, Roger. One day, not long after I discovered what Mum was doing to Dad before she left the bed, I put my hand out immediately she'd left and took Dad's cock in my hand. Moments later, I had my mouth over it, doing what Mum did. Then I stopped and ran to my room and masturbated. From then on, it was a regular thing that I did. That early sexual experience remained with me and with Dad gone, I missed it desperately.

"My mother and I now share this sexual affliction, if one can call it that. Living in the cottage right next door to you, Roger, and you sleeping late as you do, it's going to be hard, not just for Mum but for me too, not to visit you early in the mornings."

Roger was in awe of this beautiful young woman. He was also speechless. As he began to formulate a response, Serina rose slowly from her chair.

"Thank you, Roger. I better not keep you from your work any longer. Thanks for listening. I hope I haven't frightened you?"

Serina turned and smiled an appreciative smile.

"You are such an attractive man Roger. Please don't lock your doors at night. Getting through windows is something neither I or my mother are good at."

Serena gave a wicked laugh and smiled.

"Oh yes, there is one other thing, Roger. Mum knows about me just as I know about her. We support each other. We are very happy to either share, or take turns. Thanks, Roger. See you soon."

Serena glided majestically from the room and Roger slumped back in his swivel chair, his thoughts wildly trying to order themselves properly.

One question kept bobbing along in the background. How would Maria or Serina respond if Roger simply woke up and wanted to fuck one or the other? Or both of them?

Over the few weeks leading up to Caroline's arrival in Australia Roger slept peacefully, waking up late each morning as he was accustomed to do, blissfully unaware of what might have happened in his bed earlier. Only once did he wake up when something was happening. As before, the mouth on his cock felt beautiful and he just couldn't resist partly opening one eye.

Beside him Roger could see just a shapely bare leg. There was no perfume and he instinctively knew that Serina was the person lying beside him and he couldn't help but be momentarily excited at the thought of the presence of this beautiful and mysterious young woman.

His cock must have twitched, giving a warning signal that he could be about to wake up. The licking and gentle sucking ceased and he was suddenly alone.

4

HELEN'S LOVING WORLD

HELEN AND FREDERICO ALVES had welcomed the news about the new owners of Numbers 19 and 21 in Eros Crescent. They had both met Rosa Bennett's friend Maude, the new owner of Number 19, quite often over the years when visiting the Bennetts house. They knew that Maude was a music teacher with an established reputation. They also knew that she had been Rosa's lady lover for many years and that their good friend Bertie, Rosa's husband, was comfortable with that. They were very close to both of them and for that reason never asked questions that might be rightly regarded as prying.

Details about the new owner of Number 21 were not available at this point. Sufficient to say, a mutual friend of the Alveses was also a friend of the solicitor who handled the will of the deceased owner, and word had it that there were two owners, a brother and a stepsister. Both lived in London but were expected to return and take up residence in the house some time in the future.

Number 21 was a large house on a large block of land and the last residence in the crescent. It also had a small dwelling at the back, originally designed for a married couple in service when the original owners had kept a cook and a gardener.

. . .

Since Helen's first visit to her new friend Celia Ashbee, the two had not had an opportunity to meet again, though not for want of any lack of desire to renew their newly forged romantic alliance. Both women had reasons to travel away and their presence in Sydney seemed never to coincide because of their busy lives. Now the two women were finally getting to meet again, and again it would be at Celia's house.

It was the middle of February and the Australian summer was merciless in its heat and dryness. Helen had selected a bright floral summer frock and her favourite sandals for her visit. There was no place for heels and stockings in this weather.

Helen had already left home to make an early call on Rosa at the hospital before moving on to Celia's house. It was only after walking from the hospital that she got a message from Celia saying that she had been called away for a short time and would be a couple of hours late getting back to the house. She suggested that Helen delay her visit or, if she was already on her way, continue and perhaps enjoy the pool at Celia's house.

Helen thought about it and decided that it wasn't worth returning home and, as there was nothing else for her to do, she would head to Celia's place. The pool idea sounded great, although it had not occurred to her to bring her bathing togs. She reasoned that she might be able to borrow a pair from Celia.

As she knocked on the door, Helen was suddenly reminded of her last visit, particularly the moment when they were saying their farewells to each other. During Helen's visit Polly, the beautiful young maid, had acted in a very unfriendly manner towards Helen and when Helen mentioned it gently to Celia, Celia had replied: 'Poppy is wonderful and I love her dearly, but I realise now that she has become a tiny bit possessive, so I should do something about that.

Her petulance might give me a good excuse to introduce her to a little discipline. Now you and I have become lovers, I will gently lead her to the idea of us sharing ourselves with you. I'm pretty sure that when you visit next time, you will have two people waiting with their lips puckered up and yearning for you.'

Before Helen could finish thinking about this, the door opened and the beautiful Polly stood in front of her in a simple floral-halter neck dress and sandals.

"Hello Mrs Alves. So nice to see you again. Do please come in. You know that Mrs Ashbee will be a little late, but she hoped you would find something to occupy yourself with until she arrives."

Helen stepped forward out of the bright sunlight into the darkness of the vestibule and, as she did so, Polly wrapped her arms around her, put her mouth on hers and kissed her in a way much more than cursory but not long-lasting.

"Oh Polly, what a dear young woman you are. I so appreciated that kiss. It's the first I've had from a woman in many weeks."

Helen thought that lying in this instance would do more good than bad, giving the girl confidence that she was indeed special. As her eyes grew accustomed to the shadows, she thought that Polly seemed to be blushing, but she couldn't be sure that it wasn't just the hot weather.

"My word, it's cooler in here. Thank goodness for air conditioning."

Polly led Helen to the big lounge room. Helen immediately recalled her seduction by Celia and, later, their cavorting and mutual spanking on the foot stool near the piano.

"This is such a lovely room, Polly. And I have fond memories of it, as I'm sure you would too."

"Can I get you a cold drink, Mrs Alves? We have a lovely fresh lemon and ginger drink."

"That would be lovely, Polly. Oh and bring a glass for yourself. But before you go …"

Polly turned and took a quick step towards Helen, her eyes bright and questioning. "Yes, Mrs Alves?"

"Polly, I think you had better get used to calling me Helen when the two of us are alone together. "Mrs Alves" sounds a bit too formal for most situations. Is that all right with you?"

"Oh yes, Mrs Alves, I mean Helen. I would like that. And Helen, please feel free to relax and enjoy the place as you would if Mrs Ashbee were here."

Helen observed the excitement on Polly's face and concluded that

Celia had indeed presented the idea of sharing her with the two of them, and sharing was now firmly impressed on the young maid. In fact, if Helen wasn't mistaken, young Polly was very keen to begin sharing.

When Polly returned with the drinks, Helen had already made herself comfortable on the large sofa. She had picked up and was thumbing through a magazine when Polly returned.

"Mrs Ashbee phoned again. She said she is dreadfully sorry, but she won't get home now until just after three o'clock. I said you were here and she suggested you might like to wait for her but she would understand if you left and made another time. It is around midday now, Helen."

"Hmm, not sure what to do, Polly. Stay or go and come back another time?"

"Well, if you stayed, Helen we – I mean you – could spend some time in the pool. I could make some lunch and you could just relax."

Helen watched Polly closely. She seemed a little agitated.

"And if you stayed, we could get to know each other better."

Polly's voice tailed off to a whisper and she definitely blushed. Helen was excited at seeing her trying not to show her enthusiasm for some sort of encounter. The dear girl was definitely "hormonally charged" as the magazines liked to label sexual urges.

"Well, you make staying sound good, Polly. And I can't think of nicer company than you. But I didn't bring bathers so, if it doesn't bother you, I will have to skinny dip or swim in my panties."

Polly's face reddened even more.

"Oh, that would be just fine, Helen. Nobody can see the pool area from outside the property."

"You will of course come in with me, won't you, Polly. It's not much fun on your own."

"Whatever you say Helen," replied the girl, nervously clearing her throat and reaching for a drink.

Helen reasoned that is was time to put Polly out of her misery or rather reduce the poor girls hormonal fuelled tension.

"Polly?"

"Yes, Helen?"

"Before we go to the pool, would you come and sit beside me and let me kiss you? Your lips were so soft on my mouth when you kissed me at the door, I haven't been able to get over it. Please, Polly. Come here and kiss me."

Polly stood up from her chair staring at Helen and, as if in a trance, stepped over to the sofa, where Helen took her hand and gently pulled her down beside her. Then Helen put her hand behind Polly's head and brought it up close to her face, all the while staring into Polly's beautiful grey eyes.

Helen wrapped her arms around Polly's upper body and drew her close while opening her mouth and pressing it against Polly's pretty lips. Polly let out a tiny groan and melted into Helen, opening her mouth and pushing out her tongue and slowly moving it around inside Helen's mouth. Helen pulled the girl even closer, and at the same time, nestled the two of them down into the soft sofa, where they stayed for a long time, kissing and touching and holding each other very close.

When Helen had filled herself up with kissing and cuddling, she announced softly that she wanted Polly to put her hand up her frock and take off her panties.

Polly murmured a little sound and pushed her soft lips even harder on Helen's mouth. Then she turned and looked down at Helen's knees and reached out to touch them and lifted the hem of her dress. Her fingers wandered up Helen's legs which opened just enough that Polly could touch Helen's sex behind the front of her wet panties. Helen lifted herself from the sofa and Polly drew the panties down over Helen's feet.

"Now finger my pussy, you darling girl while I touch your breasts and kiss your neck."

Polly was breathing deeply and she uttered sounds that told Helen the young woman was already in a rapturous state, as indeed she knew was happening to herself. Kissing and making love slowly was the progenitor of anticipation, and anticipation rivalled orgasm as the peak of sensuous feeling.

Helen bent Polly's head forward so that she could slip the neck strap over the girl's head and let her frock fall down around her waist, exposing her small breasts to her appreciative gaze and her softly groping fingertips. Polly shuddered when Helen lightly pinched the young woman's nipple, causing Helen to enjoy a tremor in her vulva, where Polly's fingers were massaging and entering the wet special place.

Helen was now on fire and crazily wanting more of this beautiful young woman. Helen's anticipation levels were so high, she couldn't bear the thought of letting go of Polly right at this moment. Then, as if from nowhere, Helen saw her late teenage self making love with her first real lover, Miss Louise Lazarus, and immediately knew what she wanted.

At that time her small hands had become a means of pleasuring Miss Lazarus in a special way; so much so that soon her lady lover could not long do without it. On a Sunday morning, the normally severe Louise would look at the young Helen with a soft dreamy smile and say, "Please give me your hand, my pet. I'll give you whatever you want afterwards." Now it was Helen's turn to enjoy that thing that Louise had taught her to do.

"Polly?"

"Yes, Helen?"

"Reach over and get the lubricant from that cupboard beside you, sweetheart. We are going to need it."

Polly tried to read what the purpose might be on Helen's face, but then turned and fetched a bottle from the side cupboard.

"Now I want you to cover your right hand with lubricant, Polly."

"Yes, Helen."

"Now put three fingers into me and move them around inside to stretch me a little."

Helen watched as Polly did what she was told.

"Now put your other fingers in as well, and push them right up into me."

Helen looked lovingly into Polly's face, feeling the sweet young thing's hand inside her.

"Don't be scared. Now slowly move your fingers up into me. Just move them gently and keep on going. And give me your mouth. I can't live without your beautiful mouth, darling."

Polly looked at Helen with wide eyes, then down to where her hand had disappeared into Helen's vulva. She looked back up at Helen.

"Am I doing it right, Helen?"

"Yes, your hand feels wonderful. Now I want you to slowly make a fist of your hand, then just keep going up into me slowly. And kiss me Polly please, now."

Polly stopped looking at Helen's crotch, leant forward and pushed her mouth on Helen's and immediately two tongues swam around in their excited mouths.

Helen's eyes were closed and she moaned as she pulled Polly closer to her.

"Keep going up into me. I'll tell you when to stop."

While Helen spoke, Polly took a quick look at her arm. She couldn't believe how far in it had gone.

"Keep going."

Helen felt Polly's hand touch her womb.

"Yes, yes, Polly. You are there, darling. Just rest for a moment while I feel your beautiful hand in me."

Polly was in awe of what she was doing. She was in Helen's pussy so far with her arm that it was getting close to her elbow. Then Polly felt the first tiny spasm from Helen as she came and for a moment it felt as though her arm was being sucked in even further and then Polly orgasmed too, letting out a tiny scream.

"Oh, Helen you are so beautiful. I love doing this to you."

Helen's face was contorted and she looked at Polly as though she was looking right through her. In a tiny voice, Helen asked Polly to twist her fist very slightly to the left and then back again.

Polly did what she was asked and Helen let out a mighty scream and orgasmed. Polly screamed too and opened her legs wide then slapped them shut again and shuddered.

"Oh God, Helen, I've never felt like this before. I'm so in love with this. Tell me you love it too Helen."

It was as though Helen was asleep with her eyes open, staring into space without seeing. She mumbled something like "I love you, Polly. Please don't stop, Polly".

Polly felt that she should take the initiative. This beautiful older women seemed almost out of it. She was away somewhere else.

Then she decided to take the lead. She ever so lightly twisted her hand back to where it had been before and paused, and then twisted it to the right. Before she had finished, Helen exploded once again and the two of them orgasmed in unison.

It was probably at this moment that Polly, without knowing it, lost her passive, compliant little-girl attitude. Until this point she had happily accepted the role of Celia Ashby's submissive sex slave. She had basked in the pleasure of her mistress and her own accompanying orgasms. Now, for the first time, she felt that she was in charge. She was able to be the provider of the most intimate pleasure to any lover.

Polly twisted her hand inside Helen yet again and Helen screamed and they both came yet again.

When Polly eventually stopped pleasuring Helen, slowly removing her arm and hand from Helen's now limp body, the two women lay down on the sofa, their arms around each other. And when the telephone rang, Polly answered "Miss Ashbee's residence. Yes, Miss Ashbee, yes, okay. I'll tell Helen. She's asleep at the moment," Helen didn't move.

Polly brought a blanket from a cupboard nearby and covered Helen then went out onto the patio beside the pool and lay on a banana lounge in the bright warm sunlight. She closed her eyes and visualised her arm engulfed in the body of her new love, and smiled. Then she turned to let the sun shine on her pussy while her fingers found her clitoris and, while reviewing the vivid images still in her mind, she made herself come once and then a second time.

Helen jumped up from her deep sleep in a panic and looked around. She expected to see Celia or Polly, but neither was in sight and she couldn't hear anyone. She remembered what had happened and a tiny thrill ran through her, but then immediately she wondered what would be said when the mistress of the house got home and found her asleep on the sofa. Why hadn't anyone woken her up?

"Celia won't be home until after six o'clock," came a gentle voice from somewhere outside the french doors leading to the pool. "She rang and apologised and said she would call you tomorrow. I said you were asleep and that I would tell you when you woke up."

Helen shook her head wildly, trying to shake her brain and her hair into some sort of order. Then she smoothed her dress with her hands, trying to look less dishevelled, and walked out into the afternoon sunlight. Polly lay on the poolside lounge beneath a beach towel, wearing sunglasses and a straw hat.

"I'm sorry that I'll miss her. No doubt she will make another date for quite soon." Helen walked to the edge and dipped her hand in the water and splashed her face. There was silence but for the sound of doves in the big pine tree near the fence.

"I'm not sorry that you will miss her."

Polly hadn't moved since Helen arrived.

Helen was silent. She was trying to fathom what Polly meant.

"I don't want to share you with Celia."

Again Helen remained silent. Did Polly see her as a threat, a rival for Celia's affections?

"Polly, Celia loves you very much. She has told me so. There is no way that I could ever replace you in her affections. She's totally into you, so stop worrying about sharing her with me. To Celia, I am simply a friend with benefits. I think that's the correct modern description. Besides, I am totally in love with my husband Frederico, and I have a female friend whom I adore."

Helen turned and faced Polly's stretched out body.

"And now you have me, Helen," said Polly. "I'm in love with you and you won't be able to give me up. I won't let you."

Helen stared at the super gorgeous young thing declaring her love. Casually, Helen reached over and slid Polly's towel from her body. Then she lightly ran her fingers all the way down from Polly's breasts to her her toes and watched the girl involuntarily arch her back.

"I don't want to give you up Polly. I'm in love with you too."

"But how will we see each other? I don't want to only see you here with Celia. I want to have you for my very own." Polly's gasping voice was very clear and almost strident.

"You work here three or four days a week. Is that right? What do you do on the other days?"

"I'm studying at university. I work from home some of the time and I'm at classes a couple of days."

"So can we meet up? At my place, perhaps? I have the house to myself most weekdays and some weekends."

Polly's voice changed. She had sat up and removed her glasses and was suddenly more animated.

"Oh yes! I would love to do that, Helen. And even though I live at home with my mother she is often away on business, sometimes for a whole week, and I have the place to myself."

"There! Sorted already! We will be together exactly as we want to. Now, if there is any problem it is only our relationship with Celia that needs thinking through. I can never be dishonest with her and so I will have to think about what I am to say and do. By the way, Polly, I don't even know what you are studying. In fact, I know nothing about you. What you do in your spare time, for instance?"

Polly laughed. "I'm into horses, and animals generally, and for that reason I'm hoping to become a vet. I go riding with a girlfriend most weekends when I'm not volunteering at a local animal welfare centre. I sometimes socialise with Mum and her friends. There is always something going on, usually involving pool parties with her workmates or clients."

"Great! Now I know a lot more about you. But what about boys? Do you have a boyfriend?"

Again Polly laughed.

"You can imagine that, since working here, I have become a little more worldly, or should we say sexually aware. I do like some boys and older men that I meet and I do have thoughts about some of them. I haven't yet had a cock in me though. Truth is, I prefer girls."

Helen was fascinated to hear about Polly's other life and felt slightly guilty that she hadn't taken more interest in that side of things. But then she told herself that they had only just discovered each other and their intimacy so far had been exclusively about making love.

"So Polly? Do you have a special girlfriend that you can be intimate with? It sounds as though you need one."

"Belinda, my horse-riding friend started kissing me a lot and we used to cuddle up in the feed room at the stables. I got quite turned on by her. We would put our hands inside each other's shirts to touch each other's breasts while kissing and sucking each other's tongues."

Helen was intrigued. "And are you still lovers, Polly? Should I worry that you are going to ride off into the sunset with Belinda?"

Polly screamed with laughter.

"Not going to happen Helen. The stablehand got to her. She said he has a big cock just like some of the geldings get when they are brushed and very relaxed, and she wants to settle down with him and make babies.

"Belinda sometimes grabs me and sticks her tongue in my mouth and mumbles something about missing me, but that's it. I don't do anything back to her. Since being with Celia I've changed, and I don't go looking for new experiences."

Polly smiled and suddenly blushed.

"Well, that is not quite true, Helen, is it?"

Helen put her head back and laughed out loud.

"No, it's not, young lady! Thank God."

Watching Polly blushing was a turn on for Helen and she secretly looked forward to seeing her sweet new love blush more often.

"People can love more than one person, Polly. The intensity of their feelings might be different for each of the lovers in their lives. There is a woman friend of mine whom I love most dearly but in all our time as friends we have never laid a finger on each other.

"At the other end of the scale, the sexual excitement with a lover can be overwhelming and lead us into treacherous territory and eventually to unhappiness. This happened to me when I was your age and it affected me for a long time afterwards. Finding the balance is the key to our sexual happiness."

There was silence while they pondered the questions that life was currently serving up to them.

Polly had sat up and removed her glasses.

"What will I do, Helen? I want to be important to you. How will I deal with these feelings, this jealousy?"

"Polly, dearest, today you made love to me in a special way that I have not experienced with anyone. I won't let you go either."

Polly stood up and took off her hat. She came and sat beside Helen and rested her head on Helen's shoulder and sobbed. Helen waited a little while, then lifted Polly's head and kissed her gently. She then returned the girl to her shoulder and took both her hands.

"We lit a fire today and we mustn't let it get out of control and burn us. Each of us must control the feelings that can result in jealousy. It is such a destructive force.

"Seen from my point of view, you being such a beautiful young woman must result in your having many suitors – both men and women – which means that I must accept that I will one day lose you to a man and babies, or a younger woman who sweeps you off your feet.

"If we can plan our lives, things can be so much more enjoyable.

"Just so you know where I am at this moment, even though I'm very much in love with you, I'm thinking ahead. In particular I'm thinking of Freddy and Alice. If you were to like them and they liked you, then could you cope with being shared between us? It doesn't have to be a choice between you and them, but rather it would be about loving ourselves and others."

Silence prevailed. The sun sank further and the air turned cool. The two women went back into the house.

"Do Freddy and Alice know about you and Celia?"

Polly was hungry for information and Helen chose her words carefully.

"Yes, they are a little bemused and watching my movements with interest. I keep them informed simply by telling them that I like someone and it's early days. This doesn't happen very often, so I don't want you thinking silly things about me. Oh yes, and I always offer to share any new love, but so far it hasn't happened. I and the other two are very moral, good people. They both know that most of my early life was spent with women and darling Freddy understands my need for female company. He is also a wonderful lover. I so want you to meet both of them."

Polly looked up at Helen. Her eyes were dry and the sparkle had returned.

"What happens now?"

"You sexy little bitch. Kiss me like you love me, right now."

Polly's eyes lit up even more and she smiled for the first time and pushed Helen down onto the carpet and jumped on top of her, kissing her and grinding her belly against hers. Helen ran her hand up inside Polly's legs and fingered her.

In a few moments, they both shuddered and collapsed, cuddling and kissing and murmuring "I love you."

It was the day before Helen and Mary would meet in Helen's studio for their monthly "quality time" as Mary called it. Helen was restless and she wasn't sure why.

She had taken on a new lover, the very young Polly who, under instruction, had made Helen very happy. She thought that she should do more with some of the women she loved. She was the experienced, imaginative one, the initiator – the woman who would dream up things to add to everyone's pleasure as well as her own.

As Helen thought about her meeting with Mary the following day, she realised that there was something she wanted to do with Mary, which she believed could benefit all her lovers.

She telephoned Mary.

"Hi Mary! It's me. No, I'm not ringing to cancel. Of course I want to see you, you silly thing. No! What I wanted to do was to put you on notice that I've decided to ask you to do something different tomorrow, but I'm too embarrassed to tell you what it is. We've never discussed it before. No, I can't tell you now either. Just wanted you to be forewarned that your lady lover might be kinkier than you thought. That's all. No! I'm not giving you a clue. No! I'm hanging up. Love you and see you tomorrow."

Helen smiled inwardly and thought how her loving husband Freddy might well get a present out of this, if it all worked out.

. . .

Mary was already at the studio when Helen got there. They both kissed and embraced each other.

"Are you going to tell me what this special thing, is or do I have to chase you around the room with your little flagellator up there on the wall. It's 'tell Mary' time."

Helen hugged and squeezed her large lover and sat her down beside her on the bed.

"Well, it's like this, Mary. There is something I like done to me that I find particularly exciting. My darling Freddy understands and happily gives it to me pretty regularly, and that is wonderful, but I'm a bit greedy and I would like to have more of it. I haven't known how to ask you for it, Mary, fearing you might think badly of me."

Mary stared at Helen wide-eyed, all the while clutching Helen's hands.

"Darling, what is it you want from me? You know I'll do anything you ask."

Helen took a deep breath.

"I want you to bugger me, Mary. Shag my bottom. I've bought a smaller strap on dildo designed just for that purpose. Anal sex is something I crave, Mary. There! I've said it."

Mary's jaw dropped. She was speechless. What Helen had just said was taking her a few moments to process.

"Say something Mary. Put me out of my misery."

"Helen. This might surprise you and I've never told anyone until now, but I've always wanted to try it but never knew how to go about getting started.

"A woman where I worked before I was married talked about it one day. She was very good-looking and looking back now, I think I probably had a crush on her but didn't know it. We lived quite close to each other and would catch the bus home together.

"Linda was her name. She told me that her new boyfriend was giving it to her every which way and when I asked her how many ways there were, she laughed and pointed to her mouth, between her legs and then, half turning, she pointed to her bum.

"When I asked which one she enjoyed the most, she giggled and pointed down behind her. Ever since that moment I've wondered about it and longed for a chance to try it, but the opportunity has never arisen.

"Helen, after all these years you might make that wish come true. If I work out how to do it to you, Helen, would you please be so good as to try and do it to me afterwards? I'll try not to make a fuss and if it's not for me at least I'll know I've had a try."

Now it was Helen who was speechless. Mary's answer had been totally unexpected.

"I am so surprised, Mary. I never dreamt that you even suspected that people did such things. I misjudged you entirely. You have made me so happy, I feel like crying. My dear Mary is going to liberate us both. I'm so excited."

Mary looked at Helen lovingly. "Tell me what we do next, Helen. I'm ready when you are."

Helen laughed. "I guess we simply do our usual loving sexy things, darling. Once we are warmed up, I will open up my back door for you and, hopefully my bottom will seduce you and revel in your loving attention."

"Oh, Helen? You make it sound sexy just by talking about it."

Mary fell backwards onto the bed, dragging Helen on top of her. Then she ran her hand down Helen's back and pulled her skirt up. She slid her hand into Helen's panties and ran her fingers down the crack of her bottom, lightly touching and resting on her tiny wrinkled orifice murmuring, "you are going to be mine, all mine."

Helen giggled. "Oh Mary. You are a dream come true."

Helen interrupted their passionate kissing and grinding of each other's bodies against each other and announced to Mary that she was ready.

Then she reached under a pillow and handed Mary a bottle of lubricating oil. From the drawer beside the bed she produced a small pink strap-on dildo. She licked the end of it provocatively as Mary watched. Then Mary took hold of it as Helen was still mouthing it and moved it gently in and out of Helen's mouth before taking it and putting it in her own mouth.

Helen smiled lovingly at Mary with that special pleading come-hither look as she watched Mary attached the dildo to her waist. Helen then rolled over, and pushed herself up onto her knees, pushed her bottom upwards, swaying slowly from side to side.

"I'm ready, my love. Come and bugger your lover. I want to feel you heaving up and down on my bottom, you sexy bitch. Please pour in some lube and get your legs between mine, right now."

In seconds, Mary had squeezed lubricant into Helen's anus and onto the dildo. Then she slipped in a finger and wriggled it about.

"Oh, Helen? This is so exciting."

Mary positioned herself between her lover's beautiful legs up close to her now wet perfumed rear and gently slid the slippery dildo into her pink, glistening and pulsating love hole.

"Yes, Mary! Yes, you darling! I can feel it and it is wonderful. Shag me my sweet. I might make a noise and call you names as you get going but don't worry. It's because I'm in heaven."

Mary groaned appreciatively. "I'm already calling you a randy bitch, Helen. And I couldn't be more randy myself."

"Just fuck me, you big beautiful slut. Give it to me now, hard. Oh! Oh! Yes, you are such a slut, Mary. You've never had me like this before, have you, you slut? You are very naughty. This poor bottom will never be safe from you again. You will want it again won't you Mary. You do like it, don't you sweetheart. Say you like it."

Mary's heaving buttocks increased momentum.

"Yes, I love it. I've orgasmed once already just from starting to fuck you, you dirty little whore. How could I not want to push you over and get into your bum? Of course I will want to do this; for ever, Helen."

Helen was now making gurgling noises as she murmured "Yes, Yes, Oh yes! Harder you beautiful bitch. Oh yes, Mary! You can fuck me like this any time you want to. Oh my God! You feel so good, you sleazy slut. I love you, you randy bum-fucker. Just don't stop. Don't stop. I'm coming, I'm coming. Yes, Yes, Aah!"

Helen and Mary lay side by side holding hands and catching their breath after their lengthy first anal session.

"You are so good at this, Mary."

The two women laughed.

"I must have a natural talent then, Helen. I hope it works both ways. I'm a little bit nervous about my first lesson. You must be patient with me, darling. Can old bitches learn new tricks? You know what they say."

They both laughed. Then Helen slid her hand under her lover's very large backside and touched her bottom hole with an oily finger. Then she gently slid it in and slowly moved it about.

"You will be fine, darling. And if you don't like it the first time, we can always try little sessions occasionally, just for my sake. My thrills come first of course, you naughty girl."

On Helen's instructions, Mary rolled over and got up onto her knees. Helen slipped a fresh condom onto the dildo and strapped it on and positioned herself between Mary's legs, surveying her lover's magnificent backside. Then with a hand on each buttock, she moved them apart so that she could see her target. She dribbled oil on to Mary's anus and then slipped in an index finger. Mary gave a little start and took a sharp intake of breath in anticipation of what was to follow.

Helen moved her finger slowly round and round in Mary's bottom and then, when there had been no suggestion of discomfort from Mary, she oiled the dildo and slipped the first inch or two into the place for which it was intended. Then she pushed it in further and began to move backwards and forwards.

Helen loved the feeling of Mary's soft buttock cheeks flapping against the lower part of her belly and the wet, smelly pussy hair of both women rubbing together reminded her of the intense orgasm she had experienced when Mary pushed in hard in those last moments.

"I'm going to push it right in now, Mary. Hope you're comfortable with that my darling?"

"Very comfortable," came the reply.

"And then I'm going to shag you good and proper, you voluptuous whore."

"Be my guest, slut slave. I'm loving it so far. Don't hold back

Helen. I'm into it already. It feels great. I'm just waiting for my arse-fucking slut to get into it properly and stop worrying about me."

Helen slapped a buttock to let Mary know who was boss.

"Oh! Oh! Yes, all right! I'm ready for anything. Forget about me. Just do what you want with that pink prick thing."

Helen began a serious shagging of Mary's delightful backside, and as she did so the idea ran through her head that, if Mary really did enjoy this, it would be a wonderful present for both Freddy and Mary should the opportunity arise.

Helen experimented. Sometimes she climbed up higher and pushed downwards and at other times she moved down and pushed up. Mary seemed to respond more excitedly when Helen pushed down and Helen settled on that as their preferred movement.

Helen was now forgetting about Mary, concentrating instead on her own needs. She started by biting Mary's shoulders. Then she slid a hand underneath the two of them and fondled Mary's pussy. "Oh God! Yes, please my love!" Mary gasped.

It was not long before Mary screamed.

"Oh God! Yes, Yes, Yes!"

Then Helen joined in Mary's orgasm with a giant one of her own.

Mary buckled and lay on her stomach. But Helen wasn't finished yet.

"No, slut. You can't get away that easily".

Now that Mary was lying flat, she changed hands on Mary's clit and spread the fingers on her other hand around the back of Mary's neck and squeezed it tight, pushing her face down forcefully into the bed. At the same time, she pushed the pink prick especially hard into Mary's arse. Mary screamed.

"You fucking slut? Oh, God, Yes, Yes! Oh God! Yes, my bum and pussy belong to you, Helen. Oh my God! Fuck me, fuck me, oh yes. You're fucking me silly, Helen."

Helen fell to one side, pulled Mary's face around to hers and pushed her tongue into Mary's mouth, wildly rubbing her own clitoris at the same time. Then Helen screamed "Mary! Yes!" as she came, pulling Mary on top of her. They pushed their saturated pussies against each other and both women came again amid screams of passion and delight.

For these two lovers, bottom play was now firmly on the agenda.

It was only a few days after Helen became Poppy's lover when Celia Ashbee called to make another day and time for the two to get together. Her voice sounded normal enough and Helen wondered if she knew about her and Polly. Then Celia mentioned it.

"Darling, I know about Polly's strong feelings for you and I just want you to know that I am happy for her and for you. It's to be expected that young things will come and go in one's life as they mature and discover the world.

"After she confessed her feelings for you, I assured her that I still loved her and you very much and was happy for both of you. She broke down and cried, then immediately perked up and demanded a cuddle in the sitting room.

"I don't need to tell you that the remorseful but unrepentant girl did her utmost to make me happy, and she certainly did. So I should probably thank you for that, darling."

"Now, about us getting together, Helen? Given the new situation with you and Polly, I thought it only proper that you and I get together on one of her days off, so I'm suggesting you come over next Thursday or Friday. Either day suits. What do you think?"

Helen was excited and relieved to discover that her relationship with Polly was out in the open. This was great news.

"Thanks for being so understanding, Celia. I appreciate it. I know that she loves you too and I can only think that Polly's ability to share is all down to your training.

"Thursday will suit me fine. I hope Miss Ashbee will be as pleased to greet her little Helen as little Helen will be to be asked to sit on her knee."

There was much laughter from the other end.

"You're making me wet already little girl. Miss Ashbee will definitely be waiting. See you around ten-thirty. And if you are a minute late my dear, she will no doubt want to punish you."

It was Helen's turn to laugh out loud. Then speaking in her exaggerated schoolgirl voice, she said, "Oh Miss Ashbee. Please, please don't punish me. I'll try not to be late."

Little Helen was indeed late arriving at Celia's house, on purpose of course. Celia opened the door and the two women immediately fell into each others arms, mutually groping and tongue-sucking and looking longingly at each others faces, legs and feet. Then Celia spun Helen around, pinned her against the wall and slammed her abdomen against Helen's backside.

"I told you not to be late and you are. Come with me now. Miss Ashbee is waiting for you and she is not happy."

Celia took Helen by the hand and dragged her to the sitting room and closed the door. Then she dragged off Helen's top and skirt, handling her roughly, and within minutes Helen found herself lying over the piano stool pleading for forgiveness. Then Miss Ashbee inflicted her disciplinary hands on Helen's naked backside and Helen's screams drowned out any other household sounds.

Unknown to the two women inside the room, someone had an ear to the door. Aurora stood and listened to Helen's final screams of "Yes! Yes!" as she palmed her pussy in anticipation.

It was Aurora's monthly pasta-cooking day and she had stuffed her large knickers with sweet-smelling herbs. But there was something else that Aurora definitely wanted to sniff.

It was not long before Celia and Helen had fulfilled themselves and were reclining on the sofa, happily holding hands. Celia announced that it was tea and cake time.

"Do we serve ourselves as Polly isn't here?"

"No, darling. It's Aurora's pasta day today and she said earlier that she would be more than happy to serve my guest."

Celia went and pulled on the thick cord that hung from the ceiling. She pulled it three times, which she explained was the code for the request for cake and tea. Helen watched the beautiful woman walk across the room in her underwear and knew that this little Helen hadn't finished with her teacher yet.

Celia came back and slipped on her skirt and top.

"Pop your dress back on, darling. We don't want to confuse the staff do we?"

With both women looking gorgeous and very proper, Helen wondered about Aurora.

Was Celia's story about her true? Did she really have a beard of black hair between her legs and a giant clitoris? Maybe Celia was making up stories, including the one about her previous maid and the gardener. Now that Helen thought about it, it did all seem rather bizarre. And Celia was a great storyteller.

There was a knock at the door, then it opened and Aurora entered. She came across the room and placed a tray of cakes, a teapot and cups and saucers on the low table at the end of the sofa.

"Thank you, Aurora. Aurora, this is my friend Helen. Helen! This is Aurora whom I'm sure I've told you about."

Helen looked up at the strong and beautiful Italian woman. She was impressive to say the least. One would have to say that she was large in every respect, but everything was in proportion and Helen was reminded of the voluminous women often depicted in paintings by great artists.

Aurora's eyes sparkled and her aquiline nose and high cheekbones gave her face a classical beauty. Her skin colouring was a beautiful dusty tan, and the dark shadows around her eyes added to their intensity.

"Aurora! I'm so pleased to meet you. I've wanted to meet you since Celia first told me about you."

Celia beamed up at the large woman.

"Do you have time to join us for a little while? I so want to share you with my guest."

Aurora smiled and said she could and seated herself in a big chair close by. Sitting down pulled her tight black skirt even tighter, showing her large legs and a magical, sensual view of the dusky flesh peeping above the tops of her stockings.

Helen moved herself about on the sofa and crossed her legs,

offering a similar view to her lady friends. She already felt randy from the spanking Celia had given her. Helen noticed a strong smell of herbs in the room. She felt a new wetness spreading through the crotch of her panties and a wonderful feeling of anticipation.

"Aurora, my love. Can I show my friend what you have hidden between your legs? When I described you to Helen, she was very excited. Would you stand up and come closer and lift up your skirt?"

Aurora offered an all-knowing smile.

"She looks like she would enjoy more than just a look, Miss Ashbee. I'll take off my skirt. That will make it easier."

Aurora stood up and unzipped her skirt and let it drop to the floor then stepped out of it. She was wearing black silk underpants. She stepped forward and stood in front of Celia.

"Do what you always do to me, Miss Ashbee. You know how much I enjoy it."

Then she looked at Helen.

"Feel free to help her, Helen. I would like that too."

Without another word being spoken, Celia reached forward and dragged Aurora's silk pants down over her ankles. Aurora stepped out of them and moved forward to stand between Celia's legs, which were already wide apart.

Helen gasped.

"Oh my God, Aurora, you are so beautiful."

As she spoke, she moved off the sofa, dropped to her knees and knelt beside Aurora's lovely legs. The smell of herbs was wonderful and she could smell something else, something familiar, the warm sweet smell of Aurora's sex. Celia reached for Helen's hand and lifted it up to touch Aurora between her legs. Helen gasped.

In this giant tangle of black curly hair, an unusually large bright red clitoris appeared and stood out, looking for a loving pair of lips.

Celia leant across, lifted Helen's face, leant forward and kissed her.

"Aurora and I want you to share this special gift Helen. Put it in your mouth, darling, and suck it. Aurora will love you for it."

Helen looked up at Aurora's smiling face.

"Can I show you my breasts too?"

"Yes, Aurora, we want to see all of you, including your delicious backside," whispered Celia.

Helen stared upwards with her mouth open and her lips about to spread themselves around Aurora's clitoris.

Aurora had unbuttoned her top and thrown it on the floor behind her. Then she unbuckled the fastener on her bra and threw it away also.

Helen's world was turning upside down with excitement. Aurora's clitoris was pulsating in her mouth like a little penis looking for attention. Above her, Aurora's huge chest stood out firm and rounded and two giant orbs offering two very large stiff nipples were also begging for attention.

Celia saw that things should change and asked Aurora if she would kindly lie down on the carpet so that both of them could better get at all of her charms.

"But first, dearest woman, just turn and show us your beautiful backside."

Helen let go of Aurora and moved back as Aurora pirouetted to display her giant buttocks. She knelt down and wiggled her bottom at the other women, provocatively. Then she rolled over on her back, and two excited randy women collapsed on top of her. Within moments Celia was gurgling on giant stiff nipples and Helen's mouth was back, sucking and slurping on Aurora's enormous clitoris.

Now it was Aurora's turn to have what she wanted. Two beautiful wet sweet-smelling cunts, one in each hand, to do with as she wished.

Only Serge, Aurora's husband, could raise so much excitement in her at this moment. When he first came home from work each afternoon, and once he had showered and then removed Aurora's knickers and presented his hard robust cock to her, she knew exactly what to do for her husband.

First she would suck it. Then, with the addition of a little olive oil, she would lead his big cock to her welcoming bum or her cunt, and then she would enjoy this bull of a man in his quest to fulfil his matrimonial responsibilities. He and she never tired of their lovemaking.

. . .

With Helen sucking Aurora's clit and biting her nipples, along with a very lascivious well-built woman clutching two soaking cunts, these three women were in heaven together.

Having a new hand feeling her up was exciting for Helen. And it being a new hand that knew its way around her pussy, especially so.

Suddenly, she felt a pair of strong hands around her waist and before she knew it she was on her knees. Celia was suddenly kneeling in front of her with her glorious smile. She looked into Helen's eyes and whispered softly to her.

"Aurora wants to fuck us now darling. She'll start by buggering us with her clit – something she loves – then she'll have us with one of the toys from the music stool. She knows where they are."

At that moment Aurora spat on Helen's anus and shoved her engorged clitoris into the freshly lubricated hole quite roughly. Then she was still.

Helen was content with what was happening, appreciating that this was never going to be anything like Freddy's big cock getting into her at home. But then the little penis-like thing began to pulsate and she relished the sensation, looking back over her shoulder and seeing Aurora's smiling face just as the large woman orgasmed, so obviously happy with what she was having.

Then hands cupped Helen's breasts and she turned and saw the radiant Celia kneeling beside her, her bum in the air, awaiting her turn with Aurora. Moments later, Aurora left Helen and climbed onto Celia and Helen watched excitedly as the two women rubbed against each other and again Aurora suddenly pushed in harder and orgasmed. Helen realised that she was so hot for Aurora that the she could have her in whatever way she wanted.

Helen didn't need to wait very long. Aurora grabbed her once again and rolled her onto her back and pushed her legs apart. Then Helen felt a squeegee bottle on her pussy and lubricant being squeezed in. She opened her eyes and stared at the large, smiling Italian beauty between her legs, brandishing Celia's largest dildo.

Aurora rubbed the head of the strap-on against Helen's pussy then shoved it in, working her way deeper very quickly. Helen gave a little scream, then settled back as Aurora pushed and shoved and worked the instrument as if she was ploughing a field. Aurora grabbed Helen's ankles and lifted her legs up high, giving Helen the extra thrill of seeing her own legs waving in the air above her.

Aurora turned her head and bit Helen's ankle; then she looked down, smiling in a way that told Helen that Aurora was truly in heaven as well.

Helen began to gasp as this amazing woman shagged her. If Aurora was a little brutal, it worked for Helen and it was only a couple of minutes before she thrust herself upwards and screamed "Yes Aurora! Yes, Aurora! Fuck, fuck, fuck!"

Aurora yelled something in Italian as she exploded, then she fell forward onto Helen and pushed her tongue into Helen's mouth. Helen welcomed her and their mouths energetically sucked each other.

All the time this was going on Celia was behind Aurora, fondling her big beautiful buttocks, kissing them, licking them and pushing her finger into her anus, and when Aurora orgasmed and then fell forward onto Helen, Celia fastened her mouth on Aurora's newly exposed clitoris and sucked it. Then Celia pushed a hand underneath Helen and fingered her while she wrapped her other hand around the dildo still inside Helen, rocking it gently backwards and forward.

Helen and Aurora both came again.

Now it was Celia's turn.

When Aurora had finished shagging Celia, and Helen had enjoyed licking and biting Aurora's magnificent bottom, all three ladies moved up onto the sofa.

Aurora sat in the middle, her massive legs stretched out before her, wide apart. Her nipples were still very erect and she pulled both women's heads to her breasts and commanded them to bite her.

Aurora's mass of pubic hair and her protruding clitoris were a sight to behold and neither Helen nor Celia could ignore it. Each took a turn kneeling in front of Aurora with her head buried in Aurora's saturated curly carpet while lightly fingering and gently sucking her now very red clitoris.

Every few minutes, Aurora would arch her back and scream in

Italian as she enjoyed yet another orgasm and then she would pull one of whichever womens head was available to her, and mouth and suck her feverishly.

Aurora announced suddenly that she had pasta to prepare.

"You bad girls have seduced me and kept me out of my kitchen. Next time we are together I shall punish you both and you will scream for mercy."

Aurora stood up, collected her clothes and walked out of the room like the tall, upright, naked primitive goddess that she was. Celia and Helen looked at each other.

"Hope you enjoyed that, Helen."

Helen reached over and drew Celia into her arms and the two lovers kissed.

"I enjoyed it immensely, Celia, my darling woman. I will never forget it. Thank you."

Helen and Polly had started seeing each other alone, most times at Helen's house and once at Polly's mother's place when her mum was away.

Helen had been firm about the fact that she had other lovers and that Polly should embrace that as a positive, not a negative. Polly grew more secure in their relationship – even suggesting, in a teasing voice that one day Helen "might like to introduce me to some of her lovers and that it might be fun to discover what her dearest Helen so liked in these other women".

Helen had laughed out loud at the young woman's audacious suggestion; not because she disapproved of the idea, but simply because of the tone and manner of Polly's comment.

"Yes, darling, we should do that. And we must make sure we bring a tape measure and a notebook so that you can make notes. You could interview them and find out what they liked about me."

Polly squealed and pummelled Helen with her fists.

"It will serve you right if I fall in love with all of them and they fall in love with me. And then they might not have time for you any more and I will be your queen."

Helen cracked up laughing.

"Oh Polly. You get better all the time. Maybe I'll start an agency of some sort, and start marketing you and my hundreds of other lovers. In fact, I'm sure I could get a fortune just for your beautiful little thingy, my love."

Helen grabbed Polly and dragged her to the carpet, reversing herself on top of the young woman, pulling her panties aside and fastening her mouth on Polly's pussy. Polly immediately responded with the same move and the two lovingly played with each other.

"All right dear girl. I think it is time you met the most important person in my life, my husband Frederico. At the same time, you can meet a couple of other people you might like, my next-door neighbours, Mary, and her niece Sophie."

Polly was most attentive. Helen continued.

"I've invited Mary and Sophie to dinner next week. It's Mary's fiftieth birthday. It would be lovely if you would come too. I've told Freddy about you and he would love to meet you. Don't be frightened by him. He won't try to seduce you. Unless I ask him to, of course."

Helen laughed out loud as she watched Polly's face turn from a happy smile into a nervous frown.

"Just joking, my love."

"Oh, Helen. You know I'm a bit scared of men."

"Well, you'll get on with Sophie, I suspect. She has never been with a man as far as I know. She's a couple of years older than you. Oh yes! Sophie is a horsey person and has just started working at a racing stud somewhere out in the north-west suburbs."

"I would love to come, Helen."

Then Polly put on her teasing voice again, a sort of whine.

"So, other than Freddy and myself, which of the other guests are you intimate with, my darling sexpot?"

"Mary is now a lover. That was an accident, really."

"You had an accidental affair with Mary, is that what you're telling me?"

"Well yes. Mary had started an affair with a neighbour, but his wife found out very early in the piece and promptly moved them interstate. Mary was devastated.

"I had given her a key to my studio so that the two could meet and one day I discovered her alone and crying. I simply put my arms around her to console her. Well, need I go on?"

"Yes, you wayward bitch, tell me everything."

Polly feigned disapproval while searching Helen's face with obvious excitement.

"Well, Mary had stopped crying for a while and between sobs murmured that it was the kissing she would miss most. Feeling her extreme sadness, and without thinking, I answered that I might be able to fix that. So things just went from there, Polly. Mary had her first lesbian love affair and she loved it."

"Details, please, or you are in big trouble, Helen. I will dream up ways of punishing you."

Helen threw back her head and laughed.

"I love you dearly, Polly."

Then Helen recounted the story of what had happened in her studio and Polly listened intently. Helen told her then how, every so often, she met Mary in her studio.

Polly loved Helen's story and did not show any signs of jealousy, which Helen was thankful for, thinking this was a positive sign for the future.

But Polly hadn't finished.

"And who else am I likely to meet who willingly opens their legs for you, slut woman?"

Again Helen laughed out loud.

"Is this really what you want, Polly, to know about my liaisons?"

"Yes, Helen." Polly looked serious. "How else can I consider sharing with you if I'm not properly included in your world? Now, who else will I meet that might have licked you?"

"Oh, darling. I hope I deserve you, you beautiful person.

"Sophie – Mary's niece – came into my life also unexpectedly.

Mary's husband died, thankfully. He had not shown her any attention in years. He was a most unpleasant man. That was only a week or two after Mary and I had got together.

"We were due to meet in my studio that week, but her husband's passing made this impossible. Mary called me and said that she wouldn't get to see me because of all the arrangements for the funeral and so on.

"Then she said, in appreciation for my liberating her, she was sending me a present. When I asked her what she meant, she said that she had spoken to Sophie about me and that her niece had offered to come to me in place of her aunt."

Helen stopped talking to search Polly's face. She was looking at Helen in awe.

"Well there, darling. They are the only two you will meet at the party. Now lets have a snack. I'm starving."

But Polly was having none of it.

"Don't you dare leave me hanging, you awful woman. What happened with Sophie in the studio? Tell me or I'll go and fetch a kitchen knife and commit a crime of passion."

Helen moved to grab Polly but Polly jumped away.

"Not another drop of moisture from me will be had by your tongue until you tell me everything. Talk!"

"Oh my God! I sincerely hope that all of this will not be turned against me in the future if we ever fight?" Helen look suitably unhappy.

Polly frowned back at her.

"I might sulk sometimes but I will never fight with you Helen. Now, talk!"

Helen acquiesced and told Polly everything that had happened when she met Sophie in the studio.

"So there you have it, Polly. I hope you still love me and that you will still come to the party."

Polly reached across, took Helen's hand and popped it up under her blouse.

"Nothing will stop me Helen. And look out, girls, Polly is coming to the party!"

. . .

It was the day of the birthday party and Helen and Freddy had prepared a feast with a little help from the local gourmet take-away store.

This was going to be a small affair. Just the party girl, Mary, her niece Sophie and a couple of Mary's friends, including her long-time friend Janice and Mary's neighbours from the street behind Eros Park, Maria and Serina. This mother-and-daughter couple had recently taken on the job of caretakers at Number 21 just two doors down, until the new owners arrived from overseas. And, of course, Polly was coming too.

Freddy was on form, full of quips about love and lovers along with detailed insights into ingredients of cake mixes and such. Helen loved him dearly and Freddy loved her back.

"So what is it that you wanted to tell me about, darling?" Freddy inquired of Helen.

"Something about giving Mary a special present. Was that it? So what special present are we giving her? I bet it's something sexual. You girls and your toys! What is it, sweetheart? I know, one of those new strapless dildos. I hear they're all the rage."

Freddy had run out of things to do in the house and Helen wouldn't let him into his workshop for fear he might never come back in time. She knew how impossible he was when he got absorbed in things – things other than herself, of course.

Freddy had decided to sit on a stool in the kitchen and polish the silver. He was enjoying it, especially as he had his loving wife with him for company.

"Well, yes, Freddy it is sexual."

"There! I knew it. Tell me about it."

"Well, I recently introduced Mary to something new and to my surprise she really loved it. So we're giving her something I know she's desperate to try."

Freddy held up a dessert spoon and breathed heavily onto it, then continued polishing.

"Good! What is it?"

"I think we'd better say who is it?"

Helen smiled to herself as she added the cream to the pavlova.

"Who is it, then? I never know what to expect next from you except when I slip your panties down. Oh, wow, pussy and pavlova, yum. We've got a half hour before people arrive."

Helen laughed loudly, revelling in her husband's passion for her.

"Sorry, darling. You have to save yourself for someone else."

"I beg your pardon, wife. What did you just say, besides an oblique 'no thanks'?"

"We are giving you to Mary for the night, Freddy. Mary has just discovered anal sex and while she enjoys our little dildo sessions, she is desperate to try a real cock. You have always admired Mary's rear end, my love. I suppose in a way, this is a present for both my loves."

"But Helen?"

"No buts, Freddy. Well perhaps just Mary's."

Helen laughed at her play on words. Freddy looked at his wife in astonishment.

"You're not joking, are you sweetheart? I can tell when you are serious. So will you giftwrap me and tell her not to open her present until she gets home?"

Helen laughed again.

"At the end of the evening, Freddy, you will walk her home, pretty much unnoticed by anyone else still at the party. I will announce that Mary has a bit of a headache and is off home and that she asked me to thank you all for coming."

Freddy was speechless for once.

"Freddy, it's all right. I love you. I just think it's a liberating thing to do for all three of us. Can I say that I would welcome the opportunity to watch you buggering our sweet neighbour at some time in the not too distant future? I believe we could enjoy dear Mary's backside together. And I'm pretty darned sure she would, too."

Freddy was trying to think through this thing. Having accepted the personal aspect of it all, Freddy was already occupied with the logistics of it.

"Yes, darling. It is a good idea, and I believe it is doable. But don't think I'll let you get off lightly. Enjoyable though the experience may be, you have still taken liberties with my sensitivities and my emotions. I will have to find a way of punishing you."

They both burst out laughing and Helen came over to Freddie, unzipped his trousers and pulled out his rapidly rising cock. She reached over and scooped two fingers of cream and spread it on his manhood. Then Helen leant down in front of him and began to lick him, all the time looking up at him adoringly.

Then Helen spoke in her special voice she used for teasing, she said "Sorry, darling. I forgot. We have to save you for Mary, don't we sweetheart? I will have to put him back in your trousers. Still, this little moment will help you prepare for your ordeal with that 'splendid backside' as you've always called Mary's derrière."

"Oh no! A creamy interruptus! My God! I will have to find a punishment for you. That is, if I survive the night."

"Well, darling, as I've mentioned many times before, there is that little leather flagellator on the wall of the studio. And you know how I always want you to punish me properly?"

Mary's birthday party was drawing to a close. Most of the guests had said their farewells and wandered off.

Polly and Sophie had been inseparable all night and looked as though they would go on talking forever. Helen was pleased, even though she experienced slight feelings of jealousy seeing her two beautiful lovers seemingly intent on exploring each other. They can't still be talking about horse stuff, she thought.

Janice had shown great interest in Mary's new neighbours, in Number 21, Maria and her daughter Serina.

Helen had been surprised and even a little shocked when she had bent down to pick up a spoon off the floor and looked under the table to discover that both Maria and her daughter each had a hand lovingly massaging the top of one of Janice's long legs, above her stocking tops and up and beneath the hem of her very short skirt.

So Janice hadn't changed much since her therapy with Helen the year before. She was obviously still addicted to sex, and sex from anywhere. What intrigued Helen was what Janice had done or said to initiate this reaction by the two women. They had obviously responded to something that she had told them.

Fancy that! Helen thought. Was it my pavlova that got them going?

She smiled inside, and when the three women rose to say good-night Helen could see by the smiles on their faces that they hadn't even started their real party yet. She suspected that the real excitement of the night was destined to begin when the trio arrived at Number 21.

Helen walked back from saying her goodbyes and stopped in the dining room to ask if the two young women needed anything more to eat or drink. Polly and Sophie looked at her with dazed faraway looks, and thanked her, but said they couldn't eat another thing.

Helen then announced that she and Freddy were going to walk Mary home and they might not be back for a while, probably stopping to have a nightcap with her.

"Help yourselves to whatever you want. Love you both. See you later."

Polly and Sophie were obviously intensely into each other, so Helen judged it the right moment to ask Mary to pop out to the kitchen with her.

"Oh, thank you so much Helen. I love intimate dinner parties. I must say, your two loves Sophie and Polly seem to be getting on very well."

Helen smiled. "Yes, between you and me, I'm hoping for an outcome. They would make a delightful couple."

"Oh Helen! You are so generous. No wonder we all love you."

Mary took the opportunity to put her arms around Helen and kiss her, and Helen put a hand down to rub Mary between her legs.

"Oh, Helen, don't get me hot for you right now. It's not the right time, unfortunately."

Mary gave a little gasp and pushed harder on Helen's lips.

"Well, Mary, to tell you the truth, I'm just trying to warm you up ready for your birthday gift.

"Freddy and I have a present for you. Now if it is not to your liking, then it is perfectly acceptable for you to say that you don't want it. We won't be offended, I promise."

Mary looked surprised.

"Helen! What is it and where is it? I can't wait."

Helen smiled lovingly.

"Well, you will have to wait until you get him home, darling. Follow me."

Helen took Mary by the hand and led her to the little spare bedroom beside the back door. They stood outside the door while Helen told Mary what was going on.

"Freddy wants to offer himself to you for the night. He wants to walk you home now. He is in here waiting and hoping that you will say yes, my darling."

"I don't understand you, Helen. What do you mean?"

"Freddy has alway commented on your beautiful backside, Mary, and he is desperately hoping that you will oblige him with a closer inspection, if you know what I mean.

"After what you and I have been up to lately, I thought you might like to try a real cock. I'm so hoping you will try Freddy's. It would be an honour to have him in you, my love."

Helen embraced Mary and kissed her and ran her hand down over her buttocks.

"Please darling Mary? Let Freddy have you as he so often has me. Then who knows, we all three can sometimes have bottom play together in the studio."

When Helen said goodbye to Mary and Freddie, she couldn't help but shed a tear. Mary had reacted first in terror and then in lust when Helen unzipped him and took out Freddie's impressive cock to show her.

And when Helen took Mary's hand and wrapped it around Freddie's penis, Mary had let out a long low groan looking first at Freddy and then at Helen.

"Can I come home with you Mary? Please?" asked Freddy quietly.

"Oh yes, you beautiful man. Yes, you certainly can."

Helen smiled lovingly at Freddie.

"You treat her well, dear husband, or you will have me to deal with. Now Mary! There is one more thing before I push you both out through the back door."

Helen lifted Mary's dress up around her waist, quickly pulled down her panties and lifted her feet so that she could remove her undergarment properly.

"Helen! What are you doing?" Mary whispered.

"These are a security deposit, Mary. You're taking something of mine and I'm keeping something of yours. You get them back when I get him back, hopefully still in working order. It also helps my husband if you are pants free, in case he wants to grope you on the way home.

"Now kiss each other please, then bugger off the two of you. Have a nice night and I hope to see you in the morning."

Mary and Freddy had only just got past Helen's studio and through the side gate leading to Mary's house before Mary turned, puckered up her lips and pressed herself up against Freddy, putting a hand down on the front of his trousers and searching for the lump hidden there. Freddy responded, kissing her passionately and slipping his hand up her dress and grasping her large hairy pussy. Mary shook with excitement.

"Oh, Freddy. I can't believe this is happening to me. You are so beautiful, Freddy."

Freddy unzipped his trousers, took hold of Mary's hand and slipped it inside his underpants. Mary groaned and quickly found his member and squeezed him, letting go only to push down further and cup his balls in her hand.

"Oh Freddy! Quick! Get me inside the house so that we can enjoy what your beautiful Helen wants us to have. Hurry, my love."

Helen wandered about the kitchen for a little while, then she folded clothes in the laundry and headed out to her studio. She wanted to be away from the house so that the girls could feel comfortable and properly discover each other.

In her studio, Helen looked at the drawing she had made months before of Janice's legs, which she had stickytaped to the wall. Then she got out a clean piece of paper and her charcoal and began to draw.

First she drew a nearly straight line across the top of the paper. Then she began to draw Janice's long legs beneath the line, the line being the table top that Helen had peered under at dinner. She drew two arms and hands, one hand on each of Janice's legs and then a wavy line showing the hem of Janice's skirt. She added two more pairs of legs, and a skirt for each pair. Then she drew three pairs of high heeled-shoes.

A good hour had passed and Helen was feeling sleepy. She pinned up her picture and packed away her things. Looking at the picture, she could see there was still much she could do to it. She liked it, but she would do more to it later.

She wandered back to the house. She peeped into the dining room and found it empty. She thought she heard a sound coming from the lounge, and quietly went to investigate. Standing at the doorway, she looked in on a beautiful sight, one that she was already familiar with.

Sophie's long grey-stockinged legs made a large V in the air above the sofa, her ankles and feet twisting in the way she loved moving them. And directly facing Helen across the room was Polly's beautiful neat little white bottom, shining in the light of a side lamp, her panties down around her knees and the just visible back of her head and neck moving slowly up and down between Sophie's legs.

Helen put her hand up her skirt and palmed herself for just a few moments, then she smiled and left the girls and went to bed.

Freddy lifted Mary's dress over her head and threw it on the vestibule floor. Mary looked at him, her eyes moist from sobbing excitedly as Freddy dragged her along the passageway asking which room was hers while she screamed, "I want you now! Please Freddy. Just here will do."

But Freddy was particular and wanted a bed. When he found her room he knew he was ready.

Freddy pushed Mary down onto the bed and stared at her in her big blue bra, blue garter belt and stockings and blue high heels. Then he stripped off.

"I want your pussy before anything, Mary," Freddy whispered. He lifted Mary's legs, let them fall bent at the knees and moved in between them, brandishing his cock as she stared at it.

"Be my guest, Freddy. Let me suck you first, just for a few moments before you put it in."

Mary swung around and took Freddy into her mouth, slurping furiously, wanting this beautiful man in every part of her all at once.

Mary had not had a man since her short-lived one-night affair with the neighbour Charlie. Before that, she could not really remember the last time. Her husband had never touched her, nor had she wanted him to.

Mary was now so hungry for a cock she would have gladly swallowed Freddy completely. But then she stopped and swivelled back around and thrust her legs in the air.

Freddy moved up to her cunt and slid into its wet woolly undergrowth and then into her soft, welcoming vulva. He stayed motionless, letting it throb inside her before he started to shag her. But things were already working fast for Mary and she screamed and lifted herself up violently and orgasmed.

"Oh God! Oh Freddy!" But almost before Mary could finish speaking, her body threw itself up onto his cock again, wetness seeping out around her already wet pussy, and she wept.

"Shag me now please Freddy," she squeaked.

Mary's very wet warm cunt welcomed Freddy's cock as it began to slide in and out of her. She suddenly felt quiet inside for the first time since Helen had announced what was going to happen. Mary told herself that she owned what was happening, and she relaxed in the joy of knowing that she would get to have this beautiful man again, together with his beautiful wife.

An inner voice told Mary to savour the moment and that all her orgasms belonged to her and whoever she chose to share them with.

Freddy, too felt serene even as he dominated this gorgeous creature in a very loving fashion, looking down on her big curvaceous legs and thighs, tight inside her stockings and suspenders. He knew that he could do whatever he wished to Mary and that they would both be pleasured together.

Heated anticipation now gave way to a controlled fetishism and lust. Nothing was urgent. Simply being flesh together was beautiful.

Freddy withdrew and lay down on the bed beside Mary. He rubbed her thigh, he pulled her closer and murmured his request: that he would like her to get on top of him and to swing round so that her pussy was in his face, and to put his cock in her mouth.

"Yes, my love. Ask me for anything."

Then she rolled over onto him with his head between her legs and she sucked him slowly, sliding her tongue around and over his penis.

Freddy buried his face into Mary's saturated pussy and licked her pink wet lips and over and around her clitoris. He breathed in her beautiful odour and pushed his nose into her.

As the two luxuriated in their calm possession of each other, Mary reached down and found one of Freddy's hands. She lifted it slowly and laid it on a buttock, then rubbed herself with it, tenderly caressing that smooth mountain of flesh that he was yet to visit. She felt his cock throb in her mouth as she did this and she smiled inside, knowing that he appreciated what she had just done. Then she repeated the same move with Freddy's other hand, introducing it to her other buttock. Again his cock stretched upwards in her mouth and, as it did so, her pussy jerked crazily on his mouth as she came.

Slowly, Freddy moved Mary's head and turned her around so that she lay on him face-to-face. They looked lovingly into each other's eyes and Freddy touched her lips and slid a finger into her mouth. Then he kissed her and they tongued each other for what seemed like a long time. All the while, his cock nestled up against Mary's pussy which she lovingly moved up and down, keeping him in a constant state of readiness.

Freddy's hands were sweeping over Mary's large posterior, and sometimes excited anticipation resulted in Freddy arching his back and thrusting upwards causing her to orgasm and push her cunt up hard against him.

"Freddy, would you please shag me again?"

Mary rolled over onto her back and Freddy stood up and moved in between her legs, running his hands up her stocking-clad calves and caressing her thighs.

"You are so beautiful Mary."

Mary sighed as Freddy slid his cock into her again and began to shag her.

They continued like this for quite some time during which Mary came repeatedly, responding to Freddy's firm but relaxed pace. Sometimes he would shove in hard and push her about and Mary would shout "Oh yes Freddie, here I come!"

The two lovers had been having each other for nearly an hour when Mary proffered the suggestion that Freddy could take her from behind any time he wished. She wanted him to have anything he wanted. In the next breath she added that she was unsure whether he would be able to fit it in, as she had never had something as big as him in her bottom before.

Freddy smiled down at Mary and lovingly pulled her nipples upward, stretching her large breasts.

"Well, let's try. Where is the lube?"

Mary reached under a pillow and handed Freddy a bottle of lubricant. Then she rolled over onto her tummy and moved herself up onto her knees, presenting her backside for Freddy's attention.

"Oh my God! Your rear would win an international backside competition Mary. You are beautiful."

"Thank you kind sir. And I have great pleasure in presenting it you to do with as you may."

Freddy ran his fingers along the crack of Mary's bottom and when he got to the spot, he inserted the spout of the squeeze bottle and let oil flood into her bottom. He inserted a finger and moved it around inside her, and Mary pushed back against his hand and wiggled her bum.

"So far so good, Freddy. It feels beautiful."

Freddy slipped on a condom and ran a line of oil onto his erect penis, then pulled Mary up to a position where she was sitting on her heels.

"Just to keep you in the loop so to speak, hold my cock now that it is slippery so that you can have an image of what is heading into you."

Mary eagerly took hold of him and tenderly ran her hand up and down Freddy's slippery member. Then she let go of him and leaned over back onto her knees, thrusting her bum towards him and playfully wiggling it.

"Please do it to me, Freddy."

Freddy stood beside the bed with the most beautiful buttocks in the world right there waiting for him. He moved in. First he rubbed the head of his cock against Mary's well-oiled little orifice, then with his cock rigid, he slowly pushed into her magic bottom hole. And it was indeed magic. Slowly his cock slid further and further into Mary's anus.

"All good so far, darling man," gasped Mary.

Freddy eased back a little bit to give her bottom time to adjust, then he moved in even further than before, impressed that Mary had not objected once.

"It feels wonderful, Freddy. I love it. My backside loves it, and I know now why your beautiful wife loves it. It's divine."

These words, for some reason, caused Freddy's cock to twitch inside her and Mary yelled. "Oh yes! More please!"

Freddy pushed in as far as he could and as he did so, Mary groaned. Then, when he knew he was almost there, he reached right in and throbbed wildly.

"Freddy!" screamed Mary as a tiny orgasm acknowledge the happy cock in her.

Then Freddy readied himself.

"I'm going to shag your rear end now, dear Mary. Tell me to stop if you need to."

"Oh, Freddy. You are the most wonderful bottom fucker in the world, I'm sure. Bugger me Freddy, however much you want."

"Thank you, Mary."

. . .

When Freddie left the sleeping Mary and headed home, he reflected on what a wonderful evening he'd had. Even now he was still enjoying the damp odour. Hopefully, he thought, this event might now be repeated. His darling wife had organised this tryst and he believed that Helen might soon want to organise a threesome.

Freddy had passed through the gate in the fence between their two houses and decided he would have a quick visit to Helen's studio and the lovely bed she kept for herself and her lovers.

Freddy needed to lie down in a quiet spot. He had on a number of occasions wondered about a particular sensation he sometimes experienced after a long lovemaking session and he now thought it might be a good subject to bring up for discussion with Bertie in their weekly get-together when they talked about everything to do with life, love and philosophy.

In Freddy's experience, a long night of lovemaking and pleasuring a woman could, oddly enough, leave a man "unfinished" and this was best taken care of with a good wank as soon as possible after the lovemaking while the vision of one's lover was still fresh in one's mind.

As he turned the corner of the studio and reached for the door handle, a voice close by called out, "Freddy! What are you doing here?"

"Oh God, Sophie! You gave me a fright. I hadn't expected to meet anyone in the garden at this hour."

Mary's niece moved into the moonlight and Freddy saw that Sophie wore only a blouse, and that was unbuttoned and hung open. She was carrying her skirt and other clothes over her arm and in her hands, including her shoes and stockings.

"Freddy, I demand to know what Helen's husband is doing in the garden at two in the morning, and if I'm not mistaken, there is a distinct smell of warm sex. If you have been cheating on our beautiful, loving Helen, then I will personally castrate you. I work on a stud farm so I know exactly what is required. You had better have answers, Mr Alves. I'll count to ten."

Freddy groaned under the weight of this beautiful young woman's accusations. The situation was laughable but of course, on the face of it, things didn't look good.

"Damned if I do and damned if I don't. This is a very difficult moment for me, Sophie. On the one hand, I'm sworn to secrecy by Helen and on the other, I have to tell you the truth so that I retain possession of my testicles. Can I just say I've been doing something that Helen knows about and, in fact, organised?"

Sophie looked at him in disbelief.

"You men are all bastards, even nice ones like you, Freddy. I'm so glad I've never taken up with one. Women are much better. Much more considerate."

Sophie's face was alight with angry passion. Freddy admired her breasts peeping from her unbuttoned blouse and she seemed not to care that her long bare legs and belly, shining in the moonlight, were on full view to his gaze. "Maybe Sophie's right about men," Freddy mused.

"Sophie! If I tell you, please respect all of us involved so that life can go on pleasantly around here as you well know that it usually does. Helen and Mary both love you dearly. Please! If I tell you where I've been, I beg you to keep it to yourself."

Sophie's face suddenly relaxed.

"Lets go inside, Freddy. I'm getting cold. But you will tell me everything, won't you?"

Freddy followed Sophie, glancing down at her wonderful rear end but tried not to think about it. Sophie bunched herself up on the bed with her arms around her legs.

"Talk, Freddy! And it better be good."

Freddy sat down on the far edge of the bed and told Sophie about Helen's gift to Mary. He told how he had aways laughingly commented on Mary's great backside and that recently, Helen had initiated Mary into the pleasures of anal sex using a little dildo designed for that purpose, and that Mary had taken to it with gusto.

"Given our very loving situation, Helen thought she would offer Mary a real cock for her birthday and knowing that I admired her rear end would make it much easier."

Freddy paused to look at Sophie to gauge if she was responding positively to his story.

"So that's probably an anal dildo in the small parcel that arrived yesterday from the sex shop addressed to Mary!" Sophie blurted enthusiastically.

Freddy waited to hear what Sophie would say next, desperately hoping she would see the sense and the humour in what had been done.

"I believe you, Freddy. It was close. You nearly lost them. You can keep them, now that I know you've donated your services to such a worthwhile cause. Mary and Helen are my favourite people in the whole world. You're a lucky man, Freddy.

"So what were you coming in here for? Shouldn't you be getting home to Helen? It's not far, you know."

Freddy remembered Helen telling him about her long-legged country girl who asked for what she wanted and took a great interest in what people were doing. A sort of boyish naiveté, she called it, and Helen found it refreshing.

"I just needed a little time to myself, Sophie. Helen has a visitor staying over and I didn't want to bother them. I just need to … "

"Need to what, Freddy?"

Freddy was getting just a tiny bit irritated by Sophie's demanding attitude, lovely as she was.

"To wank, Sophie. Is that okay with you?"

Freddy regretted speaking in haste. But whatever Sophie thought, she wasn't going to ease up on her investigation of him.

"Why do you need to wank, Freddie? Didn't you get plenty of everything from Mary?"

Freddy closed his eyes and counted slowly to ten.

"Men who spend a lot of time pleasuring someone sometimes find they need to finish themselves off afterwards. As wonderful as it was with your aunt, I still need to just get off."

Sophie giggled and replied, "You're lucky. Us girls feel the need to finish ourselves off almost hourly."

How does Helen ever manage to quieten this girl? Freddy thought?

"Now Sophie, can we please ease up on the questions while I sort myself out? You may like to leave at this point. I care for you a lot and I don't want to offend you."

Silence ensued. Sophie wasn't going anywhere.

"Please, Freddy. Can I watch? I've never been with a man or seen a man's cock. This would be very educational."

Freddy stared at the beautiful creature sitting beside him on the bed and looking very relaxed. Is that really possible? he thought.

"Please yourself, Sophie. I don't mind."

It took only moments for Freddy to strip off. Then he lay back and began to move his hand backwards and forwards on his already half erect penis. He managed to get the image of Mary's backside and her legs back into focus in his mind's eye and was ready to tune in, heading for a quick happy ending. Or so he thought.

"Can I do that please, Freddy? Watching you is turning me on. I think I've got the idea."

Freddy stopped rubbing his cock, thinking about what the girl had just said. Given her forthright attitude, he decided he would act in the same way and see how she responded.

"If you are going to wank me, Sophie, you will need to be a part of what turns me on. You need to come a lot closer and take off your blouse. Then lie on your side facing me, with your legs apart so that I can see everything. So! Are you okay with that?"

Sophie replied straight away.

"Sure, Freddy. I understand. I have to see or imagine stuff when I wank. Tell me if I'm looking the part."

Sophie slipped her blouse off and moved over to lie beside him, all the time looking into his eyes. She pushed out her breasts and pointed one leg down, bending and lifting the other so that her mat of pubic hair was on view.

"How is that, Freddy? Oh and Freddy, considering our situation, you know, me and Helen and you, and me and Mary and you – well, even though you're a bloke, I will be more than happy if you need to touch me. Anywhere you like, Freddy. But only if you think you want to. No pressure."

Freddy looked at the naked Sophie as he processed her offer and in response his erection lifted and quivered. Sophie noticed and gave a little giggle.

"Thank you, Sophie. You are very understanding. I would love to touch you while I wank."

Freddy resumed rubbing his erection with one hand while his other hand wandered over and onto the upper inner part of Sophie's leg. The girl trembled and gave a little tiny gasp but did nothing. Then he moved his hand up to her pussy and fingered her lightly.

Sophie was quiet at long last and out of the corner of his eye Freddy noticed that she was watching him keenly. Her eyes were wide and bright and her mouth was slightly open. But as Freddy gently fingered Sophie's wet vagina, he noticed her eyes would open and shut and she would run her tongue over her lips.

Things were working for Freddy. His cock stood tall and stiff and he had started to breathe more deeply.

He closed his eyes, his fingers feeling gently inside Sophie's lovely pussy. Then he felt fingers touching his balls and he realised he had company, and moments later Sophie's tongue slowly licked the hood of his cock. She was having her way and why should he say no?

"Tell me when you are about to come, please Freddy," Sophie whispered in a slightly croaky voice.

Then the girl dragged Freddy's hand away and replaced it with her own, hardly missing a beat as she took over from him. Then he felt her mouth sucking him in tandem with her loving handwork.

Freddy looked at the girl's face. She smiled up at him and her eyes blinked open and shut as she slurped happily on his cock. It was as though she wasn't really there; away somewhere?

Then Freddy knew the moment was about to arrive.

"I will be noisy, Sophie. Don't be frightened."

Then his orgasm began deep down, and he informed Sophie.

"About to come, dear lady."

He began his deep roar way down in his chest and Sophie moved in. Without further thought, she threw herself over Freddy and dragged his cock up into her wet cunt. She planted herself firmly on him with his cock right inside and starting to burst.

"Argh! Yes Sophie. Oh yes girl. Fuck your beautiful cunt. Fuck! Fuck! Fuck!"

As Freddy came, he heaved himself upward and further into Sophie, who screamed his name, her pussy sucking him in as far as it could, while squeezing his cock with an unusually strong pelvic grip.

He swung the girl, still firmly impaled, around onto her back, pushing into her even more. Sophie's long legs reached skyward and her bare feet swivelled at the ankles. She clutched Freddy in her strong arms.

"Don't you dare leave me, Freddy. Keep fucking me. I have more orgasms on the way."

And the country girl was right. She screamed and came, pushing up on Freddy's cock; then Freddy yelled and came, pushing down into Sophie. They did it again, and then a third time. Then they stopped moving and lay still.

Sophie pulled Freddy's face to her breast and quietly whispered to him to bite her nipples.

"Like Helen does Freddy. Please, my darling?"

Freddy's mouth started seriously biting and sucking her tits and almost immediately, Sophie threw her cunt back up and the two continued their fucking, just as before.

Freddy yelled and Sophia screamed and not far away, Mary slept and Polly slept and a wide-awake Helen lay unable to sleep, thinking about her husband Freddy and about their life together.

"I will tell Helen, Freddy. I've decided that I will want a lot more of you, but I need to check with her first."

"No! She must hear from me first Sophie. I will tell her first thing in the morning when she wakes up. Please don't mention it yet to Helen or Mary, if you don't mind.

"And one more thing, Sophie, I will want to make love to you again too, but only with Helen's permission. Fucking you was truly wonderful and amazing. Helen and I trust each other and that is the only way things can work for all of us."

Sophie stared at her first male lover, and languished in this new feeling of love.

"Yes, Freddy. I'll go along with that."

Helen had thought a lot about Mary's friend Janice. Janice was an enigma. She seemed to have many lives, each completely separate from the others. Janice was a music teacher and she was one of the people Helen thought about when she went to her bed after Mary's birthday party.

Janice was a life-long friend of Mary and Mary maintained that Janice had always been very proper when they were together. Yet Mary suspected that Janice was not as innocent as she made out to be, although she had no proof.

Then there was the business at an unnamed church. Helen's friend Celia Ashbee told of the rumoured sexual goings-on between two female members of the choir and some of the choirboys on Sunday nights after church. Janice was a member of a church choir along with her friend Gertrude who played the organ. But Helen had no proof that this was happening at St John's where Janice attended.

In amongst this was the odd occasion when Janice had turned up at Helen's studio begging Helen to help her find love. On that occasion Janice had pleaded with Helen to show her some attention, as she knew Helen had shown Mary after she had lost her lover. This happened shortly after Helen and Mary had become lovers, and when Mary had discovered the benefits of Helen's strap-on dildo and immediately went and purchased one for herself.

Mary said that Janice had always expressed loving feeling for her and now that Mary was free and had discovered a new way of loving, it wasn't long before she and Janice were having their monthly coffee afternoon followed by added strap-on benefits on Mary's bed.

Earlier in the evening, during Mary's birthday party, Helen had accidentally discovered when she bent down to pick up a piece of cutlery that had dropped onto the floor, that the mother and daughter, Maria and Serina, were sitting on either side of Janice, each with a hand on one of Janice's legs, lovingly caressing her upper thighs.

Maria and Serina had just moved into Number 21, two down from Helen and Freddy's house.

Number 21 would remain empty until the new owners arrived from London in a month or two. The agent and executors of the property had employed the La Rocca family to live in the house as caretakers for however long was needed.

When Helen asked Mary about it when Mary came into the kitchen to help carry food out to the dining room, she said that they also had Maria's grandfather, Alberto living with them, and also a lodger, Giorgio, newly arrived from Italy.

When the three women were saying their goodbyes and leaving, Helen heard Serina say to Janice, "We are only two houses away, Janice. You won't have to walk far at all."

As she watched the three women head off down the driveway, she couldn't help thinking how the tall, thin Janice was like a stick insect or a praying mantis.

So why was Helen even thinking of Janice at this late hour? What mystery, if any, surrounded this woman? And in particular, what prompted these two women to put their hands on Janice's legs? And why did they leave the party early? And why were they taking Janice home to their place? She tried to put Janice out of her mind. In desperation she got up quietly, trying not to wake up Polly lying beside her, and went to the kitchen and made a cup of cocoa.

But Helen's mind wouldn't stop. Did Janice have a little-known psychological disorder? Was she able to manipulate those around her to unwittingly give her some particular kind of sexual attention? Were there different cue requirements for different sexual fantasies or desires? She had great difficulty thinking about Janice. She wished she'd never set eyes on her. Janice was an enigma. There was a mystery here that Helen might never understand.

Helen heard the back door open and close and suddenly Freddy entered the room and saw his wife sitting alone with her cocoa and a book.

"Glad you're back safe and sound, darling. I realise I have trouble sleeping when you're not in our bed. Everything all right Freddy? Is Mary okay?"

Freddy went and sat with Helen.

"Yes, darling. All is good in Mary's house, and I'm fine. Well, I'm sort of fine. Well, I'm not really fine darling. I have something I must tell you."

"Freddy! Are you really all right? What is it, darling? Tell me, sweetheart."

When Freddy had finished telling Helen about his encounter with Sophie, she took his hand.

"Freddy, I couldn't love you more than I do right now. Your devotion to me is more than a woman could possibly hope for in her lifetime. Being with Sophie was something I had wanted to explore with you both, but she was so against the idea of being with a man that I hadn't done anything about it."

She smiled while Freddy looked a little dazed and confused, accepting that he would never understand women, not in a million years.

"Now Freddy! Naturally, a wife must punish a husband for being unfaithful. I understand you are probably exhausted but you must be taught a lesson. Now I demand that you come to bed and cuddle me."

Freddie looked adoringly at Helen.

"I love you so much, Helen. I'm ready."

"Now Polly is fast asleep in our bed so we must try not to wake her. Sophie and she got together after you and Mary left and I went to work in the studio for an hour or so to get out of their way. Us cuddling won't wake her, darling. Come on, Freddy my love. It's been a busy night. I just want to fall asleep with you in my arms."

· · ·

When Polly stretched and rolled over and put her arm over Helen's belly, she realised that another arm was already occupying that space. This was the first time she had stayed overnight and Polly had unthinkingly assumed that they she and Helen would be alone in the bed. Now she realised that Helen's husband Freddy was also a regular night-time resident in the bed.

Polly lay still for a while thinking about things, especially the night before and her lovemaking with Sophie. She realised that she now had a serious crush on Sophie and she felt fairly confident that this wonderful woman felt the same way about her.

Early in the evening they had agreed to go riding together. Then they enjoyed long conversations about all things horsey. Things had just gone on from there and when the others left to take Mary home, Sophie had taken Polly's hand and led her to the sofa in the lounge room. They sat silently looking deeply into each other's eyes, then Sophie reached out and pulled Polly to her and they opened their mouths and surrendered to each other.

"That is enough talking, sweet girl."

Just as Polly was getting ready to quietly leave the bed, Helen's hand wandered over and took her hand and squeezed it.

"Love you both very much, sweetheart," came Helen's quiet murmur.

Polly hesitated to absorb the message in Helen's remark, then leant over and kissed Helen on the cheek.

"Sophie and I love and adore you too, Helen."

It was the day that Polly and Sophie were going riding. They had cancelled the event the week before because of the unseasonal and extreme wet weather.

The riding stables were just a half hour drive from Polly's mum's house. Isobel, Polly's mum, was away for most of the week and all weekend on business and Sophie had stayed the night with Polly.

Perhaps because they were close in age, they enjoyed silly times and passionate times. Being in their early twenties they were happy to be so young together.

"Just don't spend the whole weekend having pillow fights darling. Sophie is a grown woman. She's past all that," advised her mum.

The two girls laughed and assured Isobel that they would try to find other things to do.

When Isobel drove off, Sophie looked at Polly.

"Does your mum know?"

"She sure does. She's just pretending she doesn't. Keeping up appearances and being ironic at the same time is Mum's forte.

"She actually encourages me. Said she still hopes she hasn't left it too late. She thinks that at the next big conference she attends, she'll 'put herself out there', to use her words. She says there is usually a much more exciting line-up of females than males at these events."

"She's an attractive woman. If I wasn't already taken, and I met your mum at a conference I'd definitely ask her if she would like to join me for a pillow fight."

Polly pulled a face.

"Not gonna happen on my watch, my lady love. I'll never invite you to stay when Mum's home. It sounds too dangerous. My God, those legs look fantastic in jodhpurs Sophie, but they are just so tight. A girl can't get her hand inside them."

"All the more reason why a girl should practice," laughed Sophie, reaching for Polly's waist and belt.

The two had finished dressing for their horse riding-adventure. They walked out and got into Polly's car and headed for the stables.

"I guess if our darling Helen hadn't seduced us, we wouldn't be here, feeling each other up and having such a wonderful time," said Sophie.

Polly laughed out loud. "I can't bear to think about it, darling. Thank God we've got her in our lives."

The large two-story house and adjoining stables impressed Sophie.

"Wow! It's a bit different from the stables I work at. Is this where your admirer Belinda lives, sweetheart?"

"Yes. She lives with her aunt Elisha but sometimes stays a few nights with an uncle who lives somewhere in a beach suburb further north."

Polly parked the car and they got out and slowly walked around the paths that meandered through beautiful gardens and ponds. An occasional whinny could be heard from the direction of the stables.

"I think the horses know they have visitors," murmured Sophie, drawing on her long experience with horses and other animals.

Polly took Sophie's hand. "Come on. I'll show you around the back. I don't think Belinda is home. Her car isn't in its usual place. And her aunt is probably out."

The two walked around to the back of the house which faced onto a large open car space and various sheds and garages.

As the girls neared the sheds to get a better view of the back of the mansion, they suddenly heard angry voices and stopped. The sound was coming from one of the sheds in front of them.

The two looked at each other, then they crept forward to look through a half open door.

"No, Brad, it was a mistake from the very beginning. I'm not doing it any more."

Inside the shed, a woman was wrestling with a man who was trying to push her over a wooden bench that was covered with horse blankets.

"But boss lady, you know you love it."

"No! I don't love it at all. I only did it the first time because I … Let go of me."

A medium height woman suddenly broke away and ran towards the door. Sophie grabbed Polly and dragged her into an alcove between the sheds just as the woman ran out and headed towards the house.

"You fucking bitch!" yelled Brad as Sophie and Polly watched her run across the yard.

The woman disappeared into the house and the man returned to the shed.

Sophie and Polly looked at each other, trying not to make a sound as they slowly backed away. Then they turned and headed off to the stables.

"Wow! Brad's not a very happy chappie," laughed Polly while at the same time looking sad.

"He was Belinda's boyfriend and Elisha is Belinda's aunt."

"I figured that was the case. I'm feeling sorry for Belinda right now, damn it," Sophie muttered.

"Do you think we should do something?" asked Polly.

"Yes I do. If we see her, why don't you ask her if she would like to come home to your place for dinner? We have a responsibility to help her in some way, but I'm not sure how. That bitch of an aunt has really pissed me off."

Polly had not seen Sophie look this angry and formidable.

"Gosh, Sophie! I'm glad you're not pissed off with me. You seem a bit scary."

Sophie laughed in a far more relaxed fashion.

"Doesn't happen very often darling, I promise."

When Sophie and Polly got back from their pleasant but short ride around the bush track that led along and around the coastal headland, Belinda's car was parked next to Polly's.

While the two were attending their mounts, Belinda appeared and mumbled a weak hello. Polly thought how awful the girl looked. She was very pale and had black rings under her eyes.

"Hello Belinda. Good to see you. Belinda? I'd like you to meet my friend Sophie. Sophie, this is Belinda, whom I mentioned to you."

"Hello Belinda. Polly has talked about you."

Belinda stared at Sophie.

"Hello Sophie. Nice to meet you."

Belinda look confused. She hadn't expected that Polly would bring someone here, especially someone as beautiful and impressive as the woman she couldn't stop staring at. "I hope you both had a good ride. Well, I'd better let you get on with things. See you later. Nice to have met you, Sophie."

Belinda turned, about to head off to her car.

"Wait, Belinda!"

"Yes Polly, what is it?"

"I was hoping you might be able to come over to our place tonight and have dinner. Mum's away and we are getting a take-away. Please come. Oh yes, and you could bring a nightie or your pyjamas and stay over. That way you won't need to worry about driving home if you have a drink."

Belinda looked a little confused.

"Well, yes. That sounds great, Polly. Thanks. Six-thirty okay? I'm staying at my uncle's place at the moment and I need to let him know I'm going out when he gets home from work. Better if I do it face-to-face rather than by telephone. He worries about me a bit."

"Well, my dearest love. Do we have a plan?" Polly had just ordered pizzas to be delivered at seven o'clock.

Sophie put her arms around Polly and they stood in the kitchen just hugging.

"Not really, sweetheart. I have a suspicion that Belinda knows about her aunt and Brad. And I have another suspicion."

Polly looked at Sophie quizzically.

"A suspicion about what, Sophie?"

"I suspect that Elisha is jealous that her niece is bisexual. I wouldn't be at all surprised if her dear aunty had a crush on her niece."

Polly looked confused.

"Of course I can't be certain, but I'm thinking that Elisha is of an age when she probably wants something more in her life. She could be in need of a relationship with a woman. Belinda could be the one."

"That is very perceptive of you, darling. She did seem pretty emphatic that it was a mistake from the beginning, didn't she? Yes, you could be right."

"That's the clue, darling. She seemed more angry with herself, and less with Brad."

Polly answered the door and welcomed Belinda. She wanted to hug her and hold her tight and tell her that her life was going be all right, but she held back, knowing that Belinda wasn't aware of what she and Sophie had discovered about her aunt and Brad.

"So glad you came. The Pizzas are almost here and I've put Sophie in charge of drinks. I think she is concocting some sort of punch."

Belinda put her overnight bag down near the umbrella stand.

"Thanks for inviting me. Are you sure your friend Sophie doesn't mind having me around, Polly?"

"Quite sure. She said she'd like to get to know you better. I guess it's because I'd mentioned you to her a couple of times, and because you both work around horses.

"Some people find her a bit direct and full on, but she's a country girl and that might be the reason why she's not always subtle or seems a little insensitive. She's actually very sensitive."

Poppy put her arms around Belinda and gave her a hug.

"I've noticed how you seem a bit out of sorts lately, Belinda. Please just enjoy a night out with us and relax."

Belinda smiled and thanked Polly and they moved into the dining room.

Sophie had laid the table and she could be heard taking delivery of the pizzas at the front door.

Pizza followed by apple pie and cream washed down with fruit punch, not to mention the good company, was exactly what Belinda needed. She quickly warmed to Sophie's humour and direct language and thought how lucky Polly was to have a girlfriend like her. She also wondered how intimate the two women were, conscious that she found both of them sexually exciting.

The three had moved into the lounge room, each happily holding a glass of fruit punch in her hand. They had just settled down in the comfortable chairs and the sofa, when Sophie dropped a bombshell.

"How long have you known that your aunt was having an affair with Brad, Belinda?"

Both Belinda and Poppy turned and stared at Sophie. The shock on their faces reflected the impact of her words. Polly was the first to reply.

"Sophie, you can't …"

"Yes, she can," murmured Belinda in a low voice.

"Just over a month, Sophie. Can I ask you both how you know?"

Polly thought she should answer the question, thinking that Sophie might be too blunt.

"I took Sophie for a walk to show her the property before we saddled up. Your car wasn't there, so I could see you were not at work, and I thought Elisha was probably out. We heard a noise coming from one of the outbuildings, Belinda, and peeped in the door. We saw them together."

"Sorry, Belinda, but I think your aunt has been a bitch and Brad is a dumb bloody fool," added Sophie.

Belinda reached for a hanky and dabbed her eyes and blew her nose. Polly went to a drawer in the dresser and found a box of tissues, then went and sat on the sofa with Belinda. She put her arms around the girl and kissed her cheek.

"It's okay to cry, Belinda. It's what I would do, I know."

Belinda placed her head against Polly's shoulder and sobbed loudly.

Polly and Sophie looked at each other and Sophie gave an affirming nod.

Then Belinda lifted her head and blew her nose again.

"Being with you two is so wonderful. I want to say I'm jealous but the truth is I feel so loving towards you both. This just makes sense. I realise now that being with Brad never made sense."

Polly rubbed her hand between Belinda's shoulders.

"Thank you, Belinda. I want you to stay here with us for the night and just feel safe. Forget about what has happened and relax."

Belinda straightened up and turned and smiled at Sophie.

"Thank you, Sophie. I'm so glad now that it's out in the open. It's like you've shifted things for me."

Polly beckoned to Sophie to come over to the sofa and join them, and when she did, Belinda turned and put both arms around her and kissed her on the lips. Over Belinda's shoulder, Sophie winked at Polly.

"How about me please? Can I get a kiss like that too?" said Polly quietly.

A muffled reply came back from Sophie.

"Not yet, darling, I'm enjoying Belinda too much to let her go."

When she heard this comment, Belinda was immediately motivated and pushed harder on Sophie's mouth, putting a hand behind her head and pulling it too her.

"Hello! I'm over here and all puckered up if anyone is interested?" Polly pleaded good-humouredly.

Sophie unfastened her mouth long enough to speak.

"You had better go to her Belinda. But just remember, I haven't finished with you yet."

Belinda giggled and turned towards Polly's smiling face.

"Your turn, Polly."

The mouths of the two girls engulfed each other, lips were licked then sucked, then tongues moved into mouths and danced.

"While you two carry on like you've just met at long last, which could be true, I'm going to get into my pyjamas. Please feel free to do the same if either of you can find the time."

Sophie headed off to the bedroom and quickly changed. When she got back moments later, Polly and Belinda were still kissing and Belinda was tentatively touching Polly's breasts through her blouse.

Sophie smiled her most mischievous smile and unbuttoned her pyjama top and stood in front of the two kissing girls, her breasts sticking out provocatively.

"If either of you would like to change into her nightwear, I'd be more than happy to kiss you both goodnight."

Belinda and Polly stopped kissing and looked up at Sophie and her beautiful breasts. Then Belinda looked back at Polly.

"I don't know about you, dearest Polly, but I think it would be wrong to refuse this dear lady a goodnight kiss."

Polly looked up at her lover with adoring eyes. Sophie noticed and winked.

"I should warn you, Belinda. Sophie will be looking for more than a goodnight kiss. But then I can also assure you that neither of us will regret it."

. . .

When Polly and Belinda returned to the lounge room in their night-wear, Sophie had dimmed the lights and topped up their glasses with punch. Sophie who had long legs, was bent over adjusting the cushions on the sofa and Polly couldn't stop herself from going up behind her and pulling her pyjamas down around her knees.

"Quick! Look, Belinda. She loves a slap on her backside if you're into it."

With that, Polly began to spank her lover, who screamed expletives and swayed her bottom from side to side.

Belinda coloured up and smiled sheepishly.

"Can I just feel it a little bit? I want to gently rub my hand all over it. Oh Sophie, your bottom is so beautiful."

"Yes, you certainly can, Belinda. It will save me from that savage bitch. Please fondle my bottom, Belinda. I should warn you though that if you do, I will have fondling rights to your rear end."

Polly stood back enjoying the scene as Belinda stepped forward and put her hand on Sophie's beautiful buttocks. After a few moments, Polly lifted Belinda's nightdress and gently pulled her panties down, then ran her fingers gently up and down and across the girls bottom.

Without taking her hand away from Sophie, Belinda half turned and dreamily smiled at Polly, and puckered up and Polly moved her head and neck forward so that they could kiss.

"Open your legs a bit, sweetheart. I'ts time I felt your pussy and at last you're not wearing jodhpurs. I want to touch you all over and kiss you all night," whispered Polly.

"Oh yes! Yes! Please, please do that Polly."

Belinda opened her legs and Polly slid a hand between them. She felt her shaking as she felt Polly's fingers exploring her wet cunt.

Then Sophie's voice came loud and clear.

"I don't know what you two are planning back there, behind my behind, but you need to know that I'm going to eat you both."

To Belinda's surprise, Polly answered in her Little Red Riding Hood voice: "Doe's that mean you will chase these two naughty girls all the way to the bedroom Grandma?"

A croaky answer came back.

"You had both better start running now," answered the Big Bad Wolf.

The three women tumbled onto the big bed and shoved pillows into each other's faces, laughing and yelling threats about who was going to do what to whom.

"I think Miss Belinda needs to lie on her back and let us lift her nightie up around her neck and show us what she's got hidden there, don't you, Sophie?"

Polly pushed Belinda backwards and laid her down. Belinda did not object and wore an expectant smile, and her eyes were wide open. What had happened to her so far had already changed her life and she just wanted more of both Polly and Sophie, happy to give them whatever they asked for.

"I'm in love with you both. Please do whatever you want."

Belinda nestled her head in the pillow and wriggled down on top of the duvet.

"As she has been having some naughty fun with your backside Sophie, I guess it's only fair that you get a go at her first, darling."

"No! We'll have her together, Polly. Here, take this side of her nightie and I'll take the other. Now lift."

With her nightie now up around her neck and the two beautiful women staring down at her, Belinda shivered with excitement and gasped, "Oh God, yes!"

Fingers and palms wandered up and all around Belinda's beautifully shaped chubby legs, then around her crotch and up over her belly. Then she felt fingers squeezing her nipples. Her body shook. "This is heaven," she whispered.

Then she watched Sophie put her head down between her legs and Belinda felt her tongue begin to gently explore inside her mat of wet blond hair.

"Oh Sophie!"

Then Belinda looked up and watched Polly about to straddle her head and lower herself onto her face. Belinda felt Polly's wet pussy rubbing lightly against her nose and mouth, and instinctively she pushed out her tongue and lapped and then sucked on the moist soft pubic hair before pushing her head and mouth upwards and stretching out her tongue to explore Polly's vulva.

Sophie lifted her head and put two fingers into Belinda's cunt and moved them around, while her thumb, gently moved the girl's clitoris from side to side.

Belinda watched through half-closed eyes as Polly leant forward and lifted Sophie's chin, and they kissed.

Then Sophie looked at Belinda and whispered, "Rub my cunt please, Belinda."

Belinda screamed as her very first lady-to-lady orgasm erupted, setting off orgasms in the other two women in a chain reaction. Then the whole thing repeated itself moments later and the three collapsed into a heap, sighing and, in Belinda's case, sobbing.

They all rested, even while their hands leisurely caressed a part of one or more of the other bed partners' bodies. Belinda gave a little scream as she came again, then went on to sob some more.

Sophie was the first to speak.

"Thank you, Belinda and thank you, my darling Polly."

Polly suddenly giggled.

"Our first three-some, darling."

Sophie looked up at Polly.

"Yes, Polly, I think we are now in love with Belinda. Can we have associate lovers or are we going to be a monogamous couple?"

"Well, first we have to find out if Belinda wants to be an associate. Belinda?"

Belinda was now sucking on one of Sophie's breasts but managed to let go long enough to reply.

"Yes please, I do!"

"So is that it? Are we a couple but with extras on the side? I wonder what Helen would think?" Sophie added.

"Who's Helen?" asked Belinda.

"Helen is the woman who introduced us. We are both very much in love with Helen," answered Polly.

"Well, while you are both thinking about it, I've got a present for us in my bag. I'll get it."

Sophie left the room and returned with a cloth bag in her hand. Polly knew immediately what it was.

"Darling, I love the idea but we don't want to frighten Belinda do we?"

Belinda stopped licking Polly's thigh and turned to look at what was happening. She saw only that Sophie had something in her hand.

"Can you eat it?" she enquired.

Sophie looked at Polly and smiled.

"It can be fun trying, Belinda. But not really. This is a sex toy that Polly and I play with sometimes. It sort of replaces men in a way and it's apparently very useful if there are no blokes around when you need one. Would you like to try it, Belinda?"

Belinda looked at Sophie then back at Polly.

"Will I like it Polly? Do you like it?"

"I'm pretty certain you will, darling girl. Sophie is so good with it, I sometimes demand that she shags me with it."

When Belinda turned back to look at Sophie, she gasped.

Sophie had already fitted the harness when she went out of the room. Now – and in just a split second – she had inserted the dildo into it so that she now stood at the end of the bed, sporting her flesh-coloured strap-on and gently waving it from side to side.

Polly put on her Little Red Riding Hood voice.

"Oh Granny! What a big boy-thing you have!"

"All the better to shag you with, my dear," came Sophie's Big Bad Wolf reply.

"Oh my God! That is truly amazing. What are you going to do with it?"

"It's what we are going to do with it, Belinda. It is time for you to lie back and think of England or whatever, and let me show you. But first, dear lady, you must lick it."

Belinda didn't hesitate. She quickly moved forward to the end of the bed. Then she put her fingers around the pink cock and pulled it into her mouth and sucked on it.

"I can see you've got the idea. Now lie back and let's see if you like it."

Belinda scrambled back and lay with her legs wide open and her knees slightly bent. She looked up at Polly and smiled and Polly smiled back reassuringly.

Sophie moved in between Belinda's legs and rubbed the end of the dildo against her vulva and in just moments Belinda opened up and let her in. She shook in anticipation as Sophie started to move in and out.

Sophie then took hold of Belinda's ankles and lifted her feet up high.

"Are you ready for a good shagging, Belinda?"

"Oh yes, Sophie. It feels so good already. Please do it to me."

Sophie pushed the rubber dildo in and gave it to the dear girl lustfully and in no time at all, Belinda orgasmed.

Polly looked excitedly and lovingly at Sophie and asked if she could have a turn.

The two kissed and very quickly swapped over the harness and dildo.

Polly looked down into Belinda's glazed eyes, at last admitting to herself how much she had wanted to fuck her horse riding friend from the first time they had kissed, and touched each others breasts while laying on the straw in the stables.

"I'm having you now, Belinda. You okay with that?"

Belinda focused her eyes and her smiling face looked up at Polly lovingly.

"Yes, Polly, very okay. I can take much more of this, darling. Give it to me, please," Belinda whispered.

Polly shagged Belinda through two more orgasms while Sophie held Belinda's hand and kissed her lips and her breasts while her other hand gently clasped Polly's shapely thrusting backside.

The three young women slowed down, but not before letting Belinda put on the dildo and fuck her two lovers. She revelled in the feeling of power that she found it gave her and she screamed as each one came on the end of her rubber cock.

"Oh God! That was amazing. Thank you so much you darling women. Perhaps I should get one of these," she said.

When the three awoke next morning, they took turns making love to each other then, when all three were satiated, they shared the shower and bathroom. It was when all three were there, Polly and Belinda in the shower, and Sophie at the wash basin, soaping and washing the dildo, that Sophie made her second momentous statement.

"Belinda, your aunt has given Brad up. We didn't tell you what we saw but it was pretty ugly.

"What I want to tell you is this. I can't be a hundred per cent sure, but I know I'm close when I say that your aunt is in love with you and that she only took on Brad in a fit of pique. She didn't really want him; she wanted you, and it was her desperate way of stopping the two of you getting together.

"I also think that you have a soft spot for Elisha. That's why you never criticise her.

"We're leaving you a present. This strap-on might help you seduce your aunt. I'll say no more."

Polly and Belinda had stepped out from the shower and were silently watching and listening to Sophie. When Sophie stopped speaking and she and Polly looked at Belinda, they saw her very red face and self-conscious look.

"Thank you both so much for what you've done for me. I feel so much better in every way. And yes, Sophie, I do have feelings for my aunt and yes, after what you've told me I will find a way of telling her how I feel."

"Oh Belinda, you are a darling woman," answered Polly. "But just one thing. If you and Elisha get together, does this mean that we won't ever be able to be your lovers?"

Belinda answered, "If it happens, then I desperately hope that the two of you will one day be invited to a sleepover with the two of us."

And it came to pass that Belinda and Elisha did become a happy couple and they did invite Sophie and Polly for a sleepover.

5

JANICE AT LARGE

WHEN JANICE and Maria and Serina left Mary's birthday party they held hands as they walked the few yards to the front gate of Number 21. The summer night was balmy, ideal for being outdoors.

Maria and Serina gently guided Janice along a winding path to a wide covered veranda. Instead of unlocking the door, the mother and daughter asked Janice to sit down on the comfy old sofa that sat against the wall. Then the two slowly gave in to their passions, starting by lifting Janice's legs into the air, removing her panties and taking turns in licking and sucking her cunt.

"Oh my goodness, what is happening? What are you doing to me," groaned Janice?

"Just say if you want us to stop Janice. We don't want to frighten you," Maria said quietly.

"Mum and I are hungry for you Sister Janice. Please don't worry. We won't hurt you."

But Janice loved it and lay back with just her hands fumbling in the darkness, surreptitiously seeking out the bodies of the two adoring women.

Janice smiled inside. At Mary's party, she had told Maria and Serina that she was only a week out of a convent and quite lost in this modern world. She said that she had become sexually frustrated and had fallen in love with another nun, who had rejected her and reported her to the Mother Superior.

She told Maria and Serina that she had been asked to leave. It had been suggested that she could join a teaching order and become a teacher and had been told to go away and think about it.

She finished her story by shedding a tear and dabbing her eyes and, within minutes, first Maria and then Serina put a hand on a thigh and caressed her above her stockings, whispering their desire to help her, and Janice knew she was on her way.

Maria and Serina had both been boarders at convent schools and both girls had been mature for their age. As a result, both had enjoyed the sexual attention of nuns; so much so that, while Maria managed to remain a married woman, her daughter Serina found that the sexual life she shared with her husband was deficient and within a couple of years she found herself happily single again.

Now they enjoyed themselves in a variety of ways. Maria and Serina sometimes worked together as maids and kitchen hands for wealthy people, discovering that a few bored society ladies welcomed the opportunity to explore the bisexual aspect of themselves. A couple of these ladies regularly phoned and suggested it was time for one or both of them to pop over for coffee, cake and a little bit of fun. Sometimes they arranged to meet the two at a friend's beach house or some other location. One offered them her husband's cock, just for something a little different. When Maria and Serina did make visits, they took along sex toys in their bags and introduced their clients to a rich lesbian experience, although some of the woman they visited where able to teach Maria and her daughter a few things too.

They also enjoyed Grandpa Alberto, much to his appreciation. Alberto was blessed with good health and a very large and healthy cock, which both women were happy to handle lovingly. Nono Alberto slept a lot and spent much time outside in his garden.

Now they had Sister Janice, their new nun, just like the ones at school. With thoughts about their experiences with their attentive teachers, both wanted to devour Sister Janice as they had been taught to enjoy their teachers.

"Argh!" sighed Maria. "Sister Janice, you are beautiful. Say you will stay with us for a few days. Grandpa will love you as we do, and you will love him, especially his lovely cock."

Serina removed her mouth from Janice's and Janice whispered her response.

"That sounds wonderful, Maria. I'd love to spend time here, just so long as you both don't mind teaching me as much you can about sex and love. I want to make up for lost time and you are both so beautiful. And your Nono sounds exciting too. I've never seen a man's cock."

Janice was quite comfortable telling a lie or two as she moved her hand back between Maria's soft thighs and felt the wetness on her fingers. But Janice reminded herself once again that she must play the part of the innocent virgin nun who knew nothing about sex.

This masquerade she had thought up at Mary's party was already looking to be more exciting than she had imagined and Janice revelled in the idea that her two new ladies thought it was like having access to their misbehaving boarding-school nuns, from their younger days.

The delightfully lecherous Janice was intent on having every erotic stimulus that was on offer, and she would endeavour to satisfy herself and her new lovers in every way she could.

Janice awoke to the smell of fresh coffee. She felt very relaxed, probably from the fervent attention she had received the night before from her new lady friends. She leisurely touched herself between her legs, remembering the enthusiasm with which they welcomed her into their home.

She left the bed and saw that her clothes had been washed and folded and her stockings and garter belt hung from the back of a chair beside which sat her shoes.

Janice showered then wandered around as she dried herself, looking around at the sparse furnishings. Sets of drawers stood at either side of the bed. In the top drawer of one she discovered a vast array of dildos, every one designed for a specific purpose. Some had flanges on the ends making them usable with a harness. One had a finger-like appendage, which pointed to and touched a clitoris when in use. Most were coloured in pink or blue or purple. Some were translucent with gold or silver flecks set in them.

In the back of a drawer, Janice spied what looked like a box for posting bottles of wine. On the outside in big letters was written the name 'Harriet'.

Janice opened the box and discovered not one but two very long and thick black rubber dildos. She gently removed one from the box, handling it lovingly. Then Janice opened her mouth very wide and put the end of it between her lips, closed her eyes and made little sucking noises, smiling inside as she brought up fantasy images from past encounters. In the drawer below were dildo harnesses and these, too, where in bright colours, but mostly red or black.

Then she went to the other side of the bed. The first drawer was also full of sex toys. What took her eye in particular were the strapless dildos, with the large lump at one end which fitted inside a vagina. These could be held down under panties so that one could go anywhere knowing that one was prepared for sudden adventures and could spring into action the minute one pulled one's knickers aside or down.

Then there were butt plugs and small dildos designed for bottom play, along with some things she hadn't ever seen but sort of knew about. One was a smallish pink V-shaped soft thingy used for clitoral self-pleasuring and the other was a soft spongy thing with lips. The idea was that your clit went between the lips and you pumped the device with your fingers to make it suck you.

As Janice prepared to leave, she stopped to peep into a walk-in wardrobe. It was full of dresses and skirts and dress-up clothes including at least three maids' outfits and a sexy looking lady Santa outfit. Christmas party revelry, she thought. There was also a large range of shoes and boots. Then she noticed something else. Hanging behind the door were two fine leather switches and a wooden spanking paddle hung on a hook beside them.

Sister Janice was impressed. This boudoir was a pleasure centre *par excellence*.

. . .

Janice left the bedroom in search of coffee and something to eat.

"Good morning, Sister Janice! This is Father Munro. He's retired and totally deaf."

Janice had arrived in the kitchen to find Maria dressed in just a dressing gown and little Chinese slippers and standing at the stove making breakfast.

"There is muesli on the bench. Would you like bacon and eggs, or I can offer you toast with marmalade or strawberry jam? And how do you take your coffee?"

"A caffe latte would be good, Maria, and toast and marmalade please."

Janice looked at the elderly priest sitting at the breakfast bench. He was busy eating his bacon and eggs and didn't seem to notice Janice's arrival. He was a well-preserved older man, probably in his mid-seventies. Janice went and sat on a stool beside him.

Father Munro looked up and saw Janice smiling at him, he smiled back and continued eating. Maria came over with a coffee for the priest. Then she stood looking and smiling at Janice.

"Did you sleep well, Sister Janice? I hope you did. We did. I hope we didn't frighten you. Serina and I just couldn't get enough of you and we might have been a bit rough."

Janice looked back at Maria and fixed her with a gentle, loving smile, wishing she could blush on demand.

"Well, I did love it, Maria. And you were not too rough. I will look back on my first sexual encounter with the two of you as one of the luckiest and loveliest days of my life."

Maria came around the breakfast bar and put her arms out and Janice welcomed her with a loving hug. Then Janice asked Maria to kiss her and Maria did so with enthusiasm, while Janice slipped her hand inside Maria's dressing gown and caressed her breasts and felt her shudder.

"Stop it, darling. I don't want to stop, but there are things I must do. We will have time together later. I promise."

Maria smiled at Janice and moved back into the kitchen.

"Father Munro comes to visit once a month. We give him a little bit of attention, so to speak."

Maria threw Janice a knowing look.

"We enjoy it and so does he. But since we moved in here as care-takers, he hasn't been able to get an erection on any of his two visits so far. This is his third visit. I've played with it and put his hand between my legs, wriggled my bare backside in front of his face, but nothing seems to work. I don't know what more we can do, really."

Maria picked up a pencil and writing pad from the kitchen bench and started to write, speaking as she went.

"Because he's so deaf, I write him messages. I'm just letting him know who you are."

Then she took the pad and laid it beside Father Munro's plate for him to read and went back to making toast and coffee for Janice.

Janice thought for a moment and chose her words carefully. "Oh, how sad. I wonder if it's to do with your new accommodation? Maybe it just doesn't feel the same as your old place?"

Maria called back as she moved some things in the fridge.

"You could be right, Janice."

"Maria? If Father Munro hasn't got an erection, and I have never seen a penis, perhaps it would be a good opportunity for me to see his now so that I at least know what a limp one looks like. What do you think, Maria? Would it be improper for me to do that?"

Maria laughed. "You are so sweet, Sister Janice. Of course you can have a look. Have a feel too while you're there. His trousers are down around his ankles already. I'm sure he wouldn't mind."

Janice rejoiced in Maria's easygoing attitude and looked at the man sitting beside her. He was reading Maria's note. When he had finished it, he turned and looked at Janice and beamed a very big smile.

"Nice to meet you, Sister Janice," he said, holding out his hand.

Janice shook Father Munro's hand and smiled and mouthed a suit-able reply.

"Nice to meet you too, Father".

So! He believed she was a nun too. What fun. Janice was intrigued. What was going on in the elderly priest's head? She was soon to find out.

Janice dismounted from the kitchen stool and squatted down beside the priest's hairy legs, and stared into the shadows. There, nestled in between his thighs was a mass of curly hair and, almost hidden in the middle and only just visible, she could see his shrivelled penis. Janice pretended to gasp.

"Oh my God! Maria! I can see it. I'm not sure what to do next. Please advise me, Maria."

"All right Sister Janice. Don't panic. Help is at hand. I'll be there in a moment."

Maria came around the bench and looked at Janice crouched down with her tight skirt pulled up and staring at Father Munro's cock. She also stared at Janice's divine legs and feet, knowing that she and Serina would feast on Sister Janice again later.

She lifted Janice's hand and placed it on top of the priest's cock and whispered.

"There, darling. Now just run your thumb and fingers over the top of it. You can also reach in underneath and find his balls and rub those. He loves having his balls rubbed. Now I'm just about to serve your toast and coffee, so don't be too long."

After just a few moments feeling the priest's genitals, Janice surface and sat back on her stool.

"Well, Maria! That was interesting. Thank you."

Maria replied, laughing.

"We'll find you an erect one later, darling. I think you will find that far more interesting."

Not long after Janice had started eating her toast and sipping her coffee, she felt a hand sliding up her stockinged leg, a strong hand that seemed to know where it was going. She said nothing. Janice let things stay as they were for a minute or two, enjoying the experience and wondering what Father Munro had in mind. Then a finger slipped into her panties and caressed her pussy. Janice thought she should respond with some encouragement, if only to be polite.

As Janice lifted her arm and hand from the table top and moved it down towards her leg, the priest's other hand came across and took hers and carried it across and wrapped her fingers around a very serviceable boner. A sharp thrill of surprise and pleasure ran through her genitals and Janice reminded herself once again that she must, under all circumstances, maintain her innocent persona.

"Maria?"

"Yes, darling? More toast?"

"Er, not now. There are things happening under the bench that you might need to come and help me with, Maria. Father Munro has got an erection."

Maria turned and stared at Janice. "Is that a joke, Janice?"

"No, it's not. He has just put my hand on it and I need your help please, Maria."

Maria walked over and round and looked at what was happening. She bent down and looked at Janice's hand on Father Munro's cock.

"Well, that is very interesting, Sister Janice. You obviously have the touch."

"Or maybe Father has a special interest in nuns?" replied Janice. "Did you say I was a nun on your note?" Janice reached out and pulled the writing pad over and read the words "Sister Janice".

"Yes I did. I think you might be right. So what would you like to do with it, Sister Janice? It's your call. I imagine that if I tried to take over, he might not appreciate it and lose his erection."

"I wonder what he did with other nuns, if he had them?" wondered Janice, speaking quietly.

Maria laughed. "I think you need to take the lead Sister Janice. Father has the hots for a nun and you need to respond in a way that suits you."

"Advise me please, Maria. I need help now. This is all very new to me and I'm a little nervous."

"Well, your options are: rubbing his cock and masturbating him, known as a hand job; or you could suck him off, known as a blow job; or let him put his cock into your cunt and you let him fuck you. Or you could write, 'no thanks' on the pad and make sure he reads it."

Janice looked at Maria with a pleading face.

"If you turned your back on him, Maria, and I lifted your dressing gown and you bent over and I guided his erection into your pussy, he would be a happy man, I'm sure. Can we try that, Maria? Please? I'm a bit lost."

Maria looked at the worried Janice.

"Yes, let's see what we can do. I do enjoy Father Munro's cock and haven't had him for ages. Yes, we'll try that."

Maria turned around and bent forward over a bar stool and Janice lifted Maria's dressing gown right up and rested it on her shoulders. She looked at Maria's shapely legs and backside and smiled with appreciation. Then she put her hand between Maria's legs and whispered, "You are so beautiful, Maria."

"Oh, Sister Janice. Please keep me in after class and do whatever you want to do with me," whispered Maria in a mock schoolgirl voice.

Janice could not stop herself. Moving momentarily into the role of Maria's teacher was very exciting given Maria's response.

"I will, young lady. You can be assured of that. Now keep your hands away from your pussy until I can get to you."

Maria shuddered as the role-playing words from Janice found their mark.

"My God, Janice. You make role play more wonderful than the real thing. Can't wait to get more."

"Be quiet, child. Now! Try Father Munro's cock in the meantime. I promised him my sluttiest pupils pussy. Keep still, and when he yells, call out "yes Father" and "More please Father", in a loud voice." Janice's stern instructions made Maria utter a tiny scream.

"Sister Janice, you are priceless. I'm coming already."

Janice slowly dragged Father Munro onto his feet and turned him to face Maria's rear end. Then, still holding his cock, she nuzzled the end of it against the lovely woman's moist pink slit which nestled serenely in the midst of her profuse black pubic hair. Her cunt opened and Janice slipped the priest's cock into Maria.

It worked. Within moments, Father Munro was pounding Maria's vulva with gusto, yelling as he did, "There, Sister, take all of it. And make sure you come to the confessional during the week and I'll fuck you again. I know you love it."

"Yes, Father. Yes, I will! I love it. Give it to me harder, Father," Maria called out over her shoulder and in a voice loud enough for the priest to hear

Janice stood in front of Maria and the two smiled lovingly at each other. Janice had her hand up her skirt, then she lifted it and pulled her panties to her knees to let Maria see her playing with herself amidst her modest blonde curls.

Maria put out her arms and let her hands and fingers enjoy the feel of Janice's slowly rocking, mesmerising long legs, and her thighs.

Janice and Maria and Father Munro all came at the same time. The priest fell back down on his seat and the two women embraced and kissed each other.

"That was so good, Sister Janice," said a rather breathless Maria, sliding a hand over her very wet cunt.

"I thought so too, Maria. My sexual experiences are getting better every minute, thanks to you."

Maria picked up the notebook and wrote the word "Football?" and pushed it over to the now sleepy-looking priest.

"Yes, please!" called Father Munro as Maria straightened her dressing gown and headed back to the kitchen bench to put on more coffee.

Maria came over and took the priest's hand and led him through the doorway leading to a passageway that led to the sitting room and the giant television.

When she came back she looked at Janice and laughed.

"All men enjoy the simple pleasures of life, darling. Sex and football. And not always in that order."

"Now I wonder where Serina is. I expected her back by now. Father Munro's social activities officer will be here to collect him some time soon, and Serina will miss her."

Maria looked closely at Janice with a questioning look on her face.

"What is it, Maria? Is something wrong?"

Maria smiled.

"No, darling. Nothing is wrong. I was thinking whether I could ask you to stand in for Serina if she doesn't turn up, but I think you're probably not quite ready for it yet."

Janice made sure that she was looking sufficiently innocent.

"If you are thinking about something sexual, Maria, I'm up for it. Watching you shagging Father Munro gave me great confidence that I should be able to do anything you put in front of me. I'm sorry that I responded to Father's erection the way I did, but now I've seen what happens, I'm pretty much ready for anything."

Maria smiled and eyed Janice quizzically.

"Well, Janice. I don't know whether you know what a dildo is. It's a rubber cock that we women sometimes strap around our waists to fuck each other with. It feels good, better than a real cock sometimes, although not always."

Again Maria studied Janice's face for a response.

"Good heavens, Maria. It sounds wonderful. Can you show me one?"

Maria smiled.

"Yes, Sister, I can and I will. I should mention that dildos come in various sizes and shapes. You use them with plenty of lubricant.

"Serina loves me to do her with one on most mornings before she leaves her bed. She can get quite sulky sometimes if I don't give it to her. She says she needs it to wake up and face the day."

Janice listened enthusiastically.

"Perhaps she would let me try giving it to her tomorrow morning, Maria? What a wonderful experience it would be for a novice. Would you mind if I asked her?"

"Be my guest, Sister Janice. But I might have to be there to help. You can have both of us. Just to help you with your practice of course."

Both women laughed out loud.

"Now Serina still isn't here and Father Munro's welfare officer could be here any minute. Serina is Harriet's favourite. Not sure how I'll manage if she doesn't get home in time."

Janice was suddenly excited. Was this the Harriet who's name she had read on the box containing the giant dildos?

Sister Janice felt a little rush of excitement and anticipation.

The doorbell rang moments after the two women finished their conversation and Maria opened the door.

"Harriet, darling. Do come in. I have bad news. Serina hasn't got back from her cleaning job yet. I'm very sorry."

Janice stared at the biggest woman she had ever seen. Harriet was very tall, much taller than Janice, even in her regulation flat black brogues, and she must have been at least twice Janice's weight. She had cropped spiky blonde hair with random streaks of blue and red and she had piercing bright blue eyes. A vine leaf tattoo ran down her neck and disappeared under the collar of a white shirt. She wore a uniform of sorts, like a suit, a blue jacket and skirt and a man's tie, yellow with little crucifixes.

"Harriet! I'd like you to meet Sister Janice. Sister has recently left a convent to discover life, so to speak. She's not sure what to do next but luckily for her, and us, we found her so she is spending a little time here until she can find employment."

Harriet stared back at Janice, showing no emotion or clue to her thoughts.

"Well, that is interesting. But first things first Maria. I can't stay. I have an important meeting at midday, so I'll grab Father Munro and head back to the retirement centre. Tell Serina that I'm sorry I missed her but look forward to seeing her next time."

Then Harriet fixed her eyes on Janice.

"Do you have any skills other than the Church, Sister Janice? Can you type or use a computer?"

Janice was taken aback by Harriet's forthrightness, but responded quickly, once again reminding herself of her new innocent persona.

"Well yes, Harriet. I teach music, play piano and organ and yes, I can type and use a computer."

Janice smiled and the giant woman managed to smile back.

"Fine! If you would like to see me in my office on Wednesday at 3 pm, I will interview you. I'm looking for a personal assistant, but our limited budget demands that I find a multi-skilled person also capable of helping with the residents and the staff. We have around thirty priests. Are you interested?"

Maria looked back and forth at both of them.

"The retirement centre is very close to here Sister. You could board with us until you knew what you wanted to do about accommodation."

Janice thought very quickly, swiftly reorganising her other life as she did so. She had music teaching commitments, but mostly her work times were flexible. And this offer looked as if it might well afford her more sensual excitement. Janice's lustful needs always came first.

"Thank you, Harriet. Yes, I would like to come and see you. Thank you."

Harriet looked at Maria and asked her to give Janice her phone number so that she could text if need be.

"Send me your contact details, Sister."

Maria reached up and kissed Harriet.

"That is so kind of you, darling. Now let's go get the priest."

Janice arrived at the Catholic Retirement Centre for retired clergy for her job interview just before three o'clock as arranged. She felt a little unsure of herself.

Going for a job was all new to her. It was many years since she had worked in a regular job, and that had only ended when Janice was discovered in the store room, her naked breasts rubbing against another woman's naked breasts and their hands up each other's skirts. The fact that the other woman was the boss's wife made things very much worse than they might have been.

Janice smiled to herself, remembering a long-past lustful moment, triggered only because she was here for a job interview.

She found the door marked Chief Officer and knocked. Harriet opened the door and she went in.

When Janice had met Harriet at Maria's house, she had thought how scary the woman seemed. She imagined her as the classic dominatrix. Not that Janice didn't have time for such things. Being a subservient plaything for a mistress appealed to Janice's most base instincts, as did the idea of playing the role of a dominant mistress. She had enjoyed many memorable moments disciplining someone. Even the husband of the aforementioned breast rubbing wife, she recalled.

"Take a seat, Janice, and may I just say how nice you look. Now tell me, did Maria and Serina teach you about dildo's after we met?"

Janice thought quickly, then moved straight into the Sister masquerade mode, innocent but keen to know more about the real world and, in particular, sensuality.

"Oh yes, Harriet. And I most certainly enjoyed it. I think I got the hang of it but I do need more practice."

The striking figure behind the desk smiled approvingly.

"Well Sister Janice. You will be getting plenty of practice here as part of your job."

Janice's pussy trembled a little, reminding her of the pleasure she'd had on the two previous nights, when Maria and Serina had led her to the bedroom after dinner.

"Follow us Sister Janice," they whispered, laughing excitedly as they anticipated introducing the beautiful Sister Janice to her first dildo experience.

Harriet rose, reached over and took Janice's hand and led her through a doorway at the back of the office. It led to a pleasantly furnished room. With Chintz curtains, a big bed, a white fluffy carpet and an ensuite bathroom, it provided an ideal hideaway.

Harriet turned to Janice.

"I want you to take off your panties, Sister Janice so that I can properly interview you for the position I have planned for you."

Janice waited only a moment before she lifted her skirt and, with both hands, slid down her knickers and stood with a growing feeling of excitement.

Then she watched excitedly as Harriet disrobed, hanging her clothes on hangers and putting them in the wardrobe.

What an amazing sight! Harriet removed her shoes and stood up, tall and vivacious. She wore a bright red brassiere and panties set. Her extraordinarily shapely body seemed to fill the room and Janice could smell her warmth and perfume.

"Do you like what you see, Sister? This body needs servicing every morning at around nine thirty, and I'm hoping you will be the one to do it. Come here and let me feel you."

Janice moved towards Harriet. The woman put her hands down and ran them up under Janice's skirt.

"Take everything off, Janice. Let me see what I'm going to get each morning."

Janice stripped off and pirouetted in front of her new boss. Harriet stared at Janice's extraordinary bubble butt and her impossibly long slim legs.

"Beautiful! Now come on the bed and lie on top of me Janice. But first remove my bra and panties, then lay your cunt on my face so that I can smell you."

Janice did as she was told. She had expected that Harriet would be rough with her, but Harriet seemed entirely reasonable, not at all the violent, demanding monster that she had imagined.

She took off Harriet's bra and then her panties. Then she stared at Harriet's incredibly beautiful body. The vine leaf visible on her neck was part of a complete grapevine tattoo that ran down her back, around her belly, then branched into two and meandered down her thighs, ending at her ankles.

Harriet was a woman who obviously worked out, but without exhibiting the massive muscling that some women of her persuasion liked to develop. Her skin was taut all over, and her breasts were so perfect that Janice assumed that Harriet had had a boob job. But false or not, they were too impressive to ignore. They were huge and stood out and up, and her dark brown nipples were long and stiff and begged for attention.

Janice wanted to play with Harriet's tits for the rest of the day. They were truly monumental. Her nipples stood up and screamed for a willing mouth. Harriet backed onto the bed and lay down.

"Come along, Sister. I'm waiting for you."

Janice climbed on top of Harriet, turned her backside and lowered her pussy onto the woman's face. A muffled groan issued from the head between Janice's legs, and the gigantic body lying beneath her, moved like a horse rolling on the grass, as horses so often do after being unsaddled and let loose.

Janice had her arms wrapped around Harriet's abdomen with her hands clasping two gigantic taut buttocks. She searched around, inspecting every part of Harriet's legs and her beautiful belly. Then she put her head down, daring to put it between Harriet's thighs in search of her secret places.

"Yes, you beautiful bitch. Lick my cunt."

Janice was already there, pushing through a swath of blond hair, sniffing and wiggling her nose and chin in the moist undergrowth.

"Yes, Oh yes! Please! Do whatever. Just do it!"

Harriet was now lapping Janice's wet pussy and nibbling on her clit and Janice was in heaven. This was what she lived for – sensation and the anticipation of another climax. Her fingers were now working their magic inside Harriet's vulva and the woman's lower body trembled and moved dramatically, its huge size giving force to every movement.

Harriet began sobbing loudly, as if it was something she always did, and Janice felt her sexual power surge.

Knowing that Harriet was finding satisfaction made Janice decide to move forward. She placed four fingers into Harriet's giant soaking wet vulva and moved her entire hand inside her. And she didn't rest there. Slowly she moved her hand in further until her forearm was half inside Harriet's body. Then, after resting for a moment, she ever so slowly turned her now clenched fist, first a little to the left and then a little to the right.

Harriet exploded; then, moments later, she exploded again and then again. She kept on climaxing until Janice thought she might do herself an injury. In the meantime, Janice was climaxing regularly from having Harriet's mouth glued to her cunt.

A moment came when both women were lying still, just resting.

"Harriet, I'm going to take my hand out. I'm not sure whether it should be in there for that long."

There was a moments silence. Then a croaky voice spoke.

"Leave it there, darling. I haven't finished yet."

Janice smiled.

"Just as long as you're comfortable Harriet. I love having it there. And Harriet? Being with you is like being in heaven. I love it. Oh, and Harriet? I want you to lay on top of me. I would love that."

"Tomorrow, darling. I have a meeting shortly."

. . .

It didn't take Janice long to find her way around the retirement centre. After Harriet had confirmed her position and appointed Janice as her personal assistant, music and games activities administrator, staff welfare officer and, of course, her personal sex slave, Janice surveyed her new domain and she liked what she saw.

She had been given accommodation and a work area away from the residents' units, but only a short distance from the staff room. It was really a large and comfortable lounge room with two sofas and three arm chairs, and it included a piano. A bedroom was attached, containing a double bed, wardrobes and an ensuite.

Part of her round of duties was to make short visits to priests to check on their welfare. The retirement centre housed some thirty retired priests in two different wings of the building. One wing was for those requiring some form of regular care, while the other housed the healthy priests who required only feeding and a little home help.

This second group spent a lot of time socialising away from the retirement centre.

Janice began each morning with her boss, Harriet. It took only a few days of practice before Harriet declared that Sister Janice was a 'dildo natural'.

Her first day at work saw the two women naked in Harriet's special room. At first they stood with their lips glued to each other's and their hands palming each other's pussies. Then Harriet opened a drawer and brought out a giant dildo, like those Janice had seen in the drawer at Maria's house.

Harriet stood in front of Janice, then bent down and lifted each of Janice's legs to slip on the harness, tightening the buckles as she went. It was just a moment of subservience to her boss, but while Harriet fiddled with the harness she allowed Janice the opportunity to fondle her beautiful breasts, hurriedly sucking on a hard nipple before being dragged to the bed by her giant lesbian lover.

"Now Sister Janice, imagine me lying naked in front of the altar and you are the lecherous nun who came in for a quick Hail Mary and seeking forgiveness after you had just sexually abused two of your students. Your pussy is still wet and you are craving more juicy play-things. You can have me now, Sister Janice. I'm ready for you."

Janice needed no further encouragement. She hoisted herself up between Harriet's large thighs and nestled the end of the huge dildo in her mass of pubic hair.

"Put your legs in the air, you beautiful wet bitch," Janice whispered, before her mouth engulfed a stiff nipple.

Harriet lifted her legs high into the air.

"Whatever you want, Sister Janice. Do what ever you want girl, just so long as you push that fucking thing into me, right now."

Janice pushed and the giant cock slid all the way in. Then she lifted herself upwards and drove the dildo down hard, sending it much further in.

Harriet screamed.

"Oooh! My God, that feels so good, Janice. Don't ever stop doing this to me you skinny, leggy bitch."

Janice lifted herself up again and pushed down hard. Harriet screamed.

While Janice worked her dildo in and out of her sex-hungry boss, she licked, tugged and sucked Harriet's beautiful breasts. Harriet orgasmed for the umpteenth time.

"Janice, I don't want us to stop, but I must get on with running the retirement centre. I said I'd lie on top of you the other day. Would you like me to do that now, to finish off? I'm happy to do it."

Janice heard what Harriet had said and slowly extricated the dildo from her boss's cunt.

"I would love it, Harriet. I've been dreaming of it."

Janice rolled off Harriet and lay back with her legs apart. Harriet was on top of her in moments, one hand offering a breast back to Janice's mouth, the other arm around Janice's buttocks, pulling them together as she rubbed herself against her new personal assistant's pubic mound.

"There, you sexy PA. Tomorrow I'll shag you just like you shagged me. Gotta go to work now, sweetie."

"Don't go! I'm coming!"

Janice screamed and pushed upwards and Harriet joined her,

crushing her as she thrust wildly against her. Then both women sighed and slid about on their sweaty bodies, not wanting things to end.

"That was a lovely finale darling," Harriet giggled. "I didn't know I could do that."

Half a dozen or more nursing aides had fallen in love with Sister Janice in the first week. The moment these diminutive girls laid eyes on her long legs, she became the main topic of conversation.

Janice had been told how all of this group of young women had been together in the same convent school in Manila. Girls rushed to say hello in the mornings, and one girl had a picture taken of herself kneeling beside Janice's legs, her arms clasped around them and smiling cheerily.

As soon as this image appeared on the phones of her friends, every nurse wanted a similar selfie. Janice couldn't walk down the corridor without two girls rushing up to her, pleading to be allowed to kneel down and embrace her legs.

Selfies were the main focus on the young women's media posts and suddenly Sister Janice, or rather her long stockinged legs and high heels, were as popular among the girls as the latest fashion or pop star images. Janice couldn't help but enjoy the adoration.

If she had wondered about how she might enjoy these attractive young things more intimately, she didn't have to wait long for an answer.

Janice was staying in her own flat in Surrey Hills on Friday and Saturday nights, at Maria's and Serina's place on Sunday and Monday nights, and at her retirement centre apartment on the other days of the week. Everything about her life seemed to have fallen into place very quickly after she had met Maria and Serina at Mary's birthday party.

It was a Wednesday evening, and Janice was watching television in her apartment when she heard giggling outside in the passage followed moments later with a tentative knock on the door.

"Come in."

The door slowly opened just a little and two smiling faces peered around it and across the room at her.

"We brought you a plant, Sister Janice. And we thought you might be lonely too. We hope you don't mind us calling in?"

Two of her admirers came into the room, one carrying a plant pot containing an ornamental chilli plant, covered in a profusion of small red chillies.

"How nice of you both, I love having visitors, and goodness me, What a wonderful plant."

Janice waved the two to the settee across from her and switched off the television.

"Now let me see? It's Angel and Nicole, isn't it? I'm still trying to memorise all of your names."

Janice stared at the two across the room. A low diffused light came from the table lamp next to the TV, and she smiled as she looked at the girls looking at her and smiling, one behind her large-rimmed glasses, the other sporting a monumental set of white teeth.

"Yes, Sister Janice. You got our names right. It must be quite difficult remembering everybody's names to start with."

Nicole was going to be the talkative one, Janice thought.

"We seem to be so far away from you here, Sister. May we come over there and sit beside you? Please?"

"Of course you can. I was thinking the same thing. Come over here."

Janice moved to the middle of the sofa and patted a hand on either side. The two girls moved over and sat close, both with their beaming faces turned towards her.

"Do you ever get lonely, Sister Janice?"

Janice thought about what might be going on in the minds of her visitors and decided to engage the girls emotionally, earlier rather than later.

"As a matter of fact Nicole, I get very lonely at times. Especially at the end of a working day, when all you lovely ladies leave off work and I'm suddenly alone here in my room. I suppose I'm a bit spoilt. I do get a lot of loving attention during working hours so I really have no right to complain."

Janice looked at the face of each girl. Nicole with the big glasses and Angel with the big smile and a mouthful of shiny white teeth. Both had changed out of their uniforms and were now in identical pleated skirts and white blouses and long white socks.

If the members of this group of young women had been together in school in Manila, then it helped to explain their camaraderie and their familiarity with each other. It might also explain the identical clothes they were wearing.

It didn't really explain the make-up, though. Both girls had over-done the bright red lipstick and Janice could smell the face powder and heavy perfume. She guessed that they were still learning about life in the outside world, away from convent restraints and dress codes.

Nicole took Janice's hand and moved her face closer.

"We don't want you to ever feel lonely, Sister Janice, do we Angel?"

"No we don't, Sister. We could visit you regularly or whenever you want us to. We would love to spend time with you, Sister Janice."

Angel's hand closed on Janice's other hand and Janice sat admiring the two.

"Well, you two girls are just wonderful. I do so appreciate your concern. Maybe you both could call on me on a Wednesday night. I would look forward to that."

"Oh yes, Sister. We would love to have a regular date with you, wouldn't we, Angel?"

The girl with the big teeth smiled even wider.

"Oh, yes. We would love that."

"Now! Is there something you would like to do? Feel free to just relax and do whatever you want. And anything you want, just ask. And you are welcome to explore the fridge. There could be something there that you fancy."

Janice laughed and said, "And I'm quite happy if you just want to play with your smartphones. We can pretend we are a family and just do our thing, whatever."

Janice thought for just a moment before announcing, "Oh yes! To celebrate our first date, would either of you mind if I kissed you? I just want to taste your lipsticks."

They all laughed enthusiastically and the two girls moved their bodies as one, sitting up straight in anticipation.

"Please kiss us, Sister Janice. But please don't be put off if we giggle. It just means we're excited," said Nicole.

"Or nervous," added Angel.

There was a pause, then Janice turned to Nicole and removed her glasses, leaning across her and placing them on the side cupboard. She put one arm around her shoulders and then, with her other hand, lifted Nicole's face up so that she could look into her eyes.

"You are very beautiful, Nicole."

Then Janice moved her head forward and placed her lips firmly on the young woman's lips. Then she slowly ran her tongue along Nicole's bottom lip and did the same to the now trembling girl's top lip.

She felt Angel's hand looking for a spot to rest on the top of her leg.

She kept her mouth on Nicole's deliberately and was rewarded. Nicole pushed her tongue into Janice's and their tongues danced lovingly around their mouths.

"Is it my turn yet?" Angel's little voice whispered excitedly from behind Janice's head.

Janice slowly unfolded herself from the delightful Nicole and turned towards Angel.

Bright red big lips framed a huge set of beautiful white teeth. So large were the girl's molars, it seemed that she would never properly be able to close her mouth. This in no way made her less attractive; in fact, she just always looked as though she wanted to eat you, and the feeling from Janice was mutual.

Sister Janice lifted Angel's head and placed her already wet lips firmly over the girl's mouth and in no time, she and Angel were loving each other's tongues. The only sound was that of Angel's stifled sighs.

Janice had worked out where she wanted them all to go next. How to get there was now the challenge.

The three women lay back on the sofa breathing heavily. None of them wanted to stop their lovemaking, but none wished to make a move for fear of suggesting something the others might not be comfortable with.

Each had loved their kissing. But what should they do next? There was an awkward silence.

"Sister Janice? We loved being kissed by you. It was so beautiful," Nicole said quietly, looking across at her friend Angel.

"Sister Janice?"

"Yes, Angel?"

"Is there anything you would like us to do, Sister? Anything at all? We love being with you, so can we do something loving to you, Sister Janice?"

Janice looked at the two gorgeous and more than willing young ladies on either side of her, and savoured the moment. She took a little time to reply.

"Kissing you both has left me feeling something I haven't felt for years, a yearning for a closer physical bonding with women. Can I ask you both to do something to help me with these feelings? And please don't judge me harshly. I'm feeling a little vulnerable at this moment."

There was silence and then Nicole answered.

"Anything! Ask us for anything you want, Sister Janice. We would love to make you happy."

Janice looked into the dark eyes of the girl with the big teeth and smile, then she turned and looked into the doe-eyed short-sighted beauty on her left.

"I'm not sure how to say this, but here goes. I would love it if you helped me take off my panties and then let me watch each of you take off yours.

"I've always believed that at the end of the day, we can relax much better that way. But if you would prefer not to do that, I'm fine with that too. I just love being here with you both. And I also want to kiss you both some more."

There was a pause while the two girls looked at each other, and then, as one, they slid to the floor and reached their hands up beneath Sister Janice's skirt, with each planting a kiss on Janice's knees as they did so. In just moments they had her panties down. Angel took Janice by the ankles and lifted her legs and Nicole slid the panties down over her ankles and shoes and tossed them onto an armchair.

The two girls stood up and stared down at Sister Janice as she nestled down into the sofa cushions, then Janice lifted her skirt up over her belly. She watched the two girls staring at her with their wide, bright eyes. Then she put one hand down between her legs and closed her eyes.

"Thank you, Angel and Nicole. That feels so much better, but now I want your lips on mine. Hurry, my darlings, I want more kissing."

The two girls looked at each other, then instantly lifted their skirts and took down their panties and threw them away.

"Come and put your bare bottoms on my thighs, girls. I so want to feel your skin on mine."

Both the young women moved in unison, lifting their skirts as they parked their bottoms on their goddess's thighs.

Then they all embraced enthusiastically. The two girls leant towards each other, their mouths swallowing each others' tongues while Sister Janice ran her fingers up each girl's legs until she had a hand on both of their pussies, discovering that they were both exceedingly wet. Both girls moaned as Sister Janice fingered them.

"You have made me very happy and I love you both. Can I ask you if you will visit me again on a Wednesday evening, as we discussed? Tell me you will want more of this."

Both Angel and Nicole were now writhing on Sister Janice's fingers while they sucked each other's mouths. One began to undo the buttons of the other's blouse and the favour was returned. Both girls were soon able to rid themselves of another piece of clothing. Then they turned and took turns with Sister Janice's lips and mouth, unbuttoning her blouse as they went.

There was a moment when the girls separated and Nicole spoke.

"Sister Janice! We will definitely be here next Wednesday."

Then, as Nicole reached in to discover Sister Janice's breast and then her nipples, Angel added, "I think we might still be here. Oh God! I've never felt like this before in my life. You are both so beautiful."

Janice couldn't help but feel suddenly even more lustful, looking at the four tiny but shapely breasts calling to her, and her hands moved up and fondled them lovingly. The girls laughed and squealed and brazenly wriggled and pushed their breasts out to meet the mouth of their goddess.

Then Janice spread her legs wide apart and asked the girls to slide their pussies up and down on her long, stockinged legs.

Janice's legs were a source of excitement for her and for anyone who looked at them.

The two girls immediately turned over and parted their legs and each straddled one of Sister Janice's long legs, first on a bare thigh and then moving slowly downwards over Janice's silky stockings until they reached a knee. Janice's bony knees provided a sympathetic protrusion and greater traction for the two girls, and they eagerly rubbed themselves on them.

Nicole came first, along with a tiny scream, then Angel called out, "Me now! Oh God! Yes, Sister Janice!"

The two girls slumped forward onto Janice's tummy, clasping each other and kissing feverishly.

Janice was in heaven. After a minute or two, she whispered, "Would someone please lick me?"

Moments later, two mouths jostled for position, and two tongues slurped Janice's very wet pussy. Janice put her hands on the girls' heads, gently pulling them closer. Then she made a deep and lasting moaning sound and exploded.

When all had orgasmed and the girls had climbed up to lay their heads on Sister Janice's welcoming bosoms, and she was contentedly stroking their cheeks and licking each one's red lips in turn, she thought how beautiful their discovering each other had been. Janice couldn't be sure if this was the first time that the girls had so intimately touched each other, but she felt sure it wouldn't be the last, with or without her participation.

Janice languidly put a hand on Angel's bare breasts and played with a tiny erect nipple. Angel opened her eyes and smiled, her big red lips and her enormous teeth beckoning Janice's mouth to come to hers.

As Janice attached herself to the girl, losing herself in a heavenly dance of tongues, Nicole's voice whispered in her ear.

"We are in love with you, Sister Janice. Now Angel? I think it's my turn? Please?"

. . .

"We are in love with you Sister Janice."

When Janice heard those words – and appreciated where they were coming from – she didn't realise that she was about to be launched into superstardom, at least with the nurses at the retirement centre.

Janice never found out whether it was Nicole or Angel who shared information about their visit to her apartment. It didn't really matter which one. Whoever it was must have mentioned their wonderful night out to one of the other nursing staff, probably "in strict confidence, of course", describing how she and another nurse had enjoyed a wonderful evening with the long-legged goddess, Sister Janice.

And so it came to pass that on the following Tuesday night, giggles were heard outside in the passageway followed by a knock on Sister Janice's door, and Sister Janice found herself with two more sweet young things in pleated skirts and white blouses and very lipsticked lips, inquiring about her welfare and. in particular, whether or not she was lonely.

Janice was taken aback by this so obvious attempt at seduction, especially when it was apparent from the start that she wouldn't really be required to seduce anybody, but simply issue instructions. These girls were bent on seducing themselves, like groupies throwing themselves at pop stars.

"Oh, how sweet of you both. Do come in and find a seat."

Janice looked the girls over. One was plumpish and giggled nervously while the other was slightly taller and more finely built and quietly confident. They held hands, which was not uncommon among these girls. Friendships were mostly very close and much valued in their culture.

As soon as Janice got over the initial shock of the girls' arrival, she set about thinking through what she would do and then, more importantly, what she would like to do to them and what she would like them to do to her.

"Now remind me who you two are. I see you often enough during work time, but as I'm new here I haven't yet mastered remembering everyone's names."

"I'm Louise," said the chubbier one in a nervous voice.

"And I'm Tina."

Janice was thinking fast. Given that these two knew why they were here, there was no need for her to carry on with the charade that depicted her as the sad and lonely woman. That was now irrelevant. Janice was suddenly having to think of a new approach. One that made sense but, most importantly, one that would give her whatever she felt she would like.

"Well, it's so kind of you both to call in. But the truth is, girls, I've had a rotten day and I don't think even you beauties can cheer me up."

Janice was being honest. It had been a difficult day, beginning with the fire alarm going off at around nine forty-five, just as her boss was about to bring Janice to an orgasm.

"Fire alarm interruptus, darling. Sorry, Janice, I'll make it up to you later."

Then one of the bedridden priests died, and when the medics from the local hospital came to take him away, they discovered he was wearing a condom. Before anyone could do anything, the priest's niece had been informed and all hell broke loose with possible demands for an inquiry and a hint of legal action.

Janice made enquiries, then gave one of the Russian nurses time off and told her to just disappear. Then she was given the task of meeting the priest's niece.

Fortunately, Janice soon perceived her staring at her long legs and it wasn't long before she had bent over in front of the woman and then turned and smiled her special smile, successfully seducing the more than willing niece. The neatly dressed strong and shapely woman responded with great enthusiasm. In just moments, she had a hand up firmly up Sister Janice's skirt between her legs and the other hand pulling Janice's hair.

Twenty minutes on, with Janice bent over the desk, on the sofa and on the floor, the niece agreed not take the matter of the condom any further, just so long as Janice came to her house once a month for afternoon tea and a romp.

As Janice told her boss later in the day, "A tough day, but it was all in the line of duty, Harriet."

Now she had two gorgeous young dusky-skinned nurses staring at her and wanting to be entertained and she wasn't sure that she was up for it.

"If it made you feel better, Sister Janice, you could spank our bottoms. Sister Moran at school used to do it to us when she got upset, didn't she, Tina? And she always said she felt much better afterwards."

Janice looked at the cute chubby nurse with her big breasts pushing to get out of her blouse and her big red Cupid's bow lips, and thought that things might work out after all.

"We always hoped that one day she would show us her bottom and let us spank her, but it never happened did it, Louise? So, after she'd finished with us and left, we touched each others bottom's and played around with each other instead."

The two girls giggled, recalling times past.

Janice could see that they were both quite experienced and up for whatever she felt she wanted and, in this instance, it wasn't her hands on their bottoms. Well, not this week anyway.

She knew exactly what she wanted. She realised that, since the visit by Nicole and Angel, she had discovered a new fetish. Now, with these two beauties, she could have more of it.

When last week's girls had slid down Janice's legs and each one had orgasmed on a knee, she had felt the wetness soaking her stockings. And when she stripped for bed later that night, and routinely sniffed her stockings before popping them into a basin of water to wash and hang in the bathroom to dry, she discovered a wonderful odour on them that could only have come from the girls sliding their wet pussies down her leg and creaming on them.

Instead of washing them, Janice took her stockings to bed and popped them under her pillow and lay luxuriating in the scent of the girls while palming her pussy, and when she woke in the morning the girls' scent was still there. Janice loved it.

She patted the sofa on either side of her and the two new lipsticked ladies came and sat with her. Following the same routine as last week, she asked the girls to kiss her, then to take off her panties, and then to take off their own panties.

Then Janice got them to undo her top and free her breasts and then undo and throw away their own tops. Finally she instructed them to put their bare bottoms on her bare thighs and, just moments later, while they were all in a flurry of mutual kissing, Janice took each of the already damp, almost hairless pussies in her hands and fingered them gently. Janice saw how suddenly both girls were transfixed and had closed their eyes. She looked down at each ones fully exposed puffy and shiny wet and almost hairless vaginas, reminding herself that she would want to feast on them, but maybe on their next visit.

"Oh Sister, that is beautiful!" cried Tina. "Please don't stop."

Louise pushed even harder on Sister Janice's mouth while pinching her hard nipples, all the time twisting and turning her groin on her groping hand. Janice was ready and opened her legs wider.

"Now my, darlings. Sister would like you to turn yourselves over and slide slowly up and down on her legs. Please do that and don't stop until Sister tells you to."

Just as Janice had planned it, the two excited girls straddled a leg each and began rubbing, moaning gently as they hovered in a state of near orgasm. And each did orgasm. They came at the top of her stockings, well before her knees.

Janice watched their faces. Each one became contorted moments before release, then their mouths sagged open and Janice pulled a head down to her mouth. Slowly she felt the two girls' wetness, soaking the tops of her legs. Then she whispered in a croaky voice, as she too felt herself edging closer to coming:

"Don't you dare stop now, girls. Slide down a bit further. You are going to give me a lot more of your delicious juices yet."

The girls were now moving their crotches down to her knees. She moved her hands from holding their necks to the holding their bottoms. She gently ran fingers up and down each one's crack, then slowly inserted a digit into each girl's soft and sweaty little anus. Both girls gasped and rubbed themselves even harder on Janice's legs. Both came within a few moments, letting down more moisture for Janice to sniff in bed. But she still wasn't finished.

"Rub your pussies on Sister's bony knees now, please. I do love that."

Janice felt them sliding down her leg; then when each girl arrived at a knee they both paused, discovering that something special was pushing into their pussies and was even rubbing against their clitorises.

Wriggling and pushing was now the order of the day on Janice's knees with these two sexually over stimulated girls moaning and sobbing and no longer able to control themselves.

Her fingers pushed further into Louise and Tina's bottoms, causing them to jump up and down, pounding themselves on her magic knees. Suddenly she felt them both flooding on her legs as they screamed and slumped onto her bosom, each lipsticked mouth seeking out and nibbling one of her nipples.

Janet lay back and quietly ordered them onto their knees on the floor to lick her.

It was only a few minutes before Janice threw herself upwards and came as both girls attempted to keep their mouths glued to her special place.

She lay back again, feeling her saturated stockings and smiling and thinking of the night ahead, seeing her nose already nestled into the odour of today's delights. Then she heard a voice from between her legs.

"We are in love with you, Sister Janice."

"Well, girls, you are welcome to come again, but it has to be only on Tuesdays."

"We'll be here for sure next Tuesday, Sister, won't we, Louise?"

"For sure."

There were a number of Russian and Middle European nurses working in the high care section of the unit. One of them, Anna, was the carer that Janice had sent away following the condom incident, when medics had discovered a condom on the body of a heart-attack patient.

Once she had solved the problem with the priest's niece, Janice contacted Anna and told her that she could come back to work. When she returned, Janice interviewed her to try to ensure that this didn't happen again.

"Why on earth was the priest wearing a condom?" Janice asked Anna.

The skinny woman with the beautiful face and amazing cheekbones smiled.

"He said it would protect him from God's wrath."

Janice could see that the girl found the whole affair amusing, as she herself did on reflection.

"How did you come to be fucking him? From what I hear, he was unconscious most of the day and night anyway."

The girl eyed Janice, looking at her face and her legs and high heels, and came to the conclusion that Janice was probably like her, and so could be trusted.

"You might know what its like when you can't get a cock when you need one, Sister. If you see something that could do the job, you usually take it. I'm addicted to it, Sister. That is how God has made me."

Janice felt a quiver in her crotch and looked at Anna, letting her see that her sensuality was acknowledged and appreciated. Anna looked back and smiled.

"Is your appetite for cock a result of experiences you had in your younger days, Anna?"

"Probably. I lived with two older brothers and an alcoholic father and uncle. And then there were the neighbours. I was on call for pretty much twenty-four hours a day."

Janice thought about what life must have been like for Anna but couldn't imagine it. She tried to contrast it with what she knew about the convent girls she worked with. It seemed so different. Janice knew that the convent girls had early experiences with nuns and with each other, but surely it wouldn't have been so stark and unloving as the early experiences of this young woman.

"Didn't you try to get away somehow, Anna? Surely you could get help somewhere?"

Anna looked across the room and out of the window.

"I did. But not until I was sixteen. I applied for a job but then found myself being shipped off to London and locked up in a house as a sex worker.

"In some ways, playing with a man's cock at least once each day confirms my life and lets me feel complete. It's what I'm used to. Weird I know, but that's how it is."

Janice was fascinated by the young woman's story.

"You've been here in Australia for a while now Anna. Surely this new life has brought changes for you?"

Anna thought for a moment, crossing her long legs and pointing a heeled foot at Janice.

"Yes, Sister, I have discovered new feelings. I have discovered love. Well, sort of. I share my emotional life with two special women. I do love women."

"But you said you were addicted to cocks? How does that work?"

Anna laughed.

"It sounds funny, doesn't it? It's as though I have an inbuilt need to be useful somewhere. Sucking a cock or fucking one is the only useful skill I ever learnt, apart from cooking."

"So you don't do it for pleasure, Anna?"

"Satisfying my need to be useful is sort of a pleasurable experience but not like having what I now call proper emotional sex. Proper sex is what I have with women and that is where I can express and share my loving feelings."

Janice found Anna fascinating.

"So do you live with your special women friends Anna?"

Anna looked at Janice thoughtfully.

"Yes I do, Sister. You probably know them – Veronika and Dina – they both work here. We have similar backgrounds and of course we share a common language."

Janice knew the two girls. Both beautiful Russian women, similarly long-legged and skinny.

"And do they know about your need for cock?"

Anna laughed as she tended to do each time Janice asked her questions about cocks.

"We had similar experiences in our early days. Russia is a land of vodka and hopeless men. Abuse is hard to avoid for young females. While Dina had a slightly less abusive early life, Veronika suffered as I did. She, too, left home and ended up as a sex worker but in Berlin.

Both of them understand that much of their power is usually via their manipulation of men and mens cocks."

Janice started to thank Anna for coming in, deliberately smiling innocently at the beautiful girl as she thought befitted her managerial role.

"Thanks for coming in, Anna. And thanks for sharing part of your life story with me. I can only suggest that you be a little more careful with condoms in your future cock events." Anna laughed.

As Janice began to stand, Anna stood up in front of her. Then Anna leant forward and kissed her. Janice hesitated, then pushed gently back on Anna's mouth. Anna moved a hand up and spread her fingers and lightly brushed her hand across Janice's chest.

"Perhaps we could catch up again soon, Sister Janice. I have much more that I would like to share with you."

The two sensual women looked longingly into each other's eyes.

Janice surrendered herself, she hoped, with dignity.

"I will schedule another and longer appointment so that we can meet up very soon, Anna."

6

CAROLINE IN AUSTRALIA

CAROLINE ARRIVED in Sydney just a week before Maude's meet-and-greet party. Roger collected her from the airport. She was tired after her flight and her body clock was out of kilter. She really just wanted to sleep.

"I've made up a bed for you at my place. Alternatively, we could go to your parents' house so that you could spend the first night there with them and I could come over later tomorrow. What do you think?"

Caroline looked at Roger with a slightly dazed look on her face.

"My God, Roger, I can't believe I'm here with the man who is going to give me a baby. And he's so bloody caring. Not sure I deserve you, you dear man. Is this all real?"

Roger laughed. "Softly, softly catchee monkey, dear woman. I'll collect my fee when you are fully rested and able. In the meantime, I think I should deliver you to your mum and dad. Is that okay with you? You say what you want to do."

Caroline continued to stare at him.

"Oh Roger! Now I think I want you to collect your fee while I'm quietly dozing off. Sounds beautiful. But you're right and you might prefer me awake. Take me to my mum and dad, where I'll play the returning virginal daughter and introduce them to my boyfriend, who's staying at his place tonight."

Meeting Caroline's parents was a most enjoyable experience for Roger. Her mother Rosa was both gracious and beautiful and Caroline's father Bertie was a gentleman. Both were so pleased to meet him.

"You never said in your letters that your boyfriend was so good-looking, darling," commented Rosa.

As they were sitting talking, Alice arrived home from university and was welcomed and introduced to the two new arrivals.

"So pleased to meet you at long last, Caroline. Welcome home," Alice said.

Caroline looked intently at the slightly younger Alice and Alice stared back at her, equally intently.

"I hope you don't lose him to one of my beautiful slutty friends, Caroline. But then I'm sure you would know what to do about that."

Everyone chuckled at Rosa's warning. Then Roger dared to reply.

"Your slutty friends might discover that they can have their hearts broken by either of us, Rosa."

Rosa burst out laughing and Bertie's face broke into a broad smile.

Alice smiled coyly, with sufficient innocence to ignite in Caroline a sudden desire to wake up. But she was fading fast.

Caroline had long ago told her family that she was a bisexual woman and, although he had only just met them for the first time, Roger wanted them to know that he knew enough about their daughter and they could rest assured he would not be fazed by anything that Caroline did.

It was not long after Roger had left the Bennetts' house that Caroline crashed and her mother escorted to a bed in the quiet spare room in the cottage where Alice lived.

"Now, darling. This is the quietest room in the house and you will not be disturbed. And don't think you need to get up early. We'll expect you when we see you."

"Thanks so much mum. And mum? He is lovely isn't he?"

· · ·

Caroline was in a deep sleep when Alice opened the door of the bedroom and peeped in. Alice walked quietly to the side of the bed and looked down at the sleeping beauty. She bent over and kissed Caroline on her cheek, then turned and went to her own room where she slept and dreamed of a beautiful woman coming into her life.

Alice often had dreams like this.

Alice awoke to the sound of water running in the bathroom and became aware that someone was having a shower. Then she remembered that she was not alone in the flat and her thoughts immediately where of Caroline.

A short time after the water had stopped running and Alice was back enjoying her dream state, her bedroom door opened.

Alice sat up. Caroline stood naked in the doorway, staring back at Alice, then she smiled.

"I think I've got the wrong door, but I would love to come in. I'm a little bit lonely and probably disoriented from the flight, I think. Can I join you Alice? Please?"

Alice couldn't believe that the beautiful apparition at the door was real. Was she dreaming? she wondered. Then she realised that this was not a dream. She pulled the covers back on one side of the bed and wriggled over to the opposite side.

"Please come in, Caroline. Come and join me."

Without taking her eyes off Alice, Caroline walked over to the bed and lay down beside her.

"Thank you, Alice. I'm so tired. Please cuddle me. And Alice …?"

"Yes Caroline?"

"Whether I'm asleep or not, please do anything you want to me. Don't be put off just because I don't respond. I'm so sleepy, but I would love it if you did things to me. Perhaps a kiss to start with?"

Alice leant over and kissed the beautiful woman on the lips, then whispered to Caroline to close her eyes and just relax. Then, with tiny touches from her fingers, lips and tongue, she explored Caroline's body from her face to her knees.

Caroline would occasionally offer tiny sighs and little groans of pleasure, and in the early hours of the morning Caroline woke and reached out her arms and pulled Alice on top of her and each woman's mouth found the other's, and the two kissed and tongued each other as their bodies rubbed together until first one, then the other, took turns trembling and climaxing.

"So! It didn't take you two long to find each other, did it, my darlings."

It was around mid morning and Rosa had come to find out if everything was all right.

Alice and Caroline stretched and separated and lay back to look up at Rosa's smiling face.

"Hello Mum. I'm so glad to be home. In fact I'm so happy, I might just cancel my return flight."

Caroline rolled onto her side and put her arm over Alice and kissed her cheek.

Alice's face showed a pink blush and she looked lovingly at Rosa.

"Lucky that I have Tuesdays off to study. As you can see, I'm busy swatting for my final psychology exam next week."

Rosa and Caroline giggled as the two bedfellows pushed back the bedclothes and stood and stretched their naked bodies.

"I hope you're fully rested Caroline. I don't want Roger thinking that we kept you up all night. He might have plans for you."

"Hmm! Yes he might have, Mum. But I think I'm properly rested and able to be attentive to his needs."

More laughter, then Alice headed for the shower.

When Roger had collected Caroline and they had said their farewells and promised to return soon, they headed for Roger's favourite cafe.

"Now since I saw you last, we've received an invitation for dinner tonight at Freddy and Helen's place.

"It seems that your mum called Helen to tell her you were home. Freddy came around this morning to invite us. You were right. He's a great guy. It will be good to have him as a neighbour. And he told me how he and Bertie meet once a fortnight for coffee and that I would be more than welcome to join them. I was able to tell him that I had only just met Bertie and how I looked forward to seeing them both together."

"And Roger? Did Freddy mention Helen?"

"Yes, he did. He said that his wife went wild with excitement when she heard you were here. He also told me that Helen was the love of his life and that she had a number of women friends. He then went on to say how the two of them were very open in their relationship. Helen always informed her husband if she took on a new lady lover. In fact, she always offered him the option of meeting them and condoned any interaction that ensued, just so long as he told her about it.

"They believe this honest approach to their relationship is what gave it its strength."

Caroline stared across at Roger as the waiter delivered their coffees.

"I haven't told you this Roger so perhaps now is a good time to do so.

"As a young teenager, or maybe pre-teen, I was besotted with Helen, who was then in her late teens. She was always very nice to me, attentive and happy to talk to me about clothes or makeup or even boyfriend stuff. I desperately wanted something more, but didn't know what.

"Then suddenly she left home and moved to London. I've hardly seen her since. Just on one visit back for her father's funeral and another time, when her mother became ill. On that second visit, I'd left for the UK a week after she had arrived and so saw her briefly when she visited Mum and Dad. And it was during that visit home that she decided to stay in Australia, so I was denied the opportunity of seeing her in London. I was very disappointed."

Roger stared at the beautiful Caroline and thought what a remarkable woman she was.

"Well, Caroline. I'm looking forward to you two meeting. I only hope that Freddy and I will find things to do while you and Helen make up for lost time."

They shared and bit into their almond croissant and a carrot cake. Freddy thought about this sudden faster pace of life that he must accept over the next few weeks.

Roger thought about Maria and Serina and their morning visits to his bed and wondered how he should broach the subject with Caroline, which he must do soon. The alternative was to speak to his two early-morning visitors about the situation, exposing the fact that he knew about it.

One other thought suddenly jumped into his head. If Helen shared her lovers with her husband, that would mean that Caroline might have an opportunity for a moment with Freddy. Roger's mind wandered amid the logistics of impregnating and about timing and Caroline ovulating if this were to happen.

And then another thought arrived in his head. Would this mean that Caroline would then feel obliged to offer her man to the super popular Helen, who as yet he had not met?

There was much to get one's head around.

Roger looked at Caroline and found her looking at him and wearing a lazy, loving smile.

"Roger, how far is it to your place?"

"It's only five minutes away."

"So can we go home and fit in a visit to Margate darling man? I think we should practise for when I'm ovulating next week. Plus, I must admit, I'm suddenly really horny thinking about Helen. I hope you don't mind, Roger."

Roger laughed loudly.

"If duty calls, who am I to refuse?"

Helen and Freddy welcomed them at the door. Freddy looked at Roger and smiled and raised his eyebrows.

Caroline and Helen looked at each other, transfixed. Then they fell into each other's arms. Roger and Freddy heard sobs and Freddy nodded towards the lounge room and the two men headed off for a drink and some man time.

Eventually Helen came into the lounge, leading a slightly confused-looking Caroline by the hand. Roger saw Helen properly for the first time and yes, she was incredibly attractive physically and in her manner. And best of all, she had that thing that older women have that Roger responded to, regardless: a serene independence coupled with an air of happy self-confidence.

"I think we'll serve dinner sooner rather than later, Freddy. I'll go and check things in the kitchen. Look after our guests. No work talk please, otherwise our Roger and Caroline may just get up and leave."

Caroline was able to rally herself and laugh along with the others. She took Roger's hand and moved up closer to him on the sofa. Freddy excused himself on the pretext of helping Helen.

"Helen has suggested I come over tomorrow morning and visit her in her painting studio, Roger. And I'm sure you won't have any trouble guessing what will happen. I want to know if you're all right with that. I'm starting to appreciate that you are more important to me than just being a baby-maker. There is no way I would want to hurt you Roger. Is my visiting Helen okay, darling?"

Roger smiled at Caroline.

"I'm very happy that you two will get together at long last. Now that I've met Helen, I'm in love with her too, Caroline."

Caroline smiled back and cuddled up to him, kissing him on the cheek and squeezing his hand.

"I'm so pleased to hear that, Roger."

When the two got back to Roger's house, just three doors down, Caroline looked at Roger and smiled her usual disarming smile.

"Guess what, darling. I'm so hot from seeing Helen. Do you think we could run up to bed for a quickie where I can fantasise being shagged by her? And darling, now that you've met her, you could fantasise about fucking her perhaps?"

Roger grabbed her arm and took her to bed, where the two enjoyed an extraordinary lovemaking session with Caroline calling out as she orgasmed, "Yes Helen! Yes, Helen! More please, Helen" while Roger flicked through recent images of Helen along with images of past moments, including those of having his head between his aunt beautiful legs and his frantic shagging of her welcoming thin friend Sheila all those long years ago, and he thanked God for those memories.

• • •

Caroline knocked on Helen's studio door and when a voice called "Come in" she entered. Caroline wore a blouse and skirt and white socks and sandals and she had put on lipstick. Helen stared at her visitor and patted the bed, beside which she was sitting.

She had deliberately dressed in a simple light summer frock and sandals, wanting to recapture those moments years back when she would have visited the Bennett home on a hot Sydney day.

Caroline looked at Helen. Helen's choice of clothing worked for Caroline and she vividly recalled past images of the then twenty-some-thing-year-old Helen she so adored.

"Why did you never touch me all those years ago, Helen? You must have known that I ached for you. I was so in love with you and you just treated me as a child. Well, here I am, and I'm no longer a kid and I'm still in love with you."

Helen leant across and gently kissed Caroline's red lips then leant back, still looking into the younger woman's eyes.

"What would you have liked me to do Caroline? Where did your adolescent fantasies take you? Tell me, darling."

Caroline buried her face in Helen's chest and sobbed.

"I so wanted you to fondle me, anything. I wanted you to grab me and push me against my bedroom wall and put a hand between my legs and kiss me and stick your tongue in my mouth, then push me onto the bed and pull off my panties. Oh Helen, I was desperate for you."

Helen held the sobbing Caroline tight with one arm while her other hand gently rubbed the girl's back.

"I had fantasy's about you too, Caroline. I thought about you all the time, thinking of you coming home from school and finding me in your bedroom and me making you take off your uniform. Then I fantasized about making you take off your panties and ordering you to sit on my knee. Yes, darling, I thought about you a lot."

Caroline lifted her head to look at Helen and her jaw dropped and more tears welled up.

"Oh Helen, did you really have those thoughts? Oh God! You did think about me."

Helen held Caroline as she shook. Then she lifted her head and kissed her on the lips. There was a long silence before Helen spoke.

"We are older now, but I still enjoy thinking about you in the way I did then. I think we can enjoy each other and find wonderful things to do by simply remembering ourselves as those randy little sluts we longed to be back then and fantasising how it could have been."

Caroline looked at Helen and smiled.

"Oh yes, Helen. Please, let's be those two young girls who really just wanted to be hot together."

Helen rolled Caroline over so that she lay face down on the bed. Then Helen put her hands around Caroline's ankles and dragged her to the edge of the bed. She lifted Caroline's skirt up and stared at her white cotton-covered bottom and her legs.

"God! You sexy little bitch. You are so beautiful. Are you sure your mum and dad are away for the day?"

Caroline groaned with excitement at this imagined voice from long ago, and whispered in her pretend little-girl voice, "Yes Helen. There is no one home."

Caroline felt Helen's fingers slip under the top of her knickers and trembled with excitement as they slid down over her legs and feet.

"You are such a beautiful little bitch. Now get up on the bed on your knees, girl, so that I can slap your bottom and play with your pretty little pussy."

Caroline moved quickly to fulfil her mistress's wishes, spreading her legs a little as she did so.

"I've waited a long time for this, young lady. Now that you are at last old enough, I'm going to visit you in your bedroom every week when you get home from school and when your folks are out, and lick and suck your beautiful little pussy until you come on my mouth."

Helen bent and shoved her face between Caroline's legs. She opened her mouth wide and fed on the slippery young cunt that was waiting for her, listening to the loud moans of her fantasy schoolgirl Caroline.

"Now girl, are you ready for me to make you come? I want you to do that for your slutty Helen. Then, when I've finished fingering you, I will let you suck your first cunt. I know you've dreamed of it for a long time while you played with your randy self. Think about it now girl. Think about my super wet pussy between your lips. Imagine how you will go looking for my hard little clit. You randy little slut, you've made me very wet already and my pussy needs your attention. Are you ready?"

Caroline screamed out her answer.

"Yes, I'm ready to come now. Please don't stop, Helen. Do it to me!"

When Caroline cried out and orgasmed, Helen joined her and together they bucked and arched their backs, yelling each others names as they came.

Then Helen laid Caroline on the bed and gently licked her inner thighs.

"Now suck me, you darling girl."

When they had exhausted themselves and taken turns rubbing against each other's bellies, they lay back, holding hands and with their heads turned towards each other, staring into each other's eyes with glazed smiles.

"That so worked for me, Helen. You've fulfilled a missing moment in my life. I will love you forever."

Helen squeezed Caroline's hand.

"It definitely worked for me too, darling. I will want to do that again sweetheart, if you don't mind. I hadn't realised how good my slutty schoolgirl fantasy could be.

"Don't lose that schoolgirl outfit Caroline."

The two women laughed and kissed.

"You can come into my room and take off my cotton panties anytime, Helen. And you might like to spank me, if I can think of a way to make you angry. Perhaps I'll struggle with you and then bite you."

Helen put a hand down between her legs to touch herself.

"Stop it, girl, or I'll have to start all over again."

They both laughed and kissed and snuggled up.

"And by the way, my dearest new lover, I will also want your grown-up slutty version very very soon, so don't leave the country yet.

Two sluts for the price of one, methinks – the schoolgirl and the power-dressed professional bitch."

They rested and closed their eyes, but then Helen opened her eyes and looked over at Caroline.

"Or maybe three for the price of one?"

"What do you mean, Helen?"

Caroline and Helen both stretched and yawned.

"Well, Caroline. This might sound a little odd, but Freddy and I are very honest about our lovers. It's mostly me who introduces him to women and only occasionally has he suggested that I meet someone whom he's attracted to. I should add that I'm usually disappointed in his choices. They are usually not the sort of people that I would be attracted to, so I do not pursue the offer. I still can't work out what goes on in his head when he first meets them. I can only think that even the most discerning men are too easily seduced by tits and legs.

"Anyway, I should add that Freddy's assignations are very rare. I like to think it's because I fulfil all of his needs." Helen gave a wicked laugh.

"This open arrangement is wonderful and the honesty factor gives our relationship added security.

"I mention it because I'm duty bound to tell Freddy about you. Fortunately, he knew we would get together just as soon as we heard that you had arrived in Australia. The way I reacted to the news, almost orgasming in the kitchen and demanding his hand between my legs, left no doubt in his mind that sparks would fly as soon as we met.

Caroline leant over and kissed Helen, murmuring "I love you".

"I'm telling you this because, when Freddy knows that we've become lovers, he may feel romantically inclined towards you and suggest you and he have a moment together.

"There will be no pressure on you, I can promise, and you can say, "No thank you". But he has Fridays off and I am usually away that day, so if it's going to happen and you are up for it, I suggest you keep Fridays, late morning, free."

The two were silent while they each thought through what had been said. Then Caroline responded.

"I don't know that my situation is the same, because Roger and I have only recently got together and I wasn't going to tell anyone yet, but it's probably right for me to mention it to you. The agreement between Roger and me is for him to get me pregnant. I want to return to Australia and have a baby, Helen."

Helen turned and sat up and stared at Caroline in dismay.

"And why I'm saying this is that Roger was smitten with you when we all first met and he did not try to hide the fact that he would love to shag you.

"I suppose our relationship could be called open by default. I'm not sure what he thinks about me, but I'm feeling closer to him every day. Who knows, I could fall in love with him.

"He understands that I'm mainly into girls, so that is not a problem. I'm already the lover of his stepsister Jackie and her partner Miranda in London, both of whom will be moving into Number 21 to share the house with Roger towards the end of the year.

"Incidentally, Roger prefers mature women. He told me about his early experiences at age sixteen when he went to the farm of his widowed aunt, and how the aunt and the woman who cooked for her seduced him. More recently he has been living in a small town on the Italian coast while finishing his second novel and I'm pretty sure, from what his sister told me, that he discovered a plentiful supply of mature Italian women there."

Caroline laughed. "Sorry! That was probably too much information darling."

Helen was propped up on her elbow, keenly watching and listening to Caroline. She was processing what her new lover was saying, mixing images of herself shagging Roger and then thinking of Caroline having Roger's sister and her girlfriend, with the still fresh images of her pretend schoolgirl lover. And then there was the prospect of later having two new, and likely willing, women neighbours.

Helen decided that she would be ready to shag Roger if he showed interest, and she was also thinking about how Freddy might view this situation.

"Wonderful information Caroline, it so helps me to know you better. It also assures me that you are indeed a slutty little bitch. I think a five-minute kissing session is needed right now."

Caroline rolled on top of Helen and their mouths locked in mutual enjoyment.

"I'm looking forward to our grown-up slutty version, Helen. I'm travelling light, but I'm sure there is a garter belt and a corselet in the luggage somewhere, and there is a new pair of heels too. Promise you will play with my suspenders you slut, if I packed them. If not, then my garters with bows."

Helen looked at her partner lovingly.

"Yes, dear, how could I not do all of that? Plus I have to have you satisfy my secret fetish. I want to look at you on your back on the edge of the bed with your bare backside on show, wearing your heels and with your legs high in the air while you twist your ankles and feet."

Caroline thrust her abdomen upwards and whined in her little-girl voice.

"Helen! You're making me hot again. Can we just have a bit more naughty schoolgirl, please?"

Helen sat up on the edge of the bed and dragged Caroline over her knee and lifted her skirt.

"You horny little bitch. How dare you try to seduce me while I'm helping you with your homework. If I didn't know better, I'd think you were trying to get me to lick your pussy. Now take that!"

Helen had experienced a lot of spanking at the hands of her first lesbian lover, Miss Lazarus, and was an expert in administering punishment in varying intensities. As her hand fell lovingly on her victim's bare bottom, Caroline squirmed in an effort to escape and cried out.

"You fucking bitch. That hurts so much. I'm not playing any more. Let me go!"

This caused Helen to slap Caroline's bum a little harder.

"We are not playing games, you little slut. Now open your legs wide so that I can rub your wet little cunt. If you're good and do as you're told, I might let you get up. But only after you've kissed and licked me."

When the two finally rested, Caroline hugged Helen and kissed her on the lips and on her breasts and licked her neck.

"I love you so much."

"I love you too, darling girl. Now! Are we agreed that we should shag each other's blokes? I'm up for it if you are. Haven't tried another cock in ages. But we can't be sure about them. Guess we'll need to check with them first."

"Everything being equal, it sounds like a plan I could work with," replied a drowsy post-orgasmic Caroline.

7

PARTY TIME

Number 19 Eros Crescent, like Number 21, was a very large house and both houses were probably built by the same builder. They were the two biggest houses in the crescent.

Number 21 had eight bedrooms, two kitchens and three bathrooms and a cottage and Number 19 was bigger, with twelve bedrooms and six bathrooms, but not a separate cottage.

It was designed as retirement accommodation for better-off older Edwardian widows and spinsters. The only evidence of the home's past life was the large numbers – 1 to 12 – painted on each bedroom door.

Maude was a most impressive woman. She taught music, including voice. Some of her students were from country regions and in these new large premises she was intending to offer accommodation and board when they were required.

Maude had knocked on Roger's door one morning to be greeted by Maria. The two got on famously and Maria told her how the owner, Roger Robertson, worked late into the night and wouldn't rise till after midday.

Maria also explained to Maude about the recent storm and Roger's offer of accommodation for her and her daughter and Grandpa Alberto. She also informed the new neighbour of her housekeeping services, in case Maude needed help with her big house. Maude was delighted and suggested that Maria bring her daughter for afternoon tea the following week to discuss what they could do to help Maude manage the place, especially if and when she had house guests.

Maude finished by issuing invitations to Maria and her complete household and to Roger for the party she was throwing on Saturday week.

The Bennetts, Rosa and Bertie, along with their tenant Alice, received invitations. Alice's invite said to bring a friend, to which Maude had added an "s" making sure that not just Freya, but also Alice's other university pal Angie, would be able to come too. On a visit to Sydney and the Bennetts' house late the year before, Alice and her two friends had given Maude a surprise birthday party in Alice's flat where, after a few drinks, Maude had become intimately involved with all three girls and the latest member of the Feeling Sweet Club.

Maude suggested in her invitation to Rosa that, with such a large number of rooms in her new house, everyone was welcome to stay overnight.

It should be mentioned here that, as Rosa's close friend and long-time lover, Maude also had a special relationship with Rosa's husband, Bertie as well as with the three abovementioned university students.

Maude was renowned for her sensuality. Her large shapely body and, in particular, her enormous breasts were forever seeking loving attention, and she was more, often than not, well rewarded.

At Number Seventeen only Freddy was home. Maude knew Helen from meeting her a number of times at Rosa's house and she knew of Freddy, but they hadn't met until now.

"Yes, Maude, of course I know of you. Helen has spoken of you often, as has Rosa. Welcome to Eros Crescent."

Maude thanked him and offered him an invitation. He thanked her in turn and assured her that he and Helen would definitely be there. He also said that, if she needed assistance with anything, they would be only too happy to pop down and help.

Just as she was about to leave, Maude turned and asked Freddy about the occupants of Number Fifteen.

"Mary and her niece Sophie live there. They are close friends of ours and will love to meet you. Sophie works during the day, but Mary is mostly home if she isn't at her volunteer job at the Salvation Army shop."

Maude's new house boasted a vast dining room and an equally huge dining table that ran half the length of the room. It could seat around twenty-four comfortably and maybe thirty at a pinch. In its heyday, the establishment residents would sit opposite one another and still leave half the table for bowls of fruit, drink decanters, large vases of fresh flowers and a marble bust of Beethoven resting on a lace cloth.

Newspapers and the latest ladies' magazines and journals would also be placed there along with a very large brass tray on which, each day, one of the staff would leave the morning's mail.

Today the table had been placed against the wall and made home to a superb feast of food and drink and, adorned with vases of flowers, kept company by regular stacks of plates and bowls along with essential cutlery and carvery tools. Water jugs and drinking glasses sat on a small separate table close by.

There were four large glass bowls of fruit punch and a bust of Beethoven with another of Chopin reminded everyone that the owner of the house was a devotee of music. Around the rest of the room were settees and easy chairs, interspersed with ornate dining chairs and a number of music stools. In one corner, a drinks bar offered a selection of wines, soft drinks, liqueurs and spirits.

The Bennetts and their entourage made up of Alice, Freya and Angie and Angie's cousin Hayden, were the first to arrive and were shown straight into the dining room by a young man in a diner suit. A few minutes later they were joined by Helen and Freddy, who arrived with their neighbours Mary and Sophie. Also accompanying Helen and Freddy were three of Helen's friends, Polly and her friends Belinda and Elisha, none of whom had met any of the people in the Bennett contingent.

A long round of introductions and quick private assessments, especially by those women who were intimate with Helen, followed.

Just as this first flush of introductions was completed Caroline and

Roger arrived, setting off another round of who was who, and more importantly to some, who was what to their much-loved Helen. Other than Alice and the Bennett family, and close family friends, no one knew of Caroline, the gorgeous woman visiting from London and staying with her handsome partner.

Helen explained that Roger was now Maude's neighbour, having just recently taken possession of Number 21. In an incredible coincidence, Roger had met Caroline Bennett at a party in London given by his sister only a short time before he left for Australia.

For this first group of partygoers there was already so much to think about even before other people began arriving.

Maude appeared and called out a welcome to all and said how sorry she was that she hadn't been there to welcome them, but now here she was. Her extraordinarily tight black sheath dress barely held her large figure in, but it was the low-cut top, rather than the bulging thighs and backside, that kept eyes more focused. Everyone cheered and clapped as she moved among them, kissing and shaking hands and being introduced to the few whom she did not know.

Maude held up her hand, asking for a moment of quiet and announced that, although there would be two groups of people at the party who had never met – those she had known and loved for a long time and others who were staying in the house – most of whom were her students from the country, along with a number of her other country friends. She urged everyone to mingle with the other group and show them that city folk were friendly just like country folk.

When Maude had finished, everyone cheered and laughed and assured her that they would adopt a country friend. It was at that moment that other folk began to arrive along with more Sydney people, some of them relatives of Maude.

Some of the arrivals included Roger's resident family from the cottage, Maria, Serina, Grandfather Aldo and the large rustic looking man in his mid thirties who Freddy had only recently met, Maria's grandfather's distant relative, Giorgio.

Soon the mix expanded as Maude's country residents arrived back from trips into the city or from visiting city relatives. It was no longer possible for their names to be announced, and Maude asked that they all introduce themselves at random.

Freddy and Roger were standing chatting when a well-dressed man and his wife approached.

"Reverend John Cameron, and this is my wife, Edith Cameron."

"Pleased to meet you. Hope you are both enjoying Sydney? Are you staying in town for long?" asked Freddy.

"About a week, we think."

Rosa had met Mary previously, about a year before. They had been talking at the Salvation Army store and Mary had mentioned her neighbours Helen and Freddy. Discovering this connection was appreciated by both women and they enjoyed their long conversation.

Rosa was sitting in an armchair. She had eaten and now held a glass of fruit punch in her hand.

"Hello Rosa."

Rosa looked up at the large woman standing beside her and realised that not only was this Mary, it was also the woman whose butt Bertie had slyly remarked on when he murmured "What a backside" – typically his few words on such a subject – but his understanding wife had noted his interest and also noticed who the woman was.

"Oh Mary. Hello! It's so good to see you here. Of course, you are a neighbour of Maude, so we may see more of each other in the future. Maude sometimes stayed with us before she bought this house, so I will no doubt be visiting her. Hopefully, we will catch up then."

Mary stood while the two looked out at the ever-growing crowd.

"Helen and Freddy are such wonderful neighbours, Rosa. And now I think about it, their stepdaughter lives with you, doesn't she?"

"Yes, Alice is a lovely girl. It looks like she's making a lot of new friends. Not sure who they are. They could be friends of Helen's?"

Rosa looked across in Alice's direction, where she was in conversation with two young women.

"Oh yes, I met them, and for a change I remember their names.

The younger one is Belinda and the other one is Elisha. They own a riding school somewhere up past Palm Beach, I think."

"And are you a single woman, Mary?"

Mary told Rosa that she had recently become a widow. And with due respect to her late husband, she was enjoying life to the full now that he'd gone. Mary looked at Rosa oddly for a moment, then told how her life had changed dramatically since meeting Helen and Freddy.

Rosa smiled and replied. "Helen has the ability to show women that there is a lot more to life than they thought."

Mary smiled back at Rosa and they looked deeply into each other's eyes.

"She does indeed, Rosa."

"So Mary! Is there anybody here that takes your fancy? Someone you would like to know better?"

Mary laughed out loud.

"Well actually there is, Rosa but I'm sure he must have a wife somewhere here. I haven't identified her yet. Maybe I'll get lucky."

"Point him out to me Mary. Maybe I'll know if he's available."

Mary laughed again.

"You are as wicked as Helen, Rosa. Oh, there he is. That gorgeous-looking older man with the shock of silver hair. Isn't he delicious? I'd take him home at the drop of hat if I could."

Rosa couldn't contain herself. She laughed so much that Mary asked her what was so funny.

"Mary darling, that is Bertie and he is my husband."

Mary coloured up.

"Oh God, I'm so embarrassed, Rosa. I hope you'll forgive me. But you more than anyone must see how attractive he is."

"Mary, dear Mary, No apologies necessary, I can assure you. Bertie and I have been together for fifty years and now enjoy what some might call an open marriage. We have sometimes shared lovers. And if it makes you feel any better, my husband has already commented on your very attractive rear end."

Mary coloured up even more.

"Oh my God, Rosa, you are amazing. But please, let's just leave it there, shall we?"

Rosa looked at Mary intently and smiled.

"No, Mary, we won't. I've been wanting to give Bertie a present for a long time but the opportunity hasn't arisen. You might be able to help. Please Mary, I would consider it a favour if you would take Bertie down to our room and be that present. I'm confident that you would both enjoy it."

Rosa laughed, bemused by Mary's dilemma.

"Rosa, you can't mean it surely? How would it all happen?"

"It will happen much easier than you think, Mary."

Rosa beckoned to Mary to come closer. She leant forward and spoke quietly into her ear. Then she took Mary's hand and led her through the crowd until they found Bertie deep in conservation with the Reverend Cameron.

Rosa touched her husband on the shoulder and Bertie turned to his wife and smiled. Then he looked at Mary and nodded hello and Mary nervously beamed back.

"Bertie darling, this is Mary. Mary lives two houses up, next door to Helen and Freddy. She was telling me how excited she was that Maude had moved in. She is also keen to look around the house and, in particular, in the rooms.

"I told her that we're staying the night in Room Five but I have promised Helen that I will join her shortly so I wondered if you would be the gentleman and show Mary inside Number Five? Can you do that, darling?"

Bertie looked at his wife, noticing she was wearing that particular smile that she only used when she wanted him to do something special for her, usually something intimately personal.

"I would love to do that, darling. So Mary, are you ready now, dear lady?"

Mary still couldn't believe what was happening. It all seemed so unreal. A beautiful woman handing her equally beautiful husband – on a plate, so to speak. Mary squeaked a reply.

"I'm ready, Bertie. See you later then, Rosa, and thank you."

Bertie took Mary by the arm and the two disappeared through the crowd and the rear door.

Only moments later, Caroline was at Rosa's side.

"Mum! Is everything all right? I just saw Dad heading … "

Rosa interrupted her.

"Thank you, darling daughter. Yes, everything is fine. Your father has been so good while I was away in hospital I just wanted to give him a present. It was one of those moments, darling, when everything just came together."

Caroline looked at her mother in awe.

"Mum, I don't know what to say, but you sound very happy about it. I've obviously been away too long. Life for the two of you has moved into a new dimension by the look of things. I'm shocked, but also impressed."

Rosa smiled lovingly at her daughter.

"It's been this way now for a number of years, darling, but at first you were too young and then you moved away. I just never had an opportunity to talk to you about it. Remind me one day before you leave and we'll have a cup of tea and a good chat. It might also help you to understand yourself better, sweetheart. Chip off the old block?"

As she spoke, she noticed a tall, thin youth standing close by and looking as though he wanted to talk to her.

"Mum! I so love you and Dad. You never cease to amaze me. Call me over if you need me."

"Thank you, darling. Oh yes! Just one more thing. If you suddenly find me missing, don't bother looking for me. It's likely I've headed off and given myself a present."

They laughed together and, then Caroline headed off to rejoin her group, in particular Helen and Helen's super-beautiful hot young friend, Polly.

———

Rosa turned and looked at the young person standing not far away and looking a little lost. At first she though it was a young lad – one of the choirboys staying in the house – but when Rosa looked closer, she saw that it was a rather tomboyish young woman.

The young woman looked back at her. Seeing that Rosa was no longer engaged in conversation with anyone, she moved over to her.

"So! I don't think we've met. My name is Rosa. What is yours?"

The slightly nervous girl smiled and said her name was Jessica and that she was a music student from Armidale and had come with her aunt and uncle that morning to stay with Maude for the weekend. She was feeling a bit out of place here and wished she had stayed at home.

Rosa eyed her new young friend keenly.

"No, Jessica. Being here is a good thing because, especially at your age, new experiences are very important. I remember how I felt awkward when I was younger and my parents had to make me go to things. Life is a bit like learning the piano, really. You hate the practice but love it later on when you can dash off the Moonlight Sonata and impress everyone."

Jessica smiled for the first time and Rosa was rewarded by seeing this slightly unusual creature relax a little. Jessica was quite tall and very thin and showed no sign of developing breasts. Her hair was auburn and her face reminded Rosa of one of those Pre-Raphaelite paintings of young women, serene and beautiful and with a far-away look in their eyes. The girl's movements were slow and graceful, but Rosa couldn't put an age to her and only guessed that she could be anywhere between fifteen and twenty-five.

"There you are, Jessica. Thought we'd lost you, darling!"

Rosa turned and looked at a woman in her fifties who, despite the hot weather, was wearing a cardigan over a woollen dress, heavy grey lisle stockings and solid brown brogues. Her manner was constrained and she seemed a little hesitant when she spoke.

"Oh no Auntie. I'm not lost. I was trying to do what you suggested and circulate. I have just met this beautiful lady. Rosa? This is my aunt Edith who is the wife of the Reverend Cameron."

The two women looked at each other keenly and shook hands.

"Very pleased to meet you Rosa. I take it you are a friend of Maude?"

Rosa noticed that both aunt and niece made furtive glances at her hands and feet. Were they both fascinated with her lipstick perhaps, and her red-painted finger and toenails?

"Yes, we've known each other for many years and, until just recently, Maude has stayed with us on her monthly visits to town. Do you get to Sydney often, Edith?"

"Not often enough, unfortunately, Rosa. Getting away from one's husband isn't easy when you live that far away from the city. I've also been the librarian at a girls private school for many years but I will retire from that post next month.

"Getting away is not easy, but I'm planning to change things a bit if Jessica decides that she wants to come and board here. If she does, then I'll try to get down regularly to be with her. Unless of course she suddenly gets a boyfriend and doesn't want me hanging about."

The three women chuckled, enjoying the joke, but Rosa was thinking ahead. She had noticed that, although Edith laughed as she talked about getting away from her husband, she wasn't laughing inside; and having watched the Reverend Cameron talking to a man earlier at fairly close range, she had taken an instant dislike to him.

It was obvious, too, that Jessica represented a lifeline for Edith's escape from her country prison and maybe – just maybe – there was something more to the older woman's attentiveness towards her niece.

It was very hot in the room, partly because of the outside summer heat and also because of the large number of people. Jessica swished her skirt about to make a breeze and said how hot it was. Then she looked at her aunt and told Edith that she "must be boiling in all those clothes".

The impish and sensual Rosa began to plot. She took a risk.

"I'm feeling so hot that I'm thinking that I will go and find an empty unit where I can slip out of this dress and lie on a bed under a ceiling fan. Are either of you interested in joining me?"

The silence went on for so long that Rosa thought neither of the women had heard her. Just when she was about to rephrase the invitation, Jessica whispered "Yes. Let's do that," followed by the gentle voice of Edith.

"That sounds like such a good idea, Rosa. We'd love to join you. Where will we go?"

Before Rosa could answer, Jessica did.

"Number Seven is my room. We could go there. It has a ceiling fan."

Everyone smiled politely.

"Sounds good, Jessica. Lead the way."

———

Of all the people at the party, there were two who had eyes only for each other the moment they saw each other.

Sophie watched Freya standing and making a statement in her stylish Bombay bloomer shorts alongside Alice and knew that she wanted to know her better, whoever she was.

The long-legged Freya noticed Sophie looking at her. Each appraised the other's long legs and heeled sandals and interesting face from a distance, and blatantly signalled her willingness to join forces by staring at the other across the crowded room.

Little did they know that each of them had another person occupying her thoughts and that if they had known, never would have guessed that it was the same individual.

It wasn't long before Sophie and Freya were standing self-consciously side-by-side near the food table and it wasn't long before – in their hesitant but excited conversations – they discovered that they both wanted to spend time, not just with each other but with the same third person.

Freddy was quietly nibbling and drinking and thinking his usual thoughts about the meaning of life when arms encircled his waist and wet kisses were placed on each cheek. He assumed it would be Helen and maybe Polly, but he was wrong. He turned and saw the two beautiful lovers of his wife Helen and then realised that he had made love to both these charming women too. Once with each. How could he forget?

"We don't want to frighten you, Freddy, but we are here to proposition you."

Freddy turned and faced the two beauties with his eyes wide.

"What have I done wrong? Please don't kill me. Helen might miss me."

Both girls giggled.

"It's what you've done 'right', Freddy. Freya and I have just linked up and we discovered that there was something we have in common but both of us have had it only once. Now we want it a second time. We want you, Freddy!

"If you would give us a key to your house, we will go and get into your bed and discover each other. Then later in the evening, when you are bored with the party and not sure what to do with yourself, come home to us, you beautiful man, and shag us both and scream your screams. Please, Freddy?"

Freddy looked at the girls and saw that they meant business.

"Who am I, to deny two beautiful women the use of my body? Yes, Sophie, and yes Freya, I will visit you in my bed. It will be an honour to serve you both."

The two women smiled and glanced at each other with relief and excitement. Then Sophie looked around and moved up close to Freddy. She surreptitiously put a flattened hand on the front of his trousers.

"Thank you, darling man, from both of us. Just one more thing?"

"Anything Sophie! Anything at all!"

Sophie pressed harder on Freddy's trousers while Freya watched and smiled at her new audacious friend.

"Just don't fuck anyone else before you get to us. You know I work with horses and I know how to turn stallions into geldings. Thank you, Freddy. Keys please?"

Freya and Sophie quietly left the building and headed next door, excited in the knowledge that they were probably about to eat each other and that there would be a second course, and if all went well, quite possibly an encore.

"I so want to get inside your sexy bloomers, Freya. They are driving me mad."

"And I just want to get my mouth on something you've got and I haven't Sophie. Your beautiful tits."

As they arrived at the house, they found themselves looking further along to Helen's painting studio and, in the same instant, both recalled that their first seduction by Helen had been in that studio.

They wandered hand-in-hand towards the studio door.

"We could begin there," whispered Freya.

Sophie stared at Freya.

"That would be a good idea Freya. That's where my first time with Helen happened."

"Mine too."

They reached the front door and found it unlocked, and went in and threw their arms around each other. Their mouths joined for the very first time. Then they laughed and fell onto the bed.

"Freya?"

"Yes, Sophie."

"Did a certain person want to see your legs sticking high in the air?"

Freya giggled.

"Yes, that person did Sophie, and I will happily demonstrate, if you would like to remove my shorts."

Sophie turned and sat up and lovingly rolled Freya on her side so that she could get to the zip. Then she pulled Freya's shorts off and stared at the woman in her panties. She ran a hand down a leg and lifted one ankle, then the other one.

"I think she did it like this darling girl?" Freya sighed.

"Yes, Sophie. Now lie beside me and we'll stretch them up side-by-side and twist our feet in loving memory. Helen would love that."

They both laughed as they looked appreciatively at their beautiful long legs standing high up.

"Let's ask Helen if we can both come here with her one day and give her a double leg show and let her see how well she taught us."

Frey moved her arm and her hand began to unbutton Sophie's blouse.

"Yes, let's do that, Sophie. Now darling, it's time we ..."

———

Helen loved being the centre of attention, but it did make organising her personal life a little difficult. Everyone, it seemed, wanted a bit of her.

While Helen had managed to make Polly feel wanted and loved, keeping her other lovers at bay wasn't easy; it made her feel a little uncomfortable knowing that, while she loved them all, tonight wasn't to be their night with her.

But she was being overly sensitive about the whole thing. She hadn't realised how, with so many new faces and figures to choose from, everyone could find someone to enjoy.

She had very quickly noticed that Sophie and Freya had hooked up and Helen found herself fighting back a jealous twinge when she saw how quickly Alice had been welcomed by the two new lovers and friends of Polly, Belinda and Elisha.

But tonight was Polly's and Caroline's night to share the fruits of love with Helen. They, too, were obviously enchanted with each other when Helen introduced them, and as Helen moved around the crowd she would catch glimpses of the two, hand-in-hand or arm-in-arm. And again she felt emotionally confused and she realised that the sooner the two got together in a safe place, the better.

The trouble was, all the socialising was taking its toll on Helen, and she realised that what she really wanted was time out; a cup of tea and a lie down. What a dilemma for a girl in lust?

Maybe she had overdone things. But how could she possibly not do what she was doing with all the wonderful women that she was doing it with?

When Helen felt a man's arm around her waist, she knew that her beautiful husband had come to rescue her.

"Come over to an armchair and sit on my lap for just a few minutes darling. I have something to tell you and I'm also missing you."

Helen turned and threw her arms around Freddy and kissed him feverishly. She whispered "yes, master, whatever you desire, master." This was what she needed.

"Wow! I didn't know you cared that much, sweetheart. Now I want to slip my hands down the back of your knickers."

Helen laughed and for the millionth time thought how much she loved this man.

"Will I find you in our bed tonight, lovely man?"

"Well yes, but! I've been propositioned by two of your lovers, darling. Freya and Sophie have just met for the first time."

"Yes, I noticed that. Hard to believe we haven't got them together before, isn't it?"

Freddy leant forward and nibbled her ear.

"It seems that, in getting together, the clever little so-and-sos came up with the idea that they would have each other for the main course and me for dessert. I've given Sophie the key of the house and they have asked me to join them later in our bedroom."

Helen looked at Freddy with a loving smile.

"Those little hussies. I've taught them too well. Especially that lanky horse-loving slut Sophie. Encouraging her to ask for whatever she wanted could have been a mistake. I haven't had her in the studio for a couple of weeks. I'll get her in soon and give her a little something on her backside to settle her down."

Freddy looked at her appreciatively.

"So that's it, darling, are you all right with all that and have you planned your evening's playtime?"

Helen pulled him to her and kissed him.

"Yes darling, I have. It's good you've told me, so that we don't fight over who gets what bed.

"I'm planning an evening with Polly and Caroline and will probably stay here. If not, I'll bring them home and take over the lounge room.

"If I do end up at home – love of my life – we could arrange to have a half-hour interval from our respective others. I could meet you in the kitchen and you could give me a quick buggering over the table, before we head off again for regular duties."

Freddy roared laughing, drawing looks from the crowd.

Across the room, Caroline watched them and wondered whether she could ever find a man as wonderful as Freddy. But then maybe she already had one, she thought. Yes, she already had one called Roger, she remembered. What was she going to do about all that?

———

Elisha and Belinda had been a couple for only a month and were still discovering the wonderful world of the bisexual woman. Belinda's friends Polly and Sophie had brought them together.

Belinda hadn't realised that her aunt had special loving feelings towards her until Sophie and Polly made her confront the truth. When that happened, Belinda confessed to having similar feelings for Elisha.

Attending this party was the new couple's first time out in public together. They did not know anyone at the party except Polly and Sophie, and those two were busy with their other friends.

Not long after Elisha and Belinda first got together, they had invited Sophie and Polly to stay overnight and their first foursome had been a great success. Belinda had already been to bed with the two women so it was only natural that a great fuss was made of Elisha who thoroughly enjoyed being well and truly licked, sucked and shagged by all of them; her first experience after making out with her Belinda.

Polly introduced the two new lovers to Helen, of whom Belinda and Elisha had already heard much. Helen excited both of them and both confessed to an immediate crush on her. Then they were introduced by Helen to others in her group, Freddy her husband, and the older couple, Rosa and her husband Bertie.

Sophie introduced them to her Aunt Mary and Elisha commented that she thought her aunt was super sexy. To which Belinda answered with a grin, "Not as sexy as mine."

There were others, but one that attracted them both equally was Freddy's stepdaughter Alice, who boarded with Rosa and her husband, at the far end of the Eros Crescent.

After meeting Alice, Belinda asked Elisha if she too had the hots for Alice, and when Elisha replied "surely have, darling" using her cowgirl drawl, the two agreed amidst embarrassed giggles that even as novices they should risk rejection and attempt to seduce the beautiful woman.

"Oh darling, I've no idea how to do this," whispered Elisha. "What should we do?"

As the two sipped fruit punch the gods smiled on them.

The beautiful Alice wandered up and stood ladling herself a drink from the big bowl. Her delicate form in her floral summer dress and sandals and, most of all, her slow measured manner of moving and speaking, enthralled the two women.

"Hello! Belinda and Elisha, isn't it? I hope you are having a good time. Are you staying here for the night?"

The two lovers looked at each other, so wanting to be able to say yes.

"Unfortunately, we didn't think to book a room, so won't be staying," Elisha answered nervously.

"Thats not a problem, Elisha, I would love it if you both came and shared my room. The rooms have very big beds."

Alice was experiencing the lustful aspect of herself and flashed a mischievous smile at what she viewed as two inexperienced, nervous and super sensual morsels.

"I would appreciate the company of two beautiful women. I've been spending so much time studying for exams and only talking to analytical university mates, I've forgotten how to be sociable. But only if you would like to do that?"

Elisha and Belinda looked at each other and smiled and nodded. Then Elisha seized the moment and boldly answered.

"We'd love to, Alice. But we should warn you that we both picked you as the girl we'd most wanted to spend time with tonight. Having the two of us in your bed means you probably won't get much sleep, at least until we've settled down."

Alice's mouth opened as she gasped excitedly, then her sly smile returned.

"To tell you the truth, I've been trying to work out how to get to know you both better all night. I'm not very good at chatting up girls; I rarely try to do it and when I do I usually get tongue-tied. Trying to get you to my room like this was a desperate move. So please be my guests. Oh yes, and you can keep me up as late as you like. I'm sure I will love it."

The three embraced and their lips met, but only briefly in deference to the crowd around them.

"My room is down through that door whenever you want to go in.

Number Eleven. Make yourselves comfortable and I'll be there when I'm through with organising a couple of things with Rosa and Bertie. Probably won't be able to join you for an hour or so, but I will be so looking forward to it.

"Perhaps you could take some food from here. We might just get hungry later. Oh yes, and you will find nice smelly soaps in my overnight bag on the bedroom dresser and there are spare towels in the cupboard, if you decide you want to have a shower."

Elisha and Belinda thanked Alice and she turned and headed off to speak to Freya and the woman who looked as though she was going to keep her happy that night, Sophie, before they disappeared.

———

Alice walked over to the bar area just as Freya and Sophie were about to leave.

Freya kissed Alice and smiled sheepishly.

"I think you know about Sophie, but Sophie tells me that the two of you have never met, although Helen talks to her about you. Sophie, this is Alice."

Alice was impressed with this "long-legged country girl", as Helen had so often described her. Alice looked Sophie up and down, obviously assessing her as a potential lover and exaggerating the fact to amuse the two.

"Pleased to meet you at last, Sophie. Can't think why it's taken so long."

Freya and Sophie both laughed Sophie moved forward and put her arms around Alice and kissed her on the lips.

"I promise you will get her back safe and sound, Alice."

Alice regarded the two with a loving smile.

"If I don't, Sophie, then I shall be looking for a long-legged replacement and I think I know who that will be, so watch out."

———

The night was still young, but Maude had been up since daybreak getting things set up and now she was a little tired. But this super-sensual woman was not finished until she had finished off at least one man or woman, or both. Now, as things quietened down, Maude had a moment to review the evening ahead and time to think about her options.

The vicar, John Cameron, would give her a good shagging as he sometimes did back in Armidale after choir practice and they were alone. But having Edith with him was a problem. Edith and John were obviously not actively sexual, so she wasn't likely to be up for a love triangle.

The two lads from the choir could be up for some fun. She had given one of them a blow job while the Reverend was having her doggy fashion one night, after the lad had come back to the church unexpectedly to look for his phone. That youth had obviously told his friend and the next time she saw the pair was on a wet rainy day in the churchyard. The boy she'd sucked went red in the face and asked in a croaky voice if they could put their hands up her skirt. Maude had thanked them for their interest and told them "yes, but only if I can suck your cocks."

Then Maude had led them into the little shelter shed nearby and out of the rain, unbuckled their belts and pulled down their trousers and pulled out their cocks.

The wide-eyed lads had watched as Maude divested herself of her skirt and panties, then dragged the boys' hands between her thighs as she gently grasped a cock.

"This will have to be quick, boys. I need to be in the church in thirty minutes."

Nothing had seemed out of bounds, such was the sexual appetite of this extraordinary woman.

It was only when Maude looked across the room and saw Rosa heading off with the vicar's wife and her niece that she knew that the vicar would be free to have some fun. She sought him out in the crowd and whispered in his ear. He smiled and nodded and Maude knew she would not be alone that night.

———

When Bertie and Mary walked into Room 5, Mary couldn't have been more nervous. She could feel herself trembling. Bertie was so lovely, so much the gentleman. Could she really utter the words that Rosa had whispered? And he seemed so very normal. Was it possible that he was becoming forgetful, as Rosa had said?

"It's quite big as you can see, Mary. I suppose the residents spent a lot of time in their rooms, so that they did need a goodly space. And they would probably have brought pieces of their favourite furniture with them when they moved in."

Bertie continued talking, but Mary could hardly concentrate on what he was saying. She was remembering the Fifi Codes that Rosa had told her about and was wondering how and when she should utter them?

Bertie was just pulling the curtains across to stop the bright, hot sun from heating up the already hot room. Then he turned to Mary and smiled.

"Seen enough, Mary?"

Mary suddenly saw that it was now or never.

"Bertie? Fifi wants you doggy style."

Bertie was very still, processing Mary's words as he stared at the ceiling. Then he looked at her and smiled.

"That would be lovely, Mary. I would like that. Why don't you take off your frock and your knickers and get down on your knees on that nice rug over there? It looks like a comfortable spot."

Mary couldn't believe what she was hearing. She stared at Bertie's loving smile.

"Come along, Mary. Don't be shy. I'm getting excited. And my cock is too. Get them off, girl."

He leant forward and kissed her, running a hand down her back as he did so.

She looked down at Bertie's trouser front and saw that this was really happening. She flew into action, turning and lifting and removing her frock and then bending down to pull off her knickers. As she dragged them down over her knees, two hands attached themselves to her buttocks.

"How beautiful you are, Mary."

Mary uttered a little half-groan and a choking sound. Then she was on her knees, with all her glory sticking up in the air and her pussy already moistened and wanting this lovely man.

Moments later, Bertie's huge cock made a gentle but dramatic entrance and Mary began to sob. He put a hand under her and touched her and wetted his fingers, then he reached forward and took hold of a firm nipple with his sticky fingers, tugging it gently as his cock made its way right up inside the delicious woman.

"Oh, Bertie. You feel so good, you darling. Please give it to me any way you want. Your cock is divine."

Mary had never experienced a man in the way she was experiencing Bertie. With his amazing instrument inside her, it seemed that she could come whenever she wanted. His decisive attitude and loving movements engulfed her in an ecstasy that she would never experience anywhere else.

His hands caressed her back, then he would slide them up and down her large outer thighs, from the back of her knees up and around, to rub her pubic hair and then to lovingly touch her clitoris. Mary didn't want to ever stop, but she knew what she also wanted, and when the moment came she turned her head to look at Bertie and spoke.

"Fifi would like to suck you now."

Bertie kept reaching into Mary for a few more minutes, then he stopped and withdrew his cock and held it with one hand while with the other he lifted her arm and guided her around to face him.

Mary looked at the giant glistening penis, only just removed from deep inside her. Undeterred by its proportions, she took it in her hand and then in between her lips. She didn't move, letting his cock rest. She ran her tongue over the end of it causing it to jerk upwards in her mouth. Then she moved her mouth forward, finding out how far along his shaft she could get. Sucking Bertie complemented Mary's still throbbing vagina and she came every couple of minutes or just whenever she felt like it.

Bertie showed no sign of wanting anything other than that which made this big woman happy. He enjoyed the tremors in his genitals – little orgasms that developed deep down around the muscles near his prostate gland, which he had learnt about from his studies of Taoism and other ancient writings.

Rosa had informed Mary that Bertie only rarely ejaculated, believing it was detrimental to a man's health if enjoyed too often. For this reason, she should not feel inadequate in any way if he didn't come, and she could rest assured that he was enjoying himself.

Mary prepared herself for her next and final request. She reluctantly removed Bertie's cock from her mouth.

"Fifi would like bottom play, please."

Bertie swivelled Mary around to her previous position, on her knees with her bum pointing towards the ceiling. Then he rested his cock on the crack between her buttocks.

"Are you ready, Mary? Just say stop if I'm hurting you."

Mary just loved feeling Bertie's cock lying where it was, but responded in a quiet voice.

"Ready, Bertie."

Bertie spat on Mary's anus. He wetted his fingers on her wet pubic hair and then inserted a finger in her and spat on her once more. Mary's anus was already relaxed as a result of her lovemaking, so Bertie judged that she was ready. He rubbed the end of his penis against that special other splendid place that a woman could offer a man if she was so inclined.

Mary's bottom opened for Bertie as if it was a homecoming. He slid into her and stopped. Then, when Mary wriggled herself enthusiastically and her buttocks wobbled in every direction, he moved forward, and in moments he was all the way in.

"Oh, Bertie! You are wonderful. Shag my bottom please, Bertie, as hard as you can."

Bertie adjusted himself in preparation for the big adventure. Then he gave Mary the bum-shagging of her life. Or rather the first of many more to come, after Rosa later agreed that Mary could become a regular feature of her darling husband's bottom fetish.

As Mary's orgasms came and went, she pondered on what she had done to deserve this wonderful sexual life. Being such a good, well-behaved girl could have had something to do with it, she mused.

"Yes, yes, yes, Bertie. I love it!"

Jessica's room was sunny and cheerful as the three women wandered about, sharing with each other the thoughts that came into their minds about what it would have been like to be a spinster or widow living here back at the turn of the century.

"I suppose they would have been a godly lot. Hymn books, lavender bags and lots of tea and fruit cake," commented Edith.

"Oh, how wonderful! Life was so simple in those days. I wish I was alive back then," said Jessica.

Rosa smiled at her companions.

"I just think of all the buttons – no zips – and whalebone corsets. And thinking of corsets reminds me why we're here."

Rosa walked over and stood beside the bed and lifted her dress over her head, folding it and placing it over the back of a chair. Then she kicked off her shoes and rolled onto the middle of the bed.

"Anyone going to join me?"

Jessica stared in amazement at her new older friend, lying back in just her panties and bra and shiny-black choker necklace and her red-painted toenails on tiny feet. Jessica thought how wonderfully relaxed Rosa seemed, and she immediately wanted to join her. And she wasn't alone. Aunt Edith was also looking intently at the reclining Rosa. Then she looked at her niece. Together they called out that they too were far too hot and that they would join Rosa on the bed.

Rosa was delighted, although confused at having to look at two women undressing on either side of the bed.

In moments Jessica had discarded her floral dress and sandals and she seemed unconcerned that she wasn't wearing a bra. She was probably used to not wearing one. It didn't occur to her whether or not it was inappropriate to join Rosa on the bed displaying her very flat little bosoms.

Edith had a lot more to remove, so it did take longer. She was aware that two sets of eyes were watching every garment being removed, but as items of clothing came off and she felt the gaze of her companions, she began to experience an anticipatory sensation which she admitted to herself, was strangely exciting.

When she at last peeled off her heavy tights, Edith felt less the conservative librarian and more the young adventurer, and when her clothing was reduced to just a bra and pants and she tentatively moved onto the bed and lay down beside Rosa, Edith was feeling like a very different woman.

"Welcome, fellow panty brigade members. Isn't this more comfortable? My best idea all day, I think. What do you think, Edith? Are you comfortable, dear lady, lying here in your undies?"

Jessica and Edith laughed. Edith stretched and spoke.

"I feel better than I have in years, Rosa. It gives meaning to that phrase I've never understood, 'Get your gear off.' It's better than a holiday, I reckon."

Jessica and Rosa laughed.

"Well, dear Aunty, I think it is great too. In fact, I think we should get our gear off more often."

Rosa mused about these two country women. She had liberated them this far, so how far could she take them?

"I hope we don't catch a cold. Some people's bodies are hotter than others' and it depends a bit on your body heat as to whether you start sneezing or not."

Rosa began to feel herself. First she put her hand on her belly, then she lifted a leg up high and pointed her toes, quite slowly and provocatively. She ran a hand down her thigh and reached under a leg to touch her calves. Then she felt her forehead and her neck just above her chest.

"I think I'm okay. I seem very warm."

Rosa's actions hadn't gone unnoticed.

"No, Rosa, I'm sorry but you've got it wrong. We can't check our own temperature. You can only tell how warm you are when someone else touches you. Like this!"

Edith reached across with a hand and placed it gently on Rosa's belly.

Rosa smiled with a look that indicated that she knew that what Edith had just said was not really true and was in fact an excuse for the woman to put her hand on Rosa.

"There you are darling, sorry, I mean Rosa. You feel quite cool to me, but what can you feel?"

Rosa laughed loudly.

"Actually, I think you are right, Edith. Your hand feels beautiful and warm. Does that mean I'm a bit cold?"

Rosa reached down and lifted Edith's hand and placed it on her own thigh, moving it just little as though she was being rubbed.

"Yes. You still feel warm, so I must be cooler. That is interesting. Can I touch you, Edith?"

Edith left her hand on Rosa's thigh.

"Yes, Rosa."

Edith reached over and picked up Rosa's hand and placed it on the top of her thigh.

"Oh Rosa! Your hand does feel hot."

Rosa and Jessica laughed.

"At the risk of sounding naughty, Edith, I think you touching me is making me hotter, but I do like it."

Rosa knew she was pushing things along a bit, but in just moments the woman's response was positive.

Edith laughed and said, "Well, I'm glad it's not just me, Rosa. Your hand is making me feel hotter by the minute and I don't just mean my body temperature."

Then Jessica called out.

"What about me? Is anybody going to make me hot? Would someone please give me a hand?"

More laughter and all the women moved their bodies, shaking off any residual defensive posturing that they might have carried.

"What do you think Rosa? Is Jessica a bit young for this sort of grown up activity? She's led a sheltered life, you know."

Rosa thought for a moment. These lovely ladies were responding in a way that could go anywhere or nowhere. But it didn't really matter. She was quite happy just lying on the bed in their delightful presence.

"Yes, maybe she is a bit young."

Jessica screamed in disbelief.

"Rubbish. I'll be twenty in a couple of months. Just for that, I'm having both hands, thank you!"

Jessica propped herself up, reached across Rosa, lifted Edith's spare hand and dragged it across and over Rosa, placing it low down on her belly. Then she lifted Rosa's spare hand and put it on her chest, just below a breast.

The two women adjusted themselves so that they could more comfortably reach Jessica. Both moved their hands just a little on Jessica, feeling the young woman's body.

Everyone was quiet for a full minute. Then Rosa dared to speak.

"Are we all feeling really hot now, girls, or is it just me? I'm feeling very kissy and kissable. Does anyone else fancy a kiss on their bare skin? No charge and no pressure; just asking."

There was a flurry of movement and both Jessica and Edith answered simultaneously.

"Yes, I'll have just a small one please," said Edith, in a hushed voice.

"Yes please, I think I'm old enough. Is that all right aunty?"

Laughter and then silence. Then Rosa warned, "Coming to get you. Edith, you're first."

She rolled on her side and stared at Edith who stared back defiantly. Then Rosa leant towards the woman and put her lips on Edith's and kept them there. Edith closed her eyes. Rosa then moved her hand from Edith's thigh to just below her neck and above her neat, well-formed breasts.

This was the moment of truth, thought Rosa. Would Edith respond or not?

Nothing was happening and Rosa considered it might be time to leave and go back to where they were before, but then something did happen.

Edith took her hand from Rosa's thigh and put it on top of Rosa's hand. Then she gently pushed the hand down to the top of her bra and carefully lifted four fingers from the hand and pushed them under the bra until they rested on a nipple. Then, as Rosa opened her mouth slightly to gasp, Edith put out her tongue and pushed it into Rosa's open mouth and they pushed their lips hard against each other. Both women sighed as Rosa fondled the stiff little nipple beneath Edith's bra.

Rosa and Edith were now oblivious of the awestruck young woman watching their every move.

Edith's small body became agitated and squirmed a little as she acknowledged her excitement, sensing that things had moved on.

Rosa couldn't take her mouth from Edith's, such was Edith's enthusiasm. Rosa surmised that this might well be the first real lovemaking that Edith had experienced in years. If that was the case, she would need a lot of it to satisfy her.

Rosa suddenly felt fingers moving up into her bra and a little voice behind her whispered, "What about me?"

Rosa didn't want to stop what she was doing with Edith. She figured that, as things were already moving fast, Jessica had absorbed the change in mood and was open to a sensual adventure.

Rosa moved her hand from Jessica's thigh, shifting it up just little so that it rested on the front of her panties. Then, with her index finger, she found her way around the panty crotch onto a little almost hairless patch. It was already wet. Rosa felt the girl stretching and opening her legs and she heard her groan.

Then Rosa took her hand from Edith's breast, found Edith's hand and slipped it down inside her own panties, showing Edith the way to her pussy, and after just a tiny hesitation to absorb this latest move Edith pushed at Rosa's mouth even harder while her tongue thrashed about trying to swallow Rosa entirely.

Edith's fingers were quick to react. Only moments after Rosa had put Edith's hand in her panties, her fingers began exploring Rosa's wet pussy, wandering everywhere, excitedly exploring this new wet and warm place.

Rosa thought about where they should go next. Everyone seemed happy, but things would need to change, even if only to rest their overstretched arms. She decided that if she was right about Jessica's aunt, then Edith would go along with Rosa's plan. She took her mouth away from Edith's, looking at her lovingly.

"You are a very beautiful lover, Edith, but Jessica is feeling our love and wants to join in. Can I suggest that I change places with your niece? We have plenty of time and I will definitely want to kiss you again later. Just have a peep at Jessica and you will see what I mean."

Edith moved her head over to look past Rosa and saw Jessica lying with her eyes closed and Rosa's hand between her legs.

"Can I move her over here, Edith?"

"Oh yes, Rosa. Please do. I've so wanted to reach out to her lovingly for so long."

Rosa turned and spoke to Jessica.

"Jessica, darling. Edith and I want you to move over into the middle so that we can both make love to you. Is that okay?"

Jessica opened her eyes.

"Oh yes please, Rosa. And Rosa? Thank you. I love you so much."

When Jessica had moved over and settled back in between the two loving and very hot women, Rosa looked across at Edith and smiled.

"You start, Edith. Can I suggest kissing first? Everything is about kissing."

Edith smiled at Rosa.

"Thank you, Rosa."

Then Edith turned Jessica's face towards her and kissed the young woman, just as Rosa had kissed Edith, and Jessica groaned and pushed back hard on Edith's mouth.

Jessica quickly moved Edith's hand into her panties to continue where Rosa had left off.

Rosa watched with excited satisfaction as Edith removed her bra and pulled Jessica's face to her breasts.

Rosa congratulated herself, smiling with satisfaction as she contemplated the two near-naked bodies beside her, and listened to the sounds of lover's feasting on one another.

So where should Rosa go now? She already had tentative plans for these two, later in the evening, but for now she would content herself with licking and kissing Jessica's back and shoulders and touching her on any available spot without interrupting Edith in her loving efforts.

And being a woman with a voyeuristic bent, watching the two new lovers was divine and Rosa visualised those moments that, all being well, still lay ahead, when she would suck and lick both the women's pussies and watch their contorted faces as they came.

But things unexpectedly changed.

Rosa was suddenly jolted from her reverie when Edith screamed as she orgasmed and then burst into tears. Edith sobbed loudly, without any attempt to stem the flow of tears or the loud sobbing. She convulsed as she threw her body upward in a seemingly unending series of multiple orgasms.

Jessica stared at her aunt and then, instead of moving to console her, Jessica pushed Edith down onto the bed, holding her by the throat with one hand while dragging her legs apart with the other. Then she threw herself on top of her, thrusting hard against her groin and uttering incomprehensible sentences of violent love and passion.

Edith began to make a croaking attempt at speech which sounded like some multiple wave effect. Rosa could hear the one word she uttered constantly: "More!"

In all the years that Rosa had enjoyed the company of lustful lovers she had never seen the likes of what she was now witnessing. Incredibly, Rosa, who was a master of control under any circumstance, found herself being drawn into this intense whirlpool of lust and release. Without a second thought, she found herself riding atop Jessica's bare thrusting buttocks and pushing herself against her in a frantic effort to share in this sexual explosion. She could just see Edith's red face over Jessica's shoulder. Jessica's hand was rigid around her aunt's neck and Edith's eyes bulged and rolled up and down.

Suddenly Jessica rolled over, pushing Rosa onto her back, and within moments the young woman was between Rosa's legs and thrusting like a wild animal. Jessica came, then Rosa came, and as Jessica fell over to the side Edith managed to hoist herself onto Rosa where she shagged her way to heaven, coming again with screams and tears and kisses and making Rosa scream her surrender to orgasmic paradise such as she had never experienced before while the sex-crazed Jessica buried her face between her aunt's legs.

Three naked, exhausted and sheepish women stared at one another in silence. Then Jessica spoke.

"I'm going to come and live here in Sydney and you're coming with me, Aunty. And Rosa, we will want you visit us. I want us to make love like this all the time. I adore you both."

Edith and then Rosa, kissed Jessica, affirming their willingness to all be lovers. Then Jessica pulled them both tightly to her and snuggled into them and sobbed uncontrollably.

———

Freya and Sophie had shown off their long legs to each other, thrusting them up and waving them about in the air and displaying them just as Helen loved to view them.

The two young women were so excited about each other that neither of them knew what they most wanted to do first.

They took turns licking each other's legs. Then they spent a lot of time licking and playing with each other's special places. It wasn't until they had both masturbated each other for the first time, and screamed and come, that they were able to slow down and review how best to vent their passionate feelings for each other.

Talking was important. They both wanted to share their life stories and climb into each other's heads. But that was the intellectual side of things. Right now, what they needed most was the chance to express their feelings physically and above all, lustfully.

In between sudden bursts of grabbing or groping or caressing a body part, the two would reach out using language to describe what they would like.

Sophie told Freya about working at a horse stud and how one day at Mary's house she had pretended to be a mare in season and strapped herself down as they sometimes did to mares at work to stop them kicking the stallion. Then she made Helen pretend to be both the stud mistress and the stallion.

"I refused the stallion's advances, but our darling Helen eventually persuaded me to have him and she got into me with a special horse dildo that I'd bought online."

Freya screamed with excitement.

"Oh Sophie! That sounds like a wonderful fantasy. You've no idea how often I've thought about being tied up while someone has their way with me."

Freya told Sophie how she had worked as a nursing aide in a big private hospital before eventually going to university. She described how she had once secretly watched from a shared ensuite bathroom as a patient got her visiting boyfriend to tie her hands and legs to the hospital bedhead using bandages before asking him to get on top of her.

Even though Freya had not ever been with a man until later, when she had her one night with Freddy, seeing this woman tied up thrilled her beyond belief and she had wanted to be tied up ever since.

Sophie eyed her in wonder.

"Oh you sexy bitch. That's going at the top of my list of things that we will do together. I so want that too."

The two excitedly threw themselves into each other's arms and glued their mouths together while their hands explored each other's bottoms and thighs and that sensitive spot behind the knees.

"I know my tits are really little, darling Sophie, but what I do have respond to loving attention. Please bite them and lick them, sweetheart. Pretend they are big and beautiful like yours."

Sophie obeyed while Freya massaged Sophie's more than adequate breasts and nipped her nipples between her fingers.

The two eventually rested and talked about Freddy, both saying how they loved hearing him roar when he came. Then they thought about how they should get a move on and get over to the house and get into his bed.

They made cocoa and took their mugs up to bed. After a little time chatting, they decided to switch off the bed lamps and explore each other in the dark. It was like children playing spooky games.

Then Freya remembered something and told Sophie that, when she and Alice had been in bed there, and when Freddy had come to join them, he had about a half-hour rest interval between having each of them. She also spoke about how Freddy had put each of them on their knees in turn and asked the other one to put his cock in their companion's pussy.

Sophie laughed excitedly.

Freya went on to tell Sophie how Helen had described to them the ways men thought and acted, and what the girls should do and not do to get the most out of a man. She advised them to just go along with whatever Freddy wanted and that way they would be sure of getting the real Freddy.

"Sounds like great advice, Freya. I hate to think what we would all do without Helen.

"We don't know who's going to be the lucky first. But one of us will have time to read a book, I guess? And I do hope he asks me to put his cock in your pussy, darling. That would be so beautiful."

The two naked naughty ladies laughed loudly.

"I won't be reading a book, Sophie. I'll be too busy having my way with you, or rather with both of you, whatever's happening. I will be licking anything that's wet, wherever it is, so be warned."

Sophie slid down into the bed, found an ankle and dragged one of Freya's legs up and began to suck her toes.

"I love that, except why am I thinking you are about to tickle me. Promise you won't."

But her pleas came too late and Freya screamed as, beneath the sheet, Sophie gently touched the sole of her foot with her finger nails.

It was at that moment, amidst the screaming and chaos that Freddy quietly entered the darkened bedroom, switched on the bedside lamp and sat on the edge of the bed. Then he called out, in his real man voice, as Helen called it.

"Could someone please tell me if I've got the right room?"

Two heads appeared from under the sheet and stared at the figure on the edge of the bed.

"Freddy!" two voices called out as one.

"Hi to you both, sorry if I'm a bit late. Ended up helping put out the rubbish and empty bottles. I'm going to have a quick shower. I'll see you both shortly."

"Freddy?"

"Yes, Freya?"

"Can we both just have a kiss now? Please?"

"You sure can."

Freddy leant forward towards the girls and each put her arms around him and kissed him on the lips.

Freddy smiled appreciatively.

"Thank you. Don't either of you go away. I'll be back."

Sophie and Freya smiled at each other and each put her hands out to touch the other.

"It's totally weird."

"What is weird, Sophie?"

"I'm nervous, and when I'm nervous I can act strangely. Helen always laughs about how I rushed to kiss her when we first got together. I did it because I was feeling really scared and insecure."

Freya put her other hand out and turned Sophie's head towards her and kissed her.

"Oh Sophie. I know what you mean. Perhaps we should tell Freddy that we're nervous. We could tell him that we're worried that, having already exhausted ourselves with each other, we might not be as sexually responsive as he had hoped, and for his sake we would be happy to reschedule to a later date."

"Oh God! Now I'm really conflicted, Freya."

Suddenly the sheet was drawn back and Freddy stood beside the bed, holding something in his hand. Unbeknown to the two women, he had padded silently in from the bathroom and had heard their conversation.

"While you two are thinking about things, I'm here for my say. Freya, your first so on your knees please. Sophie! Put my cock into Freya, would you?"

Freddy reached out to Freya and rolled her over, then put a hand between her legs and lifted her to her knees. Then he climbed onto the bed and positioned himself behind her.

Sophie was quick to act. She rolled over to face the couple and, taking hold of Freddy's cock, drew it up to Freya's cunt and rubbed it gently against her. Then Sophie groaned and Freya moaned as Sophie slid Freddy's solid shaft into Freya and he began to shag her with great enthusiasm.

Freddy was intent on following his own agenda while the girls, remembering Helen's wise words, chose to simply follow along.

With Sophie gently touching his balls, Freddy heaved into Freya with gusto. He shagged Freya for a long time. Then, instead of the expected coming and roaring, Freddy reached over to Sophie and pulled her over.

"On your knees, Sophie. Let's see what you've got left in you. Freya, pop my cock into Sophie, would you please?"

Freddy sat up with his cock waving about and Freya turned around and grabbed it. She couldn't stop herself slipping it into her mouth and licking off her own wetness. Then she led him to Sophie's rear and put the instrument into her lover's wet pussy.

Sophie made little noises as Freddy began shagging her. She was secretly grateful for his attention, having enjoyed him so much the first time, just a few weeks ago on the night of Mary's birthday party. She had unexpectedly enjoyed her chance encounter with Freddy and now regularly visualised those moments when she masturbated, and even sometimes when she made love to a girlfriend.

Freddy stopped shagging Sophie and looked down at where Freya was licking his and Sophie's genitals.

"On your back with your legs in the air and your knees bent, Freya."

Freya rolled backwards, stealing a look at Sophie, who had turned towards her.

"Sophie? Can you do the deed?"

Without hesitating, Sophie grasped Freddy's cock again and dragged it over and pushed it into Freya and Freddy was on his way.

Freddy was now pushing into Freya much more heavily than before. Then the two women heard the beginning of Freddy's deep-down roar and suddenly he shoved into Freya like a madman and came inside her. But he didn't stop. He kept on pushing in and yelling and Freya screamed and threw herself up to meet him, then fell back and she felt Sophie's loving mouth and tongue looking for hers. Then she spent for a second time and then a third, and she sobbed loudly and Sophie's tongue licked her eyelids.

Freddy fell back on the bed and Freya rolled on top of him and lay still.

"Thank you, Freya. You are very beautiful."

Then Freddy put a hand out and took Sophie's hand.

"Don't go away, Sophie. I will want to fuck your beautiful pussy in a little while. You okay with that?"

Sophie squeezed Freddy's hand and answered in a soft, low voice.

"Very okay with that Freddy. I'm not going anywhere without either of you."

———

Helen wasn't sure how a threesome with her new lovers would go. Both Polly and Caroline were beautiful and sexy and she wanted them both to enjoy themselves. The two had just met for the first time at Maude's party and were very obviously into each other, waiting only for Helen to join them, and walk them next door to her house.

There was also the matter of where the three would spend the evening together. Helen's husband Freddy had told her that he and his two lovers, Freya and Sophie, would be using one of the bedrooms at home. Perhaps Helen's studio would do, although it would be very hot from the summer sun. There was also the lounge room.

Helen admitted to herself for the first time that she was extremely tired and unusually, found herself not fully excited by the evening's prospects. She would need to tell them the truth, she thought. Maybe they would be happy to let her just watch them discover each other. That might satisfy her lustful feelings for both of them.

When Helen was at last able to join Polly and Caroline, the pair were in an extreme state of happy excitement and she knew that they both needed each other desperately. She understood the feelings they must be experiencing, better than most people.

"Helen, darling, we've found a room here. There are a couple of empty rooms that were booked but cancelled and Maude told us to help ourselves. She suggested Room 4. Is that okay, Helen?"

"Yes Polly, that sounds great. Are you two ready?"

They both smiled at her and then at each other.

"Well, before we head down heaven's passageway to Room 4, I do have to confess something."

Caroline and Polly looked at each other and frowned.

"Oh God, Polly, Helen has double booked. She's had an offer from that bloody vicar, I bet, and she's going with the cloth rather than our silk knickers."

They all fell about laughing and Helen thought how lucky she was to have such wonderful women in her life.

"No, darlings. I want to confess in advance that I am extremely tired and I'm concerned that I may be of a bit of a dampener on our party. I thought I should mention it now so that you could send me home alone, or you could tuck me up in your bed and let me watch a coming together of two beautiful women who deserve to have their heads between each other's legs. There! I will abide by your decision."

There was silence as what Helen had just said sank in. Then Caroline and Polly looked at each other and smiled and nodded as if they were acknowledging a secret agreement. The two rose from their seats and stood on either side of Helen's chair. Then they lifted her up.

"Just come with us and don't say a word," whispered Polly.

Helen's two lovers escorted her out through the passage door as if she was a prisoner, and once they were inside Room 4 and had dimmed the lights they kissed her in turn and stripped her of her clothes, then dragged her into the bed and tucked her in.

"Now, Helen, we are going to remove each other's clothing and kiss, probably quite a lot, and even make noises, all of which you can watch, or not if you fall asleep. However, both of us will take advantage of you every once in a while and come pushing between your legs for a lick of our love's special spot. Is that clear?"

Helen looked at Caroline sleepily and smiled lovingly.

"And if by chance you do wake up, feel free to lend a hand, Helen," added Polly.

Helen smiled, and closed her eyes and spoke softly.

"Go fuck each other, you slutty bitches. I love you both."

She rolled onto her side and Polly and Caroline stretched out their arms and embraced, then their lips joined and they fell onto the bed with their hands moving about as they lifted each other's frocks and discovered each other's parts.

And when the moment arrived some time later when their two naked bodies were lying on each other and their pussies were still slowly rubbing together, something stirred next to them and a leg pushed itself in among theirs.

Another pussy pushed against them and they heard Helen's sleepy voice.

"If there is anything left over, I'd like some please."

———

When Alice arrived at Room 11, she stopped and listened. She heard the two women talking but it sounded very faint, so she quietly opened the door and peeped in.

Elisha and Belinda were beneath the duvet, giggling and talking. The usually analytical Alice tuned in to the scene, knowing her presence was as yet undetected. This triggered a frisson, an excited feeling of satisfaction, a rare momentary sensation that she had been naughty, even when she hadn't.

She heard Elisha's voice coming from somewhere in the bed.

"Oh darling, I know that you would love it. Your mum loves it and we still do it to each other sometimes. Talk to her. Tell her that Aunty wants it and you're not sure what to do. Now I've got it very slippery, darling, so just lie still and relax. Once it's in you will hardly notice it."

Alice smiled and looked across the room to where her overnight bag was lying open. Elisha had discovered Alice's emergency collection of special toys. The pink thingy in a harness and the larger of her two butt plugs lay alongside a bigger dildo and the soap container. The small bottle of lubricant stood on top of the bedside cupboard.

Alice knew immediately what she wanted to do next. In just moments she had removed her clothes and was kneeling totally naked at the foot of the bed. Slowly she lifted the end of the duvet and peered in. Two pairs of feet, with their soles facing up, appeared first. Then Alice's bells rang all at once. There, at the top of a pair of robust bare legs sat a backside like no other.

Alice's mouth sagged and she thought she was about to dribble, staring at a small and already excited glistening pussy bush topped by a pretty pink and shiny orifice nestled in a chubby but near perfect bum. At that moment, all of it offered itself to Alice and she moved forward.

There was silence from the two lovers in the bed.

"Elisha? Are you all right? Speak to me."

Elisha let out a large gasp and shook, and as she did so she must have pushed forward and down with her hand and Belinda screamed.

"Ouch! Well, it's in. I guess you're happy now, wicked woman."

There was still no word from Elisha, then as hands took hold of Belinda's ankles she knew why and screamed.

"It's all right, darling. We have company. Alice is here with us and she is making my rear end exceedingly happy. Don't panic, darling."

Alice gorged on Elisha, kissing and licking and sucking her adorable pussy. Then she wetted a finger and slipped it into Elisha's anus.

"Oh yes, yes!" screamed Elisha. "If you stop now I'll surely kill you. Oh my God!"

Belinda reached up and kissed her aunt and then pushed back the duvet to survey the scene. She stared at Alice's naked body. Then, without a second thought, she pulled her ankles free from her captor's hands and hopped from the bed. Belinda scrambled round on the carpet to Alice's rear end and knelt and glued her mouth to the totally exposed, lonely pussy.

Alice's hand reached back and grabbed Belinda's hair and pulled her head closer, then clasped it tight between her thighs. Belinda put a hand up past Alice's belly and searched until she found a stiff nipple, and she lovingly tugged at it.

Elisha screamed as she came and her body sagged. But Alice didn't stop. Alice kept licking and sucking and shoving her tongue into the slack figure until she herself screamed and fell forward, leaving just the young Belinda sucking and gasping. Moments later, Belinda screamed "Yes!" and joined the other two happy women.

All three rested, then Alice lovingly accepted each one's lips and tongue as they took turns with her mouth, wanting as much of this new lady lover as they could get. As one kissed her the other groped her tenderly, then they swapped.

Alice looked at them both and smiled.

"What beautiful girls you are. I'm so glad I found you but I must warn you though, the night is young and I intend to have you both with that black dildo over there and then get you both to fuck me.

"And Elisha, can I play with your bottom with that little pink thingy, darling? And then will you please play with mine?

"And Belinda? Are you comfortable with that butt plug in your bum?"

The two smiling women stared at Alice as she spoke, each with a hand on Alice's bosom.

"Yes, to all you have asked for, darling Alice," whispered Elisha.

Belinda put her hand around to feel her backside and reported back that all was well with her rear end and that it "felt really good when I orgasmed".

As time moved on, so did the sensual feasting of Alice and her new lovers.

She asked Elisha to bugger her first while Belinda watched the two excited women in awe. Then Alice put a new condom over the pink thingy and shagged Elisha until she cried. And when Belinda asked her if she was okay, she smiled.

"Oh yes, darling, I'm so okay that I'm crying with happiness."

It was at a quiet moment, when they were all resting, that Alice asked about Belinda's mother, desperately wanting answers to what had sounded quite mysterious when she had listened at the door earlier and overheard Elisha tell Belinda that her mum loved it. Alice was fascinated with what Elisha related.

"Belinda's and my relationship may seem a little creepy to some people; a taboo in their eyes. In fact, we are not related. I'm really her step-aunt, but it is more easily understood when you know that I and Belinda's mother Ruth are identical twins. Belinda knows all that I'm about to tell you, so she won't be shocked.

"People who know or have studied twins know that they can be exceedingly close and that they share things. Ruth and I have always shared things.

"We were in our mid-twenties when Ruth met the man she eventually married. He was a widower with a five-year-old daughter, and had lost his wife to cancer two years earlier. When Ruth married James, it was only a short time before she invited me to share the marital bed and James seemed to enjoy us both equally.

"James was taken from us in a tragic road accident. We were distraught and both of us felt the loss and I suppose we tended to dote on Belinda, who couldn't understand why her father had disappeared. After a year or so, Ruth and I found ourselves cuddling up on cold winter's nights with Belinda in a little bed nearby. We were indeed a family.

"One warm spring evening, after we had put Belinda to bed and were sitting on the sofa in the lounge, Ruth asked me if I would like to do that thing we did as teenagers. I had thought about it too and said I would."

Alice and Belinda nestled down on the bed and listened attentively.

"So to clarify things. The two of us shared a room until our late teens and, as I've said, we shared everything. We were of an age when we had noticed boys and, although we were very innocent, we couldn't help but think and talk about them.

"One night, Ruth produced a book she had taken from our mother's room. I think it was called 'The Joy of Sex' and it had just been published. We were fascinated and, I should add, turned on by what we read and what the drawings depicted.

"Each night I would hop into Ruth's bed and we would devour the book. It wasn't long before we were kissing each other in a special way, kissing each other's breasts and nipples, and touching each other between our legs and comparing the length of our pubic hair. Finally, we discovered how to give ourselves, and then each other, orgasms, most often while staring at a drawing in the book.

"In our everyday school life we had learnt that boys could get girls pregnant if they made love, so girls should avoid doing rude things with boys. Ruth and I talked about it and then she remembered that there was something in Mum's book that we should have another look at.

"That night, as we lay turning the pages and giggling, she found the section. It discussed anal sex. It said that most men liked it, and some women liked it even more than when boys put it in their other place. But of particular interest to us was that boys sticking their thingies into girls' bums didn't result in the girls getting pregnant.

"We got very excited thinking about the benefits of anal sex. The more we thought about it the more we realised that we didn't need a boy to do it with. We could easily do it to each other. If we practised, we'd be ready for boys when the time came and so would avoid getting into trouble."

Alice was fascinated with the story, as was Belinda, who already knew some of the details but not all.

"So what did you both do, Elisha? I doubt that you had access to a little pink thingy in those days?"

Elisha laughed.

"No, we didn't, Alice, but we did have lots of candles in the house. We took three or four to our bedroom and set about trying to shape the ends to look like the erect men's penises drawn in Mum's book. Then, with a cup of cooking oil we'd taken from the kitchen, we began our adventure and it worked.

"Slippery candles can be amazingly exciting for a couple of hormonally charged adolescent girls. Our original ideas about using them anally was soon moved to second place when we discovered where else we could put them, pushing them into each others vaginas while perusing the drawings in the pages of Mum's erotic sex book.

"Perhaps because we are so close and can so easily predict or understand what each of us wants, we soon found that we could get a lot of satisfaction from making love with our candles and when one evening Ruth and then I actually orgasmed, well, we never looked back.

"And so here we are today. Sometimes, when I visited my sister at her apartment, and before she met her new partner, we often enjoyed playing around with each other using the wonderful toys that are now available. We still enjoy giving each other a good shagging, both back and front."

. . .

The three women ate some of the food they had brought from the party. Then they lay back and relaxed.

"So can I ask both of you how you ended up in bed together? It's probably rude of me, I know but I'm so turned on by you both that I feel I need to know the full story."

It was Belinda who spoke this time.

"Elisha was a part of my life from the beginning, so I don't know a life without her. She was like a second mother and she helped Mum and shared all the duties involved in my upbringing.

"When I reached my teens I had boyfriends, but these relationships didn't last long. They just didn't seem right. I didn't understand my feelings, but I did know that I felt best when I was with Mum or Elisha, or just girls generally.

"I was a virgin and confused, and I wanted to be like everyone else. The girls at school always talked about one day getting married and having babies and I thought that I should be thinking that way too. I liked boys a bit, but it all seemed a bit silly and difficult.

"One Sunday evening, when I was in my late teens, I was lying on Mum's bed. We were both in our shorty pyjamas reading and just as she had all through my childhood, Mum was stroking my hair.

"Without realising what I was doing, I began running my fingers up and down the top of Mum's leg, which was lying beside me. A little while later I heard a sound and looked up from my book. Mum had her eyes closed and was breathing heavily and she had her hand in her pyjama pants. A moment later she uttered a little scream and pulled me to her chest and held me very tight.

"I suddenly felt an urge to put my hand with hers in her pyjamas and I did so. Mum opened her eyes and stared at me and smiled and told me she loved me.

"My hand felt her wetness and her beautiful pussy and I was so enlivened I pulled her head down and kissed her as I had never kissed anyone before.

"Suddenly she screamed and jumped out of bed, yelling that we mustn't do this terrible thing. I was confused and I cried."

Elisha leant over and kissed Belinda and patted her head.

"Mum disappeared a few days later and didn't return for nearly a month. Elisha came and looked after me and told me that a relative of a friend that Mum had gone to school with was very sick in Western Australia and that mum had gone to help out.

"I was even more confused.

"Mum eventually came home and things went back to normal, but Elisha had just purchased the stables, so there was a lot going on.

"With my love of horses and having just finished school, it was agreed that it would be good for me to go and help Elisha and live on the property with her and, of course, I jumped at the chance.

"Not long afterwards Mum met the person who was to become her lover, Genevieve, and the two bought a house and settled down."

Alice caressed Belinda's arm and ran her fingers lightly over Elisha's knees.

"And you two only recently became lovers, is that right?"

Elisha looked intently at Belinda.

"Yes, because of the stigma associated with these sorts of relationships, it has taken a long time for it to happen. But after much difficulty we have, and we are no longer worried about what people think."

Alice smiled at them.

"I so admire you both. From the little I've seen, you are very good together. How does your sister Ruth, Belinda's mother, see things?"

"The close twin sister bond that exists between us means it works well. The truth is that Belinda and I now visit Ruth and Genevieve. We sometimes stay over and we've all become lovers, well sort of.

"Ruth has got over those conflicted moments with Belinda that she once ran away from and happily makes love to her with extraordinary tenderness and affection but only as a part of our foursome. I explore my sexuality further by making love with my sister's partner Genevieve.

"Yes, things may well change in the future. Now that Belinda has reached her early twenties, she may want to try a heterosexual life and have a family. The good thing is that I am happy for her if that happens, just so long as she is safe and happy. I'm sure Ruth and I will be happy grannies if that comes about."

Alice looked at the time and noticed Belinda yawning.

"I'm going to suggest that we get some rest. Let's all snuggle up and be together and if any of you wake up feeling randy, feel free to put your hand wherever you want on me and I'm sure you will get a loving response."

They all laughed and kissed and planted their mouths on each others' breasts as a final goodnight.

"Elisha?"

"Yes, darling?"

"Should I take this thing out now?"

Elisha and Alice giggled and looked at her with a mischievous smile.

"Roll onto your tummy, Belinda. Aunty will fix it. You might like to help me Alice?"

———

Alice lay thinking. She wondered about the lack of eligible men in her life and what she would do about having a family. Having the fabulous love life she had now was one thing, but fitting in the demands of that ticking clock was another.

Analytical Alice's world might be about to change.

———

Maude was not amused when the Reverend Cameron didn't show up and that, as she discovered later, he had disappeared with a young man named Hayden and the two choirboys. Suddenly Maude was alone with no one to play with.

It was only when she was confronted with two young women dressed in bunny costumes that she remembered the daughters of the Sydney family, both of whom had attended her open day earlier in the week and were looking to enrol for singing and voice lessons.

Sylvia and Stella had arrived at the party quite late, pushing a large suitcase and hoping to find accommodation for the night. By that time Maude had enjoyed a few drinks and had generously offered the girls the only option available.

"I can only suggest that you make yourselves comfortable in my room, Number 1 just inside that door over there. There is a big bed and a smaller one. I won't be going to bed until quite late, so I'm happy to take the single bed. Please yourselves. It's all I can offer you, I'm afraid."

The two young women accepted enthusiastically.

When Maude at last walked into her room she was confronted by two girls in bunny costumes, both giggling. One was putting on makeup in front of the mirror. She had already applied pink lipstick to her nose in the shape of a small dot. Now she was drawing long, straight whiskers on her cheeks with an eyeliner pencil.

The second girl was hopping and prancing around, mimicking her version of an exuberant rabbit.

"Oh hello, Mrs Spicer. Hope you don't mind us doing this. Stella and I received parcels just as we were leaving the house. They contained our fancy dress outfits that we will wear at the university student break-up, so of course we wanted to try them on. Do you like them?"

Just for that moment Maude was speechless, staring lustfully at the two super-sexy young women. They were all legs and their tiny powder-blue panties were each adorned with a white fluffy tail. Their thigh-high blue and white striped stockings ended in blue-flecked silver trainers.

"We had trouble getting the ears to stand up, but we read the instructions and now they are perfect. The fluffy bras seem a bit ticklish, but otherwise fine. What do you think, Mrs Spicer?"

Maude continued staring at the girls.

"Oh please, call me Maude. Your outfits are incredible, girls. I haven't seen anything this sexy since ... "

"Since when, Mrs Spicer?"

Sylvia and Stella both stared at Maude, waiting and smiling mischievously.

"Er, well um, I'll just say that, some time back, I had to help two young women put on their bridesmaids' dresses and ... "

"And what, Maude?"

Stella was the more forward of the two and she was keen to hear the rest of Maude's little tale.

"Well. I'll just say that when I was helping to adjust their underwear they got a bit excited. So much so, they were almost late for the wedding."

Stella and Sylvia looked at each other and giggled.

"We would love it if you would check our outfits, Maude. We think we've got them right but your expertise would be very welcome."

Stella crossed the room to stand smiling in front of Maude. She pulled herself up straight and pushed out her chest.

"I can't work out why this bra is so tight, Maude. I've loosened it twice already. Perhaps you can help me. And Maude, can I ask you what size your bra is. You certainly look amazing."

They both looked at Maude then at each other, smiling inquisitively. Maude was now fully alert to what the young things had in mind, even if they themselves were not yet sure what to do.

Many people longed to see Maude's breasts let loose. What were contained inside her bra was a major selling point, followed only by her curvaceous backside and winning smile. Stella's willingness to present herself to Maude was exciting, but Maude considered it better if she held back a little and let the girls set the pace.

"I have my bras made specially for me, so I'm not sure what regular sizes would fit. I imagine a very large size, obviously?"

The two girls laughed excitedly and looked at each other and then back at Maude. Sylvia came across and stood beside her friend and the two stared at Maude's barely covered bosom. Maude asked them to twirl around to show her their costumes.

"Well, I'm sure you will both be a big hit at the break-up. I think there will be many young men wanting to go rabbiting that night. And of course we know what rabbits are supposed to be good at."

The giggling bunnies were starting to get excited.

"Maude, we have another outfit in our case. It is for our friend Valerie whom we will give it to later when we see her. She older and is a number of sizes bigger than us. We'd love it if you modelled it for us. You could slip off your dress and we would take care of the rest. It would be such fun. Please, Maude?"

It didn't take long for Maude to agree, though she showed a degree of hesitation just for appearances' sake.

"Just help me with this, girls. I have trouble reaching the zip."

In just seconds, Stella was unzipping the large lady; then with Sylvia helping, the two peeled Maude's close-fitting black dress up over her head. The two stood back and, with eyes wide, stared at the vision of Maude in her black silk panties, garter belt and black stockings and of course, her enormous black bra.

"Oh Maude! You are so beautiful. I want to put my arms around you and kiss you all over."

The removal of Maude's dress had shifted her own excitement up a notch, and she was ready for anything she could get. She whispered to the girls and smiled.

"Be my guest. I would love my bunnies to cuddle up."

Stella came and put her arms around Maude from the front while Sylvia stood behind, sliding her hands slowly up and down Maude's silk-covered buttocks. Then Stella put her mouth to Maude's and the two pushed equally hard against each other, presenting their tongues, softly sucking and licking each other's lips and inside their mouths.

Maude felt Sylvia's fingers unfastening the giant brassiere, then felt the bra sliding down. She heard Stella gasp when she looked down at Maude's huge stiff nipples. Then Stella croaked an instruction to Sylvia.

"Come around here and see these Sylvia. You won't believe your eyes."

Maude closed her eyes and her jaw sagged as she felt that exquisite sensation she always felt when her breasts were played with. Then the two bunnies started nibbling her nipples and Maude cried out "Yes, yes, don't stop!"

The sucking and licking of Maude's breasts was beginning to have a deeper effect on the two women and Maude felt hands exploring her, caressing her thighs and buttocks. Sylvia wanted more of Maude's backside and gently slid a hand down into her panties, rubbed a buttock and fingered the crack of her bum. Then a hand from Stella ventured between her legs and gently rubbed the crotch of her panties.

"Pull my knickers down please girls," Maude gasped.

Four eager hands obliged, sliding her knickers down over Maude's solid stockinged legs and over her heeled shoes, removing them altogether. Then Stella knelt down and discovered the giant clitoris that Maude was also renowned for.

"Oh my God! Get here, Sylvia. Heaven has sent us a rare present. I didn't believe these really existed."

The two stared at Maude's extraordinary appendage. Then Stella pushed out her tongue and touched it and Maude gave a tiny scream.

"Oh yes!"

As the two girls licked and sucked her clitoris, Maude thought about what she wanted to happen next. The large bed nearby, beckoned. She looked down at the girls beautiful face as they stared up at her adoringly, each taking turns to suck and swallow her special gift.

"I want my beautiful bunnies on their knees on the bed now. Let's go."

She gently moved the girls' heads away and lifted each one by an arm. The two stared at her with dazed expressions, then each one turned and knelt on the bed, instinctively knowing that Maude was wanting to feast on them as they had on her. Maude gazed at the two perfect backsides adorned with fluffy white tails and thrust up before her, and she licked her lips.

The girls looked at each other and smiled lazily, gasping as they felt Maude's hands removing their knickers. Then one sighed and the other groaned as the woman with the amazing tits palmed their pussies and pushed stiff nipples and large, soft breasts against their vaginas.

Then Maude put her fingers inside each of the girls, pushing them in quite hard while she gently worked her thumbs over their clitorises. She knew her way around female genitalia and it wasn't very long before first Sylvia, and then Stella, arched their backs and screamed and fell forward onto the bed.

Maude looked down at the two beautiful bunnies as they lay face down in their post orgasmic stupor, their long legs bent at the knees. She knew she could have them which ever way she wanted.

She first slid her hands over the young things' perfect bottoms and leant over and licked the backs of their legs. Then she ran a hand between each ones legs and fondled their wet hairy pussies, then licked her very sticky fingers.

The very large lady then moved her body onto the bed in between the tailless bunnies, and lay back with her legs slightly apart. Finally she spoke to her two sleepy new lovers.

"Your music teacher is as horny as hell and wants her slutty bunnies hopping all over her. You can lick her when you're ready. In fact right now would be really good! "

———

The party crowd had begun to thin and Roger found himself alone at the bar in the corner, finishing off his last drink for the night. He started chatting to the bartender, but he excused himself a few minutes later to collect empty glasses from around the empty room.

A woman's voice spoke softly from the other end of the bar, asking him if he would like to join her.

He turned and looked at a short, plump younger woman, sitting alone with her glass and smiling at him. He smiled back then went over and sat down on the sofa beside her.

"Hello! My name is Roger. It seems we might be the last ones standing."

He looked at the sweet, smiling face sitting alluringly above a large bosom.

"I'm Angela but you can call me Angie. And you are the last one standing, Roger, because I think I'd have difficulty."

Roger laughed, realising that Angela was quite inebriated. He put her age at the late twenties or early thirties.

"Well, Angie, I know what it's like. Best you find somewhere close by and have a nap. You'll feel better after that."

Angie stared back at him with a fixed-looking smile that seemed to accompany her slightly drunken state.

"If you would be so kind as to help me get to my car, I'll have a sleep there. It's a warm night."

She hiccuped loudly and moved her short, plump legs about on her low heels as she contemplated rising from the seat.

"Shall we go now Roger?"

Roger hadn't even agreed to the idea of leaving together but he figured that the woman was past being able to clearly understand the situation. He had thought about going out into the garden for some fresh air and this seemed like an opportunity to do so.

"Sure, Angie. Let's go."

He reached out, took her arm and helped her to stand. She wobbled a bit but managed to hang onto him long enough to find her balance.

As the two of them wandered slowly down the driveway Angie attempted to make conversation, but she constantly failed to finish sentences and more than once Roger had to catch her in his arms to stop her falling over.

The last time she slipped and he held her up, Angie held onto him and stared up at his face.

"Men usually say I've got nice tits, Roger. Tell me I've got nice tits, you lovely man."

Roger wondered whether he should pretend he hadn't heard Angie, but then found himself looking down at her large bosom rising up out of her low-cut dress.

"Your tits are beautiful, Angie."

Angie giggled and hiccupped some more.

As the pair got closer to the gate, Angie spotted a garden seat on the lawn. She pushed against Roger and indicated that she wanted to sit down.

Roger held her arm, lowering her gently to the seat, and sat down beside her. He felt her hand on his trousers and he knew things were going to get tricky.

"Show it to me, lovely man. Damn it! Where's it gone?"

Angie was having trouble with his zipper, so to avoid problems he helped by letting his cock out. She grabbed it and had it in her mouth in moments.

Roger contemplated his situation. That this young woman was giving him her attention was very pleasant, but he was acutely aware that she wasn't his preferred mature woman. But then that wasn't preventing him from getting a hard-on.

"Come and fuck me, lovely man."

Angie's speech wasn't getting any less slurred, but she wasn't having any trouble getting her message across. She dragged Roger up by his cock and lay down on the grass. She let go of him and took off her knickers. Then she reached up and pulled Roger down on top of her. In no time at all she had put Roger's cock against her cunt.

"Fuck me, lovely man. Fuck me silly. Come on!"

Roger pushed into Angie's surprisingly tight little pussy while she was still trying to make herself comfortable. Then she slipped her dress down to expose her breasts.

"You can suck my tits now, lovely man."

It occurred to Roger that Angie had forgotten his name, probably the minute they left the house, but under the circumstance it didn't seem like a problem.

A shadow suddenly appeared as someone stood between the shagging couple and the full moon. Roger looked up and to the side. A pair of woman's legs in black stockings and high heels confronted him and as he raised his head to look up, the legs shone in the moonlight and seemed to go on forever.

Suddenly the strange woman dropped down onto her knees and Roger felt fingers gripping the base of his shaft. As he half knelt trying to comprehend what was happening, the hand pulled him out from Angie's cunt and a woman's head pushed in between him and the girl and he heard the mystery person sucking and slurping. Then he heard Angie.

"Christ! Who's that?"

Then Angie screamed and lifted herself up and came. The person removed her head and put Roger's cock back inside the cunt, then stood up and turned and looked at Roger in the darkness.

"Get into her really hard now and she'll come again, straight away."

Then the stranger walked away towards the gate and looking back, called out.

"Thank you!"

Immediately, Angie responded in her slurred voice.

"Our pleasure. Any time, darling."

Roger pulled himself together and, heeding the mystery woman's advice, shoved hard into Angie's tight little cunt and, as predicted, she came immediately, screaming as she did so.

"Yes, you clever lovely man. Yes, Yes!"

Roger had manoeuvred Angie back onto the garden seat and he had pulled up her dress to cover her breasts. Angie held her panties in her hand.

"Thanks, lovely man. I do hope we meet again."

Angie attempted to stand but, whether it was the alcohol, or having just been shagged, she fell onto the grass. As Roger picked her up and put her back on the seat, he heard voices.

"Hello Roger. Fancy finding you here."

The smiling faces of Maria and Serina stared first at Roger and then at Angie. The two women had worked in the kitchen, helping mainly with cleaning pots and dishes. Now they were homeward bound.

"Hi Maria and hello Serina. Are you both going home, by any chance?"

"Yes, we've just finished and we're going home."

Both women were staring at Angie, noticing her slightly odd behaviour. Then they both looked at Roger and smiled.

"Got your hands full, Roger? Can we help?"

Roger smiled at his two tenants.

"This is Angela, but she prefers Angie. I've suggested that it would not be a good idea for her to drive home right now. I was thinking that she could rest up in that little front bedroom downstairs at my place, but I promised to go and check on Rosa's husband Bertie very soon. Is there any chance you two could take Angie home with you and put her to bed?"

Angie hiccuped for the umpteenth time as she stared at Maria and Serina.

"Lovely ladies, thanks for what you did before. That was beautiful."

Angie was mistakenly thinking these women were responsible for her recent licking and her orgasms.

Roger laughed.

"It's all right. Mistaken identity. Can you help?"

Maria and Serina laughed loudly.

"It must have been good, whatever it was. Yes, we can help, can't we Serina?"

The mother and daughter looked knowingly at each other, which reminded Roger that he had every intention of fucking both of them, but probably not until Caroline had left to go back to London.

"Sure, Roger, we'll take Angie home for you. Don't worry about her. We might even take her to the cottage, where we can keep an eye on her. That way you won't have to deal with it early in the morning."

Roger thanked the pair, then turned to Angie and told her that the nice ladies had a bed made up at the house next door and she should go with them.

Angie giggled.

"I hope they give it to me like before."

As Roger began his walk back to the party, Maria and Serina took Angie's arms, lifted her up and began to walk her down the drive and to their house.

"Now remind us, Angie? Tell us what we did to you before so that we can give it to you all over again."

Angie couldn't have been in better hands.

———

In the bright moonlight, a late arrival at the party moved quietly around the garden. Many of the guests had either left or were having loving moments in their respective quarters.

The figure of the latecomer tottered on high heels and wavered from side to side. She stopped every few moments to listen, like a hunter in the forest at night. Then she heard a sound and turned towards it, walking more surely, knowing what she was looking for. She stopped to listen and there it was again.

"In vino veritas."

Then silence. Janice saw a cigarette burning not far away in the direction from which the sound had come and she headed towards it.

The summer house doors were wide open. Alberto was lying on the floor, bathed in moonlight and holding a bottle in his hand. He was happy. Nearby, his nephew Giorgio, recently arrived from Naples, sat smoking, thinking of who knows what.

Janice slid into view and stood between the two of them with her long thin silky stockinged legs and shiny black high heels catching the moonlight.

Janice stared first at old Alberto on the floor, then turned her head and stared at the younger man, still sitting and smoking a cigarette.

Speechless, both men stared back.

Without saying a word, Janice slowly pointed towards her crotch. She began to slowly unzip her dress, letting it fall to her feet. Next she pulled down her black silk panties over her suspenders and stepped out of them.

She lay down first beside Alberto, then Janice lifted herself up onto her elbows and indicated with a beckoning hand to Giorgio to come and put himself between her legs.

Giorgio, mesmerised by what he was seeing, stood up and undid his belt. As he moved towards her, Janice licked her fingers and wetted herself and spread her legs in preparation for his cock. In just moments, Giorgio had pushed his way into her wet cunt as she let out a satisfied moan.

Then Janice put her hand over towards Alberto, discovered he had already let his member out, clasped hold of it, and sighed.

"Rallenta, rallenta," Janice called out in her limited Italian. She wanted Giorgio to slow down. She wanted a shagging that could go on for hours.

Alberto was wanting to do something with his cock. He was enjoying Janice's hand, but was intent on finding other parts of her body. Without losing Giorgio, Janice lifted herself and slid across onto Alberto, and before he knew it, was rubbing his cock against her willing anus.

"Culo! Culo!"

Moments later Alberto was in Janice's bottom, pushing upward as

Giorgio pushed down. This was what Janice lived for and her body sang as it moved rhythmically on the two attentive cocks.

When Janice had enjoyed a long session with the men working for her in unison, she issued another instruction.

"Spingi più forte! Spingi più forte!" It worked, and both men pushed into her harder than ever.

They had been fucking Janice energetically for quite some time when she pushed both of them away and rolled over onto her knees.

"Cambiare!"

Janice was now poised with her cunt hovering above Alberto's solid member. Giorgio's throbbing penis waved from side to side and lifted itself up and down like a drawbridge, readying itself for Janice's backside. Janice's Italian language had worked and the two men had changed places. Alberto pushed his cock up into her just as Giorgio found the already open slippery orifice in Janice's rear. Janice crouched, fully impaled, staring into space and feeling those things which she mysteriously craved each day.

Finally both men, unable to withhold any longer, came in unison, filling her with cum in pulsating explosions. Satiated, she stood up and, without a word or a sign, picked up her panties and her frock and walked off into the shadowy garden, heading down to her car at the bottom of the drive.

As she got closer to the gate she noticed a couple in the moonlight, making love on the grass.

Without thinking, she walked over to them, knelt down and put her hand between their crotches, and took hold of the base of the man's shaft.

Janice removed it from the woman and put her head down and energetically licked the woman's cunt, thrusting her tongue in and eagerly biting a hard little clit as she savoured the flavours. Then she licked the man's cock, nibbling the end of it before she slipped it back in and stood up.

"Thanks," Janice murmured in her faraway voice as she walked away.

"Our pleasure!" came a woman's slurred voice. "Any time, darling."

Janice spread a hand towel on the driver's seat, knowing that she would be wet on the way home. There was only one thing left to do now and that was to get home and make a cup of cocoa, get into a bath and then go to bed. Tomorrow was her therapy day. Her sister paid for it, but only on condition that Janice never missed a session.

Janice loved Benjamin Bauer's voice. His Viennese accent and soft vowels excited her beyond belief, and Janice loved the fact that he refused to fuck her. He asked only that she pull her skirt up high and stretch her long legs out and far apart, and touch herself while he watched her as he played with his cock and then masturbated.

That was enough for Janice, but only as long as Mr Bauer kept on talking. Sometimes he ran out of things to say while stroking himself; then he would panic and repeat things he had already said. He knew that if he stopped talking, his sexual fantasy would end. Janice would simply get up and leave.

Janice lay in her bath holding her mug of cocoa and not thinking about very much.

Then she remembered the shoes. Oh yes, she must wear her special heels tomorrow. Benji's shoes, she called them. Styled in Europe and worn by fancy ladies. She was certain that they kept Mr Bauer talking for much longer, and she liked that very much.

8

LOOSE ENDS

CAROLINE HAD RARELY GONE this length of time in the company of another person without speaking. Roger's tale of the two morning visitors to his bed, Maria and Serina, defied belief, but Caroline believed him.

"So I've told you at last, darling. You've been so busy up until now, and I didn't want to confuse you with my bed problems."

Caroline continued to stare at the man she had selected to father her child.

"I doubt there are many men who would call it a bed problem, Roger. Far from it. And I'm fascinated with your resolve not to acknowledge them in your bed. Some folk might even think that you had an even greater bed problem."

Roger smiled and took Caroline's hand in his.

"You – I hope – remember that when I arrived here, I had already committed to becoming a dad. This decision carried responsibilities, one of which was to keep myself nice in preparation for that big trip to Margate when the proposed mother-to-be of my child turned up. Without that commitment, my morning adventures might have turned out differently."

Caroline laughed at Roger's serious attempt to divert her enquiries.

Understandably, he had omitted to mention in his long story that he had thought numerous times about the possibility of fucking both of the ladies in question.

"So my darling man. I will need to sign up for early morning bedroom sentry duty to protect our future child's interests. Is that what has to happen?"

More laughter and a fond kiss joined the two in harmonious agreement. Roger looked at Caroline lovingly and smiled.

"Given that we haven't yet worked out our sleeping arrangements, it might be tricky. We've given you your own room as befitting a virginal girl staying with her boyfriend, but the real reason being of course that neither he nor she knows if they could ever be in the same bed with another person for a whole night.

"Under these circumstances, sentry duty might not work. And, of course, not ignoring the possibility that you might also sleep through their visit and miss the whole event anyway. And then, what would you do if you did wake up and find one of them on the end of my member?"

Things were becoming more hilarious as the two explored this odd situation.

"We could of course, swap beds, with you being the recipient of the early morning attention of one of the ladies instead of me. Do you think they'd notice the difference?"

Caroline looked serious for a moment.

"Hmm! If I had brought a strapless dildo, one that fits inside me, our morning visitor might settle for that. Though come to think of it, I wouldn't be fooled by it."

"Oh, at last, I've been assured that women do know the difference. Yippee!"

Caroline suddenly giggled and yelled.

"I've got it! We will go to the bondage counter at our local friendly sex shop and buy you a chastity belt. There Roger, isn't that a good idea?

"And now that I think about it, your value has gone up significantly as a result of this conversation so that I will keep the keys and not give you one.

"I can't be sure one of my mother's so-called slut friends won't drop by when I'm out and about. I'm sure phones have been running hot all over Sydney as Mum spreads the word about her daughter's handsome man-friend.

"There! We will be totally safe from predatory females. I feel much better now. Problem solved. Happy, darling?"

Roger dragged Caroline down onto the carpet.

"I've just got tickets to Margate, you sexy bitch, and I'm having a pre-chastity belt event, just like a prisoner's last meal before going to the gallows."

Roger had Caroline's skirt up almost over her breasts, only to be denied his lustful advances.

"Sorry, darling, love to, but I'm ovulating tomorrow. Must save the seed. Sorry, lovely man."

Roger fell back against the front of the sofa and stared at this delightful woman who ticked all of his boxes.

"Now Roger. About tomorrow. We need to synchronise our agendas so that we make ourselves available for the seed deed. Accepted wisdom is that we should do it on at least two occasions during the day and, if possible, another one at night.

"Is there anything special you would like me to wear, Roger? I'll dress in anyway you want. I'll be busy organising my ovaries, but you can fulfil your fantasies however you wish my love. I'll dress and act out in any way that will help float your boat darling.

"So black silk panties and garter belt and stockings and heels? Or a schoolgirl look, perhaps? Or naked but for my sneakers? Plastic poncho over a legless jumpsuit? Your sister Jackie and Miranda like me in onesies or a cat suit when I have a stay over with them. Your call, darling."

Roger managed to not laugh but instead fired back with the air of a man who knew what he wanted, answering her nonchalantly and with a hint of a frown.

"Just the librarian look will do, darling. Tweed skirt, hair up in a classic career bun. Clear nail polish. White blouse with a plain neck and buttoned right up and over either a cream or white corselette. No knickers, and with preferably, heavy brown or tan stockings, one hundred and twenty denier or higher, with beige or cream suspenders and finished off with low heels or, if you can manage it, brown brogues. Yes, that will do, Caroline. Oh, and I almost forgot. Large glasses with heavy frames. Oh, and I forgot the half slip. But don't go to too much trouble, sweetheart. I'm sure I'll manage. Whatever you want to wear will do just fine.

"You're really quite sexy anyway." Roger finished, with a wry smile.

Caroline was agog. She stared at Roger with wide eyes and an open mouth. Then she reached out her hand and held his arm and in a super-soft voice she answered him.

"That was a real woman, Roger. You definitely just described an ex lover and she had certainly floated your boat darling. You even bought her stockings. What was her name?"

"Was it that obvious? Sorry! Agnes, a librarian I met at a book signing in London. At Selfridge's book department actually, and my first lesbian lover. Agnes was also a poet and a tiny bit older than me. Then she met a Scottish woman and ran off to Edinburgh. She got a job working for the Edinburgh Festival Committee.

"I had no idea, darling. Now I'm really hot thinking of Agnes and I bloody well want you in me right this minute. Oh, and by the way Roger, just for the record, Agnes probably wasn't your first lesbian lover. Women of that persuasion don't usually bother explaining these things to men. Most men just wouldn't understand."

Roger smiled lovingly at the beautiful woman.

"Thank you, darling, I'll remember that. Meanwhile, you sexy leso, we're not allowed to go to Margate until tomorrow. Remember? But now you might like to indulge me with something a little different that I really enjoy. Just lie back and think of Agnes. I'll channel her for you, complete with the fine hairs of her auburn pussy."

He made Caroline sit up on the sofa and she stared at him in seeming disbelief. Then he pulled her to the edge and slid his hands up her dress and pulled down and removed her panties.

He settled back and began to lick Caroline gently and put a finger into her vagina, but he only inserted it a tiny bit, enough to trigger a wonderful sensation of anticipation. Then, Roger gave what he hoped would be an exhibition grade cunnilingus performance *par excellence*.

It wasn't just lessons in cooking pasta that the memorable Italian woman in Positano had given Roger. Martina had instructed him in the affairs of love over a few months, each night after she finished work, when she would call around to see him in his tiny cottage.

Not only that, she would send him to visit her women friends, supposedly for coffee or a glass of Sangiovese and to help him with his Italian language learning. But Martina was really making him available for her friends' entertainment.

Martina had little trouble convincing Roger that it was all to help him understand the culture and the people. And she assured him that despite his often expressed exhaustion, it would benefit his future love life. Cunnilingus was a popular sexual pastime for these super sensual women and Roger suspected that it was practised between many of Martina's ladies – who only ever wore black – on each other. He was never refused by any of them and they would all immediately pull up their tight black skirts and lay back and position themselves for his loving advances with obvious prior knowledge of what they were about to receive. And if they then wanted something more to finish off with, they well knew that he would be instantly ready for that from his prior excitement and that they only need offer him that special smile and lean forward and let him out.

Caroline sighed and moaned and sometimes called out and pushed herself up towards Roger's mouth before pulling back sharply in order to do it all over again.

Roger was really enjoying making love to Caroline. He hadn't made love to anyone in this way since his time in Italy. He looked at Caroline's beautiful thighs and legs on either side of him and up at his lady's flat little belly and down to her fine ankles and feet.

Then he thought about Caroline being pregnant and with a big belly and maybe asking him to do things like this to her often if regular sex was judged to be too difficult or, in late term, inappropriate.

She came many times, and when Roger thought she might be getting tired and started to move his head away, the delicious woman would grab his hair and pull him closer into her and murmur lovingly, "Not yet, Agnes."

———

"For a woman, penetration is not an essential ingredient of good and enjoyable sex. There is so much more to lovemaking than having a cock inside them. Playing with a cock can, or might be fun but most times, it is more for the benefit of a man's enjoyment or to ensure that the female gets his attention for the simple purpose of eventually making a child."

Then Bertie ended his monologue on love and sex with the following words. "Are either of you ordering a cake?"

Freddy and Roger stared at their older friend and laughed. Bertie was well known for his rigorous commitment to a healthy diet, except when he was out in a cafe with Freddy.

It was Bertie and Freddy's fortnightly get-together at their regular bookstore cafe in Paddington. It was Roger's first time with then and he was enjoying it immensely.

"So what happens to men if they are needed less, Bertie? If women begin to realise that they can enjoy life without men playing a role that was once accepted as normal? Do men just sit and watch ancient re-runs on television or maybe pornography, and yearn for the good old days?"

"Well Roger, it's too early to tell, but things are already happening. The rise in the numbers of women working in the new computerised workplace is staggering, as is the number of working women who happily attend retraining courses. Also, industries that traditionally employed men are disappearing; either becoming obsolete or moving offshore where costs are lower.

"Men, in the Western world at least, seem to be stuck. Probably as a result of childhood conditioning, they have greater difficulty in refashioning their future when they find themselves out of work, or the profession they trained for is no longer required. Often these jobs are taken over by more adaptable and empathetic females. Women readily show up for classes or retraining workshops when these are offered. They are simply more adaptable. Men, less so.

"There have been many good books published recently that discuss these changes. In fact I've only recently finished one, *The End of Men and the Rise of Women* by Hanna Rosin. There is much to be considered in just this one book, but there are many other things too. And yes Roger, what will men do? That's the big question."

The three ordered another round of coffee and Bertie looked longingly at the apple pie and cream that the waiter had just served up to Freddy.

"The studies of sexuality in various cultures that I made many years ago led me to Tantric sex, Taoism and other Eastern and Middle Eastern philosophies. I don't claim to be a master of these things but they offer sound advice which we can all benefit from. They can improve our health, and our sex lives.

"For Roger's sake, I'll repeat what Freddy already knows about me.

"The most important thing I learnt is that I should not ejaculate every time I make love. I must save my '*chi*', as the mystics called it. Regular and constant ejaculation can seriously weaken a man and reduce his ability to enjoys a full life of sexual activity.

"Retaining their *chi* was a technique used by men who had access to, or responsibility for – depending on your point of view – a number of wives or concubines. It allowed them to pleasure all of their female partners whenever the urge took them, or when females sought them out for a little male attention. Holding on to his semen meant that a man could make love all night to a number of women without becoming exhausted."

Bertie reached over for another smidgin of Freddy's apple pie.

"Another important thing is diet; in particular, the amount we eat. Staying lean is important. Alcohol, sugar and drugs are a definite no no."

Roger listened with interest.

"If I understand you correctly then, Bertie, over the long term the future of men in a modern society looks decidedly uncertain. What do you think will happen?"

The waiter came and suggested they order anything they wanted now, as the kitchen was closing shortly. The three thanked him and Freddy said they would be leaving soon.

"The rate of change is so different in different parts of the world, as cultures vary tremendously and various religions repress people's ability to think for themselves. It is hard to know what will happen. In the past, the numbers of men have often been reduced by war. Now one man can destroy an enemy from a distance by pressing a button and sending a drone or a rocket.

"Men also have notoriously self-destructed by their own hand, usually from fighting, alcohol, drugs or dangerous adventures.

"Historically, going way, way back to Greek and Roman times, and also to Middle and Far Eastern cultures, men often took male lovers; usually young boys. This subject is a huge area of study if one has a spare lifetime to do the research. But we do know that, for various reasons, men would often forgo the opportunity to enjoy the love of a woman in favour of a man. Some studies suggest that men have historically been afraid of women. Be that as it may, it is my opinion that learning to love a woman both physically and emotionally is the most important activity that a man can pursue.

"Things are now looking very different. We are moving into an era where women and medical science have come together to produce children from sperm banks and women's lifestyle choices have been liberated by the contraceptive pill. Men will become far less important both to the economy and to the new women.

"Already, an increasing number of men are earning less money than their partners and this trend looks likely to continue. This rising economic disparity and the new independence of women have militated against the idea of partnering with a man. Many women are choosing not to enter into a permanent live-in relationship, both for financial reasons and also because they can better enjoy a single life with a wide network of friends.

"In short, the penis will no longer be a source of power. This will bring about changes that are difficult for us to imagine, but I believe that the revolution will lead to a new awareness. Despite the difficulties, this change is likely to reduce violence amongst men and against women and be a benefit to mankind generally.

"Let us hope that the global environmental crisis doesn't kill us all first."

———

Freddy came home early on Thursdays. It was his night to cook dinner, but when he walked through the front door he could smell a roast dinner already in the making.

"Hello darling. I thought I'd cook tonight so that you could relax."

Helen spoke as she walked past him on the way to the dining room carrying plates and cutlery, only stopping for a moment, to kiss him on the lips.

"It won't be long. Settle down on the sofa, darling, and I'll bring you a drink."

Freddy smiled after her as she walked back into the kitchen. He watched her walk past, lovingly noticing her frock and shoes and he wondering why she was dressed up just a little bit more than usual for a weeknight.

"This is a surprise, darling. Have I done one of those things that men sometimes do that their wives like but their husbands don't know what it was?"

"Maybe, darling. Now, are you sitting down yet?" Helen called back.

She appeared carrying a tray with their drinks and the open bottle of red wine. Freddy sat beside her on the sofa and asked about her day.

"Mary and Sophie came over this afternoon for coffee. Sophie had the day off from work."

Freddy smiled.

"And what scandal did Mary bring? Has one of the neighbours been caught embezzling the local flower show funds or something?"

Helen looked lovingly at her husband. She was going to enjoy this moment.

"Well darling! It's interesting that you ask. Given your intimate knowledge of the local gossip collected from fellow front lawn mowing males on Sundays; who would you guess was pregnant darling?"

Freddy laughed and sipped his drink and closed his eyes.

"Let me guess. Oh, that's easy. Jack from over the back got over the fence again and got the neighbours' fluffy yappy little bitch up the duff? I bet that shut her up for a few minutes."

The Jack Russell dog in the next street was notorious for his ability to escape from his walled garden, usually only when he caught a whiff of a nearby bitch in season.

"Nope! Try again, darling. You are sort of close about getting out and getting up to something, though. Tease it out a bit. I'm sure you'll get there eventually."

He looked lovingly at Helen.

"Give me a clue, darling. My brain is still not quite here yet. It was a busy day at work."

Helen was getting silently excited. This was such fun.

"Two legged. That's all I'll give you."

Freddy's forehead wrinkled in a frown.

"No! I can't think of anything, Helen. Just tell me, sweetheart, so that we can get on with dinner. I'm starving."

Helen took Freddy's other hand and looked into his eyes, smiling her beautiful smile.

"You are going to be a daddy, Freddy."

Freddy put his glass down on the tray and turned to face his wife.

"Sorry, darling. I can't play games until I've eaten. What you just said doesn't make any sense to me, but I'm sure a bellyful of roast beef will help me to understand."

Helen felt a pang of remorse, teasing her lovely husband like this. But such a rare opportunity could not be missed.

"Sophie is going to have your baby, Frederico. Congratulations, darling. Our lives are about to change and we are all excitedly looking forward to it."

The look on Freddy's face was not one that his wife had ever seen before.

"Darling? Are you okay?"

Freddy did not reply. His well organised life flashed before him. He had rarely had unplanned events happen to him. He just wasn't that sort of man. This was indeed a moment of truth that would affect him and his wife far into the future. It was too much to take in at this moment.

He sat up and looked at Helen. She seemed so serene. What was going on in her head?

"More important to me is knowing if you're okay, Helen?"

Helen put down her drink and put her arms around her husband.

"Yes, Freddy, I'm very okay with it. In fact, darling, I'm beside myself with excitement; a baby at last!"

Freddy pushed Helen back and stared at her. He suddenly realised that this wasn't just about Sophie and him.

For the very first time Helen, and Mary, Sophie's aunt, were going to be what one could call grandmothers, and for them this was to be a celebration of life.

Helen kissed him lovingly on the lips.

"Come and have dinner darling. We should celebrate, and Freddy…?"

"Yes, Helen?"

"Let's have an early night, darling. I so want to show you how much I love you."

————

Alice had passed her university exams with honours and had been offered a job tutoring in the psychology department she had studied in for the past four years.

As a first job, she couldn't really refuse it. It paid well, she knew the people she was working with, and most of all, she loved her work. She had considered applying for jobs in other universities, but something held her here. It wasn't that Alice was unsure of her ability to find employment somewhere else. Being at the same place that she had been at all this time, just made sense.

When Freya came for her usual Sunday night sleep-over, the two invariably discussed their futures.

Freya had opted to become a psychologist and guidance officer at the large co-ed private school, where she had gone for her complete pre university education, and which was close to where she lived in the leafy suburb of Vaucluse.

Freya had moved into a self-contained flat when she started university. The flat was in a large house owned by her aunt. It was the closest thing to moving out of home and her family all enjoyed teasing her about it because it was only a couple of streets away from her parents house.

Family was important to Freya and she could not imagine moving far away from where she lived.

For reasons neither woman really understood, they were both single and at around thirty years of age, things were just beginning to look a little serious in regard to settling and having a family.

"Alice?"

"Yes, Freya?"

"I've been thinking about us."

Alice lowered her cocoa mug and looked at the love of her life.

"In what way, sweetheart?"

"I think we should live together. My apartment is huge and I'm likely to inherit the whole house and property in a few years. Aunt Phoebe is pushing ninety. She's wonderfully fit physically and mentally, but she will pass eventually, as we all do.

"Deep down, I can't see myself meeting someone else who I could love like I love you, and I've long given up looking for a man, especially now that we have Freddy in our lives. It's just a thought that I've had that's been growing stronger lately. You can disagree with me and I promise I won't go into a funk.

"Oh and there is another thing I should mention. I haven't had a period lately. As you know I'm not very regular with it anyway but given that we had that night with Freddy, I'm thinking I should check things out. Because I've only been with a man once, my head still thinks I can't get pregnant. But realistically, once is enough I suppose. I'll go to the chemist in the morning.

Alice put her mug on the bedside table and put her arm through Freya's and leant over and kissed her on the cheek.

"Gosh! So much to think about Freya. Let me know how things go. Promise you will ring me immediately you get the results."

Freya wriggled down into the bed.

"Will do, Alice."

"It must be the hot weather. I've been thinking weird thoughts lately, thoughts that I'm not sure I should talk about."

Freya frowned and looked at Alice.

"Tell me about your weird thoughts darling. Sounds interesting."

"All right I will, but promise you won't panic, although if you were pregnant, that would make life really weird, in a wonderful way though.?"

"Well, I keep thinking about wanting to have a child; even having a lot of them; and I've even been planning how this could happen."

Frey stared at Alice, her mouth open with surprise.

"Please go on."

"Well, firstly I need to change my life, and finishing university and starting work has already brought big changes. But I need to do more, and most of all, I need to move out of here and away from the Bennett's, even though I love them very much. It is time we got out of each other's lives, even if only in a small way.

Freya kept looking at Alice.

"It's a lot to do with your relationship with Bertie too, isn't it Alice? Rosa warned you that he could become addictive."

"Yes, Freya, it is."

There was silence as the two women thought about all of the things that seemed to be lining up for their attention.

"So how would you get pregnant Alice? Virgin births are not common these days."

Alice didn't reply straight away.

"I had thought about Freddy, and he is still the main contender. I would have to talk to him and Helen first of course.

"But someone else has come up. I had a conversation with Caroline, Rosa and Bertie's daughter and who you met at Maude's party."

Freya screamed. "Yes, I was sure I was going to loose you to that sophisticated super attractive woman. But I worked out that you had probably tried her, then decided that my tiny tits were more to your liking."

Alice yelled and pulled Freya over her lap and pretended she was about to give her a spanking.

"Yes! And just like I thought you were about to ride off into the distance with that thoroughbred mare, Sophie, you no-good little slut."

The two women yelled and squirmed and bit and kissed each other.

"Now, beloved, if you bothered to take your eyes off of Sophie for just a minute at the party, you might have noticed Caroline's attractive male friend, Roger.

"Caroline confided in me over marmalade toast and coffee only yesterday, that Roger and she were not yet a couple but rather that he had agreed to father a child with her. He knows that she is the lover of his step sister, Jackie, back in London. That was how Caroline first got to know about him and decided to proposition him after she met him when he returned from a lengthy working holiday in Italy.

"Caroline told me that she thought she was falling in love with Roger, something which she had not expected to happen. She also talked about her longtime infatuation with Helen, which has just been consummated after so many years.

"Helen told Caroline that Freddy's and Helen's relationship was successful because they told each other about any intimate interactions that they might have with other people. Helen also told her how the two were happy to share those other people with each other.

"When I inquired about how Caroline felt about sharing Roger given that she had crawled into my bed the night she arrived, she laughed and said she would need time to think things through but seeing how successful Helen and Freddy's arrangement looked, following their example was a strong a possibility. But she also insisted that given her relationship with Roger was still very new, she wasn't about to offer him to anyone yet."

The two women sipped their hot chocolates, staring into space and thinking about their lives.

"Gosh Alice, there is a lot to think about isn't there? All I said was that I thought we should live together. Now, if we both started having babies, I'm wondering whether aunt Phoebe's house is going to be big enough?

"So can I ask again? Will you come and live with me Alice? It would be a start and we can sort out our baby thing from there?"

Alice parked her mug and snuggled down beside Freya.

"Yes, my darling, I would love to come and live with you. Let's do it. And maybe one day we could even get married and all our children will be flower girls and page boys?"

———

Freddy often had déjà vu moments but tonight seemed decidedly real.

Freddy came home early on Thursdays. It was his night to cook dinner, but when he walked through the front door he could smell dinner already in the making.

"Hello darling. I thought I'd cook tonight so that you could relax."

Helen spoke as she walked past Freddie on the way to the dining room carrying plates and cutlery, only stopping for a moment, to kiss him on the lips.

"It won't be long. Settle down on the sofa darling and I'll bring you a drink."

Freddy fought back the scary feeling that he was in some sort of time warp. Maybe he had spent too much time playing with the mathematics of time travel, or the just averted crisis at his work as an airline traffic controller earlier in the day, involving more than fifty planes in a holding pattern above Brisbane. Perhaps the strain had got to him.

"This is a surprise darling. Have I done one of those things that men sometimes do that their wives like but their husbands don't know what it was?"

"Maybe, darling, now, are you sitting down yet?" Helen called back.

Helen appeared carrying a tray with their drinks and an open bottle of red wine.

Freddy sat beside Helen on the sofa and, as usual, asked about her day. Then he asked if there was any news from next door, Freddie's way of enquiring about Sophie and her recently announced pregnancy.

Helen looked lovingly at her husband.

"Well, darling husband! No news from next door, but there is from a suburb just a little further away. So, darling, it will not surprise you when I ask you to guess who you think is going to be a father? And yes, we've gone down this road before, haven't we sweetheart?"

Helen beamed her sweetest all-knowing smile at her hapless husband.

Frederico Alves found himself speechless. He sensed that things were about to head in a direction that he could never have foreseen. He found himself reviewing his life over the past couple of months, looking for clues to where Helen was heading, but without success.

"Freya rang me today, darling. She has discovered that she is going to have a baby, and … "

"Don't say another word Helen. How could this be happening to me? Why me? I'm not the only bloody man in the world. Should Freya consider a DNA test, just to keep the records straight? And for her sake and the sake of the baby?"

Helen took Freddy's hand and with the other, lifted his chin and looked deeply into his eyes.

"Freddy, you are the only man Freya has ever been with. You are a lucky man and she is a lucky woman and the baby is a lucky baby and I am your lucky loving wife who is so excited about another child coming into the family. Everyone loves you Freddy and we are all over the moon about what has happened. And Sophie is beside herself with excitement, knowing the two babies will grow up together."

Freddie stared at his ecstatic wife. Sometimes he thought that for just a moment, the mysteries of womanhood would be revealed to him, but his brain would suddenly be full of male thoughts about the wheel sizes on modern prams or the arguments for and against breast feeding. If only he could just be at one with the universe and enjoy the moment.

"I've invited Sophie and Freya and Mary for dinner tomorrow night, and of course Alice will be here too. I spoke to Alice this afternoon. Freya had told her the news. Apparently, Freya and Alice have recently decided to live together and Alice will move in with Freya. There is so much happening Freddy, thanks to you."

Helen reached out and embraced her husband.

"Roast pork tonight darling, with apple sauce and roast potatoes. Then I think we should go early to bed. You've had another big day, I can see."

"Are either of you ordering a cake?" asked Bertie.

Roger ordered carrot cake with cream along with an extra spoon.

Roger and Freddy were with Bertie for their fortnightly coffee get together and philosophical chat at Bertie's favourite cafe in Paddington.

"What is the latest on the arrival of your sister and her friend, Roger? I win brownie points with Helen if I bring her news about the new girls. Mind you, I don't think she can fit another girlfriend into her life."

"Well, it seems as though they will get here in July. They both finish their work contracts at the end of June, so will be free to head on over here.

However, Jackie is planning a quick trip to view the property the week after next so hopefully she will have time to also meet the neighbours.

The visit is pretty much for her to view and make preliminary arrangements for any major renovations she would like done before they arrives. Caroline will be about to leave for the UK as she arrives, but they will no doubt spend time together when my sister gets back there.

"In the meantime, Maria and her family move out of the adjacent cottage this week. The house repairs at their place are complete. This means that I can now move in at my leisure. I'm really looking forward to it. My very own little house in the woods."

"So! What is Caroline going to do? Is she happy about living in the cottage? I know you two are still working things through so I really shouldn't ask.

"Alice has announced that she is moving out to live with Freya so that Caroline's parents cottage will become vacant. I think that is right, isn't it Bertie?"

Bertie was just collecting another piece of cake and his mouth was full.

"We sure will miss Alice. I suspect that Rosa already has a new tenant in mind. She introduced me to a lovely woman and her niece the other day who I think she wants to move in. I guess she will need to talk to Caroline first. No doubt she will make an announce about the direction in which we will all travel at number one in the not too distant future."

Freddy wasn't going to let Roger off the hook totally.

"What do you want Roger? Apart from peace and quiet while you write? Are you ready to be part of a couple?"

Roger stared at his near-empty plate and frowned at Bertie who was helping himself to another fork-load of Roger's cake.

"I'm feeling very good about what we are doing, Freddy. I think we are both ready to commit to a relationship. We just need to reorganise our lives a bit and she needs to return to London to clear out her flat and finish up at her job. There is a possibility that she can work for the same UK company here in Sydney.

"You and Helen are her role model for relationships, Freddy. She calls it the F & H Sharing model.

"We need to do the fine tuning. Neither of us have ever shared a bed with anyone on a regular basis so what sounds like small things are in fact big things. Add to that my work habits which see's me heading to bed at midnight or later and not getting up until late morning.

"Caroline also reserves the right to stay out at a girlfriends place if she gets side-tracked. I have no problems with that. Just so long as she lets me know and I know that she's safe."

Roger looked at Bertie and asked, "I'm getting another piece of carrot cake, Bertie. Can I order a piece for you while I'm at it?"

"No thanks Roger. Mustn't overdo the sugars you know."

Freddy and Roger exchanged knowing smiles.

"So Roger, when do you think Caroline will leave Australia. Helen will want to know."

"Well it depends a bit on Jackie's visit and we still have a couple of things to sort out."

"Like making a baby perhaps? It's all right. Helen can't keep secrets from me. At least I don't think she can."

Roger laughed at Freddy's comment.

"Okay, yes, but we put that one to bed – forgive the pun – finally yesterday. It's been a busy few days indeed. Just waiting for the test results. Then she will be off and hopefully back here very soon afterwards. Oh yes, Freddy, there is just one other thing you can advise me about. Caroline is talking about sharing me if she tests positive and when we are sure that she is pregnant. I fail to see what her being pregnant has to do with sharing me. Any thoughts on that, Freddy?"

———

Alice welcomed Helen when she arrived for her regular Wednesday luncheon visit. Even though Alice was now working, she was still able to fit Helen in and they continued to enjoy each other as they had when she was studying.

"Rain at last," Helen gasped as she parked her umbrella in the brolly bucket near the door.

"Cuddling up weather, my love. But only after coffee, methinks."

The two kissed and Alice took Helen's hand, led her to the kitchen table and served the fresh coffee she had just made.

"So when are you moving, darling and more importantly, will it change things for us?"

The two women held hands and looked at each other and smiled.

"Well Helen, things shouldn't change that much, given that we're both so close to Freya. However, I do have something I need to discuss with you which I hope you will understand."

"Goodness, Alice. You sound a bit serious. Should I be worried?"

Alice laughed nervously.

"I hope not, darling."

"Well! What is it?"

"I want to have a baby, Helen. There, I've told you now. It's nothing to do with Freya and Sophie both being pregnant. I've been thinking about it for some time and given, that there is little likelihood of me meeting the right man, you will not have any trouble working out whose baby I would most want to have. But given that Freddy has already become dad of the month amongst my friends, I'm wondering how you and he would feel about doing the deed. I could understand it if you both thought things had gone far enough in the baby department."

Helen stared at Alice in astonishment and hesitated before giving her reply.

"Darling, I'm shocked. I had picked you as the career woman and for that reason I'm finding this a little confusing."

"I'm sorry, Helen. It would have been a good idea to have mentioned it earlier, before the unexpected baby boom. Now I feel a bit silly and guilty for wanting Freddy's baby. I've tried thinking of other ways. Between the two of us, I can tell you that two names came to me. One was Bertie, but the more I thought about it the more it seemed unfair to him and to Rosa. The other person is your neighbour Roger.

"Caroline said that because the relationship was so new, and even though she thought that she would like to model their relationship on yours and Freddy's, she wasn't ready to share Roger yet, at least not until they were definitely pregnant and she was more established here in Sydney and in the relationship. As you probably know, once she is pregnant she will make a quick trip back to London to settle things there and clear out her flat. By the time she returns, Roger will have moved into the cottage at the back. In short, they have a lot of working out to do so best I not get involved there."

While Alice talked, Helen was thinking through the situation. Ultimately it would depend on Freddy's response. Helen had almost immediately decided that Alice having his baby was fine with her, but the thought of fathering three children in just twelve months might be more than her wonderful husband could cope with.

"You needn't say any more, darling. I'm all for it. The question will be whether Freddy can fit you in."

The two laughed at the idea of Freddy fitting her in.

"Thank you Helen. I know the arrival of babies is going to affect both of your lives quite dramatically. Are you still feeling good about it? You were most excited when we last spoke."

"Yes, all is fine. Freddy is even joking about being a dad while thinking more like a grandpa. He's already planning baby projects for his shed. I just hope he doesn't overdo it. You know what he's like once he gets excited about something he's building."

"There is just one more thing, Helen."

"Tell me, darling."

"Well, if Freddy agrees to do the deed, I would like you to be with us as a threesome. I can't think of a more exciting and loving way to get pregnant than being with the two of you. Please say you will?"

Helen again stared at Alice in astonishment. Then she took Alice's hand in hers.

"If and how things will happen will depend on Freddy, but yes, darling. I would love to be with you at conception. I've never made a baby before."

The two women laughed and hugged each other.

"If it's okay with you Alice, I could ask Rosa to mention it to Bertie, whom she could instruct to tell Freddy at their fortnightly cafe get together, that the best things in life come in threes. I'm sure Bertie can come up with an ancient Chinese saying confirming this and he does have an influence on Freddy's thinking."

"I'll leave it in your capable hands, wicked stepmother. I'm handing it all over to you, darling."

"I can't wait to see the look on Freddy's face, Alice. Call me cruel if you like, but being with and watching a man trying to think straight can be such fun sometimes."

"Now my love, talking about making babies has made me feel a little horny. As you've agreed to help out, maybe we should wander to my bed and practise. We can pretend Freddy's there. I'm sure you can impersonate his roar."

CONTACT

Publisher or review enquiries should include your full name and details in all correspondence.

Email address:
admin@richardlee.biz

RICHARD LEE PUBLISHING

Erotic Fiction

The Eros Crescent trilogy in separate volumes:

The Fifi Code

ISBN - 978-0-909431-02-0

Eros Crescent

ISBN - 978-0-909431-05-1

Mount Eros

ISBN - 978-0-909431-08-2

The Eros Crescent trilogy in one volume:

Eros Crescent Omnibus (Trilogy due mid 2020)

ISBN - 978-0-909431-09-9

———

Literary Fiction

Australian Short Stories

ISBN - 978-0-909431-00-6

Restless: A novel about two young men growing up
in Australia between 1900 and 1936 (Publication date unknown.)

———

Out of Print Titles

Mathematics for Young Children by Helen Western

ISBN - 978-0-909431-01-3

Currajong: For Those Whom Schools Have Failed
by Bruce Wicking
ISBN - 978-0-909431-03-7

The Puppetry Handbook by Anita Sinclair
ISBN - 978-0-909431-04-4

Wordswork by Chris Davidson & Bruce Wicking
ISBN - 978-0-909431-06-8

Sheep Production by Murray Elliott
ISBN - 978-0-909431-07-5

Ducks for Starters: A Practical Guide to
Backyard Duck Keeping by Bruce Wicking
ISBN - 978-1-875207-00-8

Sweethearts by Colin Talbot
ISBN - 978-1-875207-02-2

www.ingramcontent.com/pod-product-compliance
Lightning Source LLC
Chambersburg PA
CBHW031316170626
46807CB00002B/445